INCONVENIENTLY
WED

BOOK ONE

Secrets
AND A Scandal

By Jane Maguire

Secrets and a Scandal

Copyright © 2022 Jane Maguire

Cover design by Holly Perret
Edited by Kyleigh Poultney

ISBN: 978-17778926-0-9

www.janemaguireauthor.com

To my three special C's.

-Love, JM

Chapter 1

July 1818

Edward Adderley had once sworn he would never set foot in England again. Yet here he stood, six years later, on the doorstep of his family's ancestral home in Kent. Darkness had already fallen, accompanied by a misty rain, turning the familiar facade of Highfield Park into an imposing shadow. If the rumors of his father's ill health were to be believed, Edward would soon become the earl and its master. The thought filled him with dread.

The front door flew open in response to Edward's knock, revealing the astonished face of Higgins, the house's long-serving butler.

"Why, Lord Camden," he exclaimed. "Is that truly you? This is certainly a surprise! Please, my lord, step inside out of the rain at once. Your father hoped, of course, that you would come, but we received no confirmation. The staff would have been out to greet you, but as I said, we had no idea of your coming …"

This marked the first time in Edward's thirty years he could recall ever seeing the old butler flustered.

"It is of no matter, Higgins," he assured him as he set aside his hat and greatcoat, both crumpled after the long journey. "I want no fuss or ceremony. Only pray, tell me, how is my father? Is it true that—"

"Edward!" A soft cry from above was followed by the sound of footsteps pattering down the stairs.

He looked up, and now it was his turn to be astonished as he caught sight of his sister, Catherine, rushing toward him in her dressing gown and nightcap. The sister he had left behind six years ago had been a girl of eleven, still rambling about the house with childlike clumsiness. The figure rushing toward him was a young woman of seventeen, an undeniable golden-haired beauty who had inherited their mother's height and grace.

"Oh, Edward, you truly came!" She hurried forward, although she stopped short of approaching him, as if suddenly wary of what his reaction would be after all this time of separation.

"Catherine," he said, stepping toward her and pulling her into a quick embrace. There was much he should have said to her in the moment, words of reassurance or affection after his long absence with no communication at all. But being back at Highfield left him stiff and uncomfortable, and all he could muster was, "I didn't know if you would be here."

"I arrived just last week," she replied. "It was only when news of Papa's health became increasingly dire that I was finally allowed to return home. Do you recall Papa's friends Lord and Lady Bathurst? I've been in London with them and their daughters for the Season. I did not wish to go, but Papa insisted. I am not yet out in society, of course, but there are still certain entertainments deemed appropriate, which I was forced to endure.

"But forgive my impudence," she said, stepping back a little and flushing. "That is all of no consequence now. You received my letter, then? About Papa?"

Edward gave a curt nod. "But are you really certain his condition is as serious as he makes it out to be? You know how he tends to exaggerate."

While over the past few years, he had occasionally wondered if his contempt for England and the people of his acquaintance were at least somewhat unfounded, he felt entirely justified in his skepticism regarding his father's health complaints. The elder Edward Adderley, Earl of Ashton, had long been prone to episodes of overindulgence with food and drink, followed by bouts of severe indigestion and gout. He had often referenced his own mortality, certain he would not survive another fortnight, until some tonic or powder, or simply the passage of time, eased his symptoms, and the cycle began again.

Catherine looked at him solemnly. "I believe it is quite serious this time. He has not left his room since I arrived last week, and it seems unlikely he will ever have the strength to do so again. Why, he no longer even cares to eat! Dr. Livingston has tended to him frequently and prescribed numerous treatments, but none seem to be working. His heart has weakened beyond repair."

Edward gave a heavy sigh. "I suppose all that remains is for me to go upstairs and see him myself. The hour is late, but perhaps it would be best to speak to him right away."

"Yes, do," affirmed Catherine. "Even if he is already asleep, I'm certain he would want you to wake him. I've tried my best to be a comfort to him since my return, but you are the one he truly wishes to see. He has asked for you every day without fail, saying he cannot rest easy until he speaks with you one more time." She had kept her voice free of emotion, but melancholy clouded her dark eyes.

"Very well, I will go up directly. Thank you for coming to speak with me, and I apologize for having disturbed you so late at night." He gave her a small bow and turned his attention to Higgins, who, having regained his composure, was still standing in the entrance hall, eager to be of use. "Higgins, see that my old room is made up. I will retire as soon as I've finished speaking with the earl."

"I'll rouse the housemaids to attend to it right away, my lord," came his reply, and he hurried off at once.

Edward started heading toward the staircase when abruptly he stopped, and on second thought, called over his shoulder, "Oh, and Higgins? See that a decanter of brandy is placed in my room." He only hoped these last instructions had been heard.

He began trudging up each step, his legs leaden. He would give a fortune to be anywhere in this moment but here. This whole ordeal left him out of sorts, and as his fingers slid over the gilded balustrade, a new emotion nudged its way into the mix: guilt.

He had been on the Continent about six months, traveling from city to city in a stupor of rage and grief, when his father's letters had started to reach him. Once he had settled in Florence, after the Peace had been declared, the letters, beseeching missives insisting that he return home and do his duty to his family, had become all the more frequent. He had thrown them in the fire without a second thought. It was his burning of the other letters, the ones written in Catherine's then-childish hand, stating how much she missed him and looked forward to his return to Highfield Park, that now gave him a moment of regret. Apparently, she hadn't shared their father's persistence, for, after about a year of sending letters to which she received no reply, her correspondence had ceased. It hadn't been well done of him; he could see that now. Yet in those early days, with his hurt still so raw, he had placed his desire to escape all association with his former life above everything else.

But maybe it had all been for the best. At least, that's what he tried to convince himself. For when he had received Catherine's most recent letter after five years of silence, the words brief but imploring, he had listened in a fashion he perhaps would not have done had her letters been as frequent as their father's. In its rarity, the letter had served its intended purpose of finally bringing him back home. And now that he was here, it was time to face whatever lay before him.

He paused only a moment as he reached the door of his father's bedroom before quietly letting himself in. The fire had burned to embers, and he had to hold out his candle to see clearly before him. As the flame illuminated his father's sleeping figure, he let out a gasp. The earl's fondness for food and drink had always been reflected in his substantial frame, but the man lying still in the vast four-poster bed was diminished and frail. Sallow skin hung slackly from his once-robust frame, and his eyelids sat dark and sunken on his listless face. There was no longer any question of the earl exaggerating his condition. His numerous past predictions of not living another fortnight would certainly be correct this time.

Edward approached the bedside, unsure if he should call out his father's name or attempt to rouse him with a soft shake. However, he was spared pondering any further as the earl suddenly opened his eyes, and they immediately widened. "Edward? Do I dream?" he rasped.

Edward gave his father's hand a swift touch. "No, Father, it's me, in the flesh."

The earl's weathered face broke into a smile, his voice sounding stronger as he said, "God be praised. I knew you wouldn't desert me in the end." He struggled into a partial sitting position, leaning his graying head against the pillows. The effort left him gasping for breath, and he gave his head an impatient shake as he waited for his ability to speak to return.

"But let's not waste time with idle chatter," he finally uttered. "There are things I must say to you, things you need to understand before I depart this earth."

Edward lowered himself to sit at the foot of the bed, peering into the once-familiar face that was no longer familiar at all. "Then, by all means, speak what needs to be said."

The earl paused to clear his throat, then said, without meeting Edward's gaze, "It seems we have found ourselves in some degree of difficulty."

Edward couldn't help the wave of indignation that rose in him. "What do you mean *we* have found ourselves in difficulty? How could *we* have difficulties when *I* have not set foot in England nor associated with anyone there for more than six years?"

His father's face colored with a flush of rage. "Never mind your impertinence!" he snapped. "What I must tell you is important, and I'm too weary for constant interruptions. You *will*, therefore, hold your tongue until I have finished speaking with you." His voice was nowhere near the boisterous bellow he had used when angered in his earlier years, but authority still lingered behind his words.

"Very well," said Edward with a sigh, thinking it unwise to further agitate his father given his fragile condition. "Continue, and I'll say no more."

"Good, good." The earl took in a deep, wheezing breath. "As you are so troubled over semantics, *I* have found myself in financial difficulty. Rather serious, I'm afraid."

True to his word, Edward said nothing, although an uncomfortable coldness began trickling through him.

His father raised his eyes to look at him imploringly. "You know how it is. A few bad hands of cards, a series of poor runs at the hazard table …"

Edward thought wryly of how his own gambling ventures on the Continent had made a significant contribution to funding his living there, through some stroke of luck. However, there would be no benefit to him pointing this out. So, while there were many remarks he wished to make, he tried to keep his face expressionless as he merely uttered, "Indeed."

Encouraged, the earl continued. "But you needn't trouble yourself too much over it. While the situation is quite grave, I will not simply leave you drowning in debts from which you have no escape. On the contrary, I've devised a solution to the problem, and it is of this to which you must listen very carefully."

"Yes, go on," prodded Edward, although his father's reassurances had done nothing to quell his anxiety.

"I made a new acquaintance in London earlier in the year, a Mr. Thomas Wright. Unfortunately, I cannot refer to him as a true gentleman, as he's quite low born, but he puts on a good enough show of it. He has had significant success as a cotton merchant—exceedingly wealthy. He was even decent enough to pay my way out of a bind at the gaming hell before my health necessitated my early retirement from London."

"How very generous of him."

If his father detected the sarcasm, he gave no indication of it and resumed his speech. "It's quite fortunate that you will soon become acquainted with Wright. For you see, after spending years dividing his time between his house in Liverpool and his rented rooms in London, Wright developed a desire to have a place in the country, while still a convenient distance from London, to call his own. What a fortunate coincidence that Sir Walter recently put Hinshaw House for lease. Wright, of course, must purchase the property if he truly wishes to establish himself as a gentleman, but for now, he believes Hinshaw House will do quite nicely. He has spent the Season mainly in London, but with it soon drawing to a close, I'm sure you will see him around here often, now that you're to be neighbors. I believe an alliance with him will serve you very well."

"I see," was the only comment Edward made, although a flurry of thoughts tumbled through his tired brain. Hinshaw House? Why, that was a mere three miles from Highfield Park. Fortunate indeed that Wright had chosen it as the perfect location for his new home. Something was amiss about the whole situation, and Edward could no longer stay quiet on the matter. "There is a question which, in my mind, yet remains unanswered. If Wright has turned himself into a merchant of considerable success and wealth, he's surely no fool. What, then, does he seek to gain from his association with you? For he is not offering you charity out of the sheer goodness of his heart, I'm certain."

At this, the earl blanched a little. "Yes, well, there is something he hopes to gain, although it will benefit you just as much, if not more. It seems Wright has a daughter, a Miss Eliza Wright, who is in want of a husband."

"No." Edward's response was immediate, the word hard as iron.

"No?" The earl raised an eyebrow. "Why, you did not even take a moment to consider the matter. Are you concerned about Miss Wright's low breeding? You needn't be. It seems Wright made an advantageous marriage to a baronet's granddaughter. As I understand it, with Wright traveling so often, on account of his trade ventures, the girl was brought up almost exclusively in the company of her mother's family. I, therefore, cannot imagine you would find her lacking in that way."

"The girl's breeding is not the problem," Edward exclaimed. "You know I swore never to remarry."

"Nonsense," said his father dismissively. "I realize you voiced such sentiments long ago, but you cannot still be dwelling on it all six years later. You had a difficult time of things with Julia, to be sure, but you're long past the point where you should allow that to have any bearing on your actions."

"Do not," cut in Edward, "speak that name to me." He jumped from his seat and began pacing the room, dragging his hands through his unruly hair. "Surely there's something else to be done. Why not sell the London house? Or the lodges? I certainly have no use for them."

The earl glanced at him with a slow shake of his head. "Already sold, I'm afraid."

Edward tried his best to contain his expression of shock. "And Highfield Park?" he mumbled, although he was already aware of what the response would be.

"Entailed, as you well know. Although, if you look around the house, you may notice that certain furnishings, pieces of artwork, and the like are … missing. Sadly, it couldn't be helped."

"Blast it all!" Edward swore. It was against his better judgment that he had returned home, and to be welcomed back with the news that his father had bankrupted the family with his careless gambling was almost too much to endure.

He and his father didn't bear any great affection for each other, the earl being too self-indulgent and egotistical to truly love another. However, his father had always taken a certain pride in the son and heir he had created, and Edward had felt he owed him one last act of obedience to fulfill his final wish by listening to his dying words.

However, it became clearer by the minute that he would have been far better off ignoring that annoying sense of duty and remaining in Florence. And with that, a new realization dawned on him.

"I will return to the Continent at once." As the idea took form, he felt silly for having let himself get so overwrought. "Yes, I'll make a swift and permanent departure from England," he said, his outlook brightening considerably, "and be under no obligation to settle any debts that remain here. Highfield Park needn't give me cause for concern. Someday, some distant cousin will inherit it, along with the earldom. And if, by that time, the estate has crumbled to the ground, then so be it."

His father regarded him with a mixture of astonishment and outrage. "Do you mean to say you care nothing for your birthright? For your home, your title, or your responsibility to carry on the Ashton earldom that has been in the Adderley family for generations?"

"Not a farthing."

"You ungrateful ass!" spluttered the earl. Had he enough strength, he surely would have yelled the words at the top of his lungs, possibly while throwing the nearest breakable object across the room. Instead, he slumped farther back into his pillows in angry defeat. He lay in silence for a moment, his lips twisted in a quivering scowl, when a sudden brightness spread over his face, and his eyes glittered guilefully.

"Very well," he said, almost too calmly. "If you feel no sense of obligation to the estate, to the place in society that is rightfully yours, and think you can simply cast it all aside without a backward glance, then so much the better for you, I suppose. However, have you spared a moment to consider what will happen to poor Catherine? Would you truly feel at ease leaving her behind with no home, no close relations, and most importantly, no dowry? Surely you would not be so heartless."

This speech did indeed give Edward pause. In his desperation to untangle himself from this convoluted web, he had cast aside all thoughts of Catherine. For the second time that evening, a pang of guilt hit him for his treatment of his sister.

The earl took Edward's hesitation as an opportunity to resume his persuasion. "You really shouldn't be so quick to turn down the idea of marriage. If the thought of Miss Wright as a wife is unappealing, I suppose you could try to find another. However, that will take considerably more time, especially with the Season nearing its end, and it would be difficult to find her match in wealth. I believe she is staying at her uncle's house in Lancashire at present, but Wright plans to have her join him at Hinshaw House any day now so that you can become acquainted with her directly. If good fortune deigns to present itself on your doorstep, why turn it away? In any case, from what Wright has told me, I cannot see any way in which you would find Miss Wright objection-able. He says she is quite gentle-natured and more than adequate in appearance and skills."

While his father had intended to reassure him with these words, Edward was once more suspicious of Mr. Wright's intentions. The earl put a great deal of trust in his recent acquaintance, but it seemed that certain things about the situation yet remained unsaid. With that in mind, Edward couldn't help but pose a question. "If Miss Wright is such a lovely, charming creature, why is her father allowing her to be shut away in Lancashire instead of flaunting her on the London marriage mart?"

"Oh, she made her London debut at the start of the Season," answered the earl. "However, along the way, it seems there was a bit of a scandal, and her father thought it best she retreat to Lancashire until all the silly chatter sur-rounding her died away."

"Scandal?" Edward's ears had perked up at the word. "What sort of scandal?"

"It seems there was a suggestion of … impropriety on her part. Some sort of forwardness with a household serv-ant, which her father insists was a complete fabrication. It was born of the ridiculous ramblings of a scorned suitor, a man of little importance. Pay it no heed."

It didn't surprise Edward in the least that Wright had downplayed the severity of the matter. Of course he wouldn't openly admit that his daughter had been involved in wrongdoing.

It all made sense now. While having a close friendship with the earl was no doubt beneficial to Wright in itself, having his daughter marry the earl's successor to help elevate her above scandal was indubitably even more advantageous. Nevertheless, Edward was all too aware that being of high rank did not make one immune to scandal. He thought back to the whisperings that had surrounded him when he'd last been in England and how deep his humiliation had been on account of them.

"No," insisted Edward, "for though Miss Wright may be rich as Croesus, I will not go through with a marriage that will subject me to scrutiny and gossip."

His father waved his hand flippantly. "You worry for naught. You know what the ton is like—they latch on to rumors like pigs to a trough. However, any particular rumor only circulates until a new, more salacious one comes along. Keep to Highfield Park for a few months, and by the time the Season arrives again, no one will even remember the silly business with Miss Wright. As for the girl, having been banished to Lancashire amidst her first Season, she should be especially inclined to act with more prudence from now on so that such a fate does not befall her again."

Seeing that Edward was about to protest, the earl continued speaking, although his voice was becoming a tired rasp. "If that still does not satisfy you, then content yourself with the knowledge that you need not even see Miss Wright often after your marriage. Once an heir has been sired, you may go and do as you please as long as you exhibit discretion."

To this, Edward could make no reply as a fit of coughing seized the earl. It was a horrible sound rattling from deep within his chest. When the fit subsided, he was visibly exhausted, sinking flat against the bed as he drew in heavy breaths.

"I believe we must stop our conversation here," he sighed, his eyelids drooping despite his best efforts to keep them open. "I grow weary."

"Rest," Edward urged him. "You have already communicated your message most clearly."

The earl weakly motioned for his son to draw nearer to him, his face imploring. "You will do as I've told you, then? You will take the necessary steps to set things right?"

"I will give your words all due consideration," replied Edward carefully, unwilling to make promises he wasn't sure he could keep.

"Good," muttered the earl, and though his eyes were now shut, he turned his mouth up in a slight smile. Had he been his former self, Edward's vague words surely wouldn't have been enough to satisfy him, but in his deteriorated state, he seemed appeased.

"I will leave you now," said Edward in a voice close to a whisper. "I bid you a good night."

As he moved toward the door, he pictured himself bolting through it, running back down the stairs, fetching a horse from the stables, and riding swiftly away, not stopping until he was safely on board a ship bound for some faraway destination. But recognizing the impossibility of it, he instead walked slowly and closed the door behind him with a quiet click. All the while, he wondered how to even begin managing the blow fate had dealt him.

Chapter 2

It was fortunate that Edward hadn't run from his father's room in all haste, for in the hallway, outside the door, stood the shadowy figure of his sister.

"Catherine," he exclaimed, jumping back a step, "what on earth are you doing here?"

"Do not be angry with me." She moved the candle she held to better illuminate her face, revealing her large and imploring eyes. "I wasn't listening at the door, I promise. I just found I could not rest without knowing of your meeting with Papa. Did he awaken? Were you able to speak with him?"

"Yes, we spoke," replied Edward, his mind working so hard to process all the information he had just learned that he was disinclined to disclose anything further.

"I'm so glad." Relief washed over her face. "I was hoping, of course, that seeing you might revive him a little, but I was unsure how it would transpire. In my encounters with him over the past week, he has often seemed so listless and even confused at times."

"On the contrary, tonight, he had moments when he was actually rather—animated."

"I'm so glad," repeated Catherine. She looked away from him and began to shuffle her feet, although she made no move to depart from the middle of the hallway.

After they both stood for a moment in awkward silence, Edward asked, "Was there something else you wished to say?" He immediately regretted the unintended sharpness of his tone, especially when it caused his sister to flinch. Her delicate face reminded him of a startled deer. "You may speak plainly with me," he assured her, careful this time to keep his voice gentle.

"It's only …" She hesitated for a moment longer before her words came pouring out. "It's only that Papa was so adamant that he speak with you. He said matters for us had taken a very bad turn but that your coming home would remedy the situation entirely if only he had the chance to explain things to you."

"Pray, do not distress yourself over this," he replied quickly. "As you said, Father has experienced moments of confusion lately and likely knew not of what he spoke." Hopefully, nothing in his expression or voice had betrayed his inner worry. For what good would it do to relay the details of his conversation with the earl to Catherine? There was no need to trouble her unnecessarily, especially when he had yet to fully make sense of the situation himself.

"You are certain all is well?" Her mouth twisted in a small smile, but it didn't hide the lingering doubt in her eyes.

"Quite well," he lied, forcing himself to smile reassuringly at her in return. Before she could question him any further, he added, "But I'm rather fatigued after my long journey and must retire now."

"Of course," she answered at once. "Forgive me for taking up so much of your time."

They both started walking down the corridor in silence, but as Edward turned the corner toward his old bedroom, she called out to him once more. "Edward?"

He looked back at her, and she smiled at him anew, appearing more certain this time. "Good night. I'm very glad you're home."

"Good night, Catherine," he replied, his tone adopting a hint of its former brusqueness. "Sleep well." With that, he hurried away, anxious to forget the look of hopeful innocence on his sister's face.

Upon reaching his bedroom, he let his body sag against the closed door as he took in the familiar mahogany furnishings, illuminated by a newly laid fire. At least the brandy he had requested was sitting on the bedside table. He hastily poured himself a glass and set to unfastening his cravat and waistcoat and pulling off his Hessians. No longer so constrained by clothing, he flopped onto his old bed with a sigh, although the long-awaited repose brought little comfort.

His journey home to Highfield Park had been a hasty one, and he no longer remembered how many hours he had been awake; he only knew that he desperately needed sleep. Yet, try as he might to rest, he couldn't stop thoughts of how to remedy this whole awful situation from turning over and over in his mind. He couldn't marry Miss Wright. He wouldn't. Surely there was another way he could secure a dowry for Catherine and leave this mess behind him. Wasn't there?

Two weeks later, the matter still plagued him. The fact that he was now the Earl of Ashton and all debts accrued by the former earl were exclusively his only exacerbated the problem.

From the evening of his arrival home, his father had lived only another three days and never regained his ability to speak more than a few words at a time. It was as though the old earl had saved all his strength for that one conversation, and having seen it through to his satisfaction, had no more strength left to give.

After the funeral, a somber affair at which Edward had exchanged stiff conversation with old acquaintances, he had journeyed at once to London for meetings with his solicitor and bank. Unfortunately, they had revealed the situation to be precisely as dire as his father indicated. Disheartened, he returned to Kent to better assess the situation at Highfield Park and had been pleased to see that, aside from a few missing decorations and furniture pieces, the house itself looked in relatively good repair. However, as he had ridden about the rest of the estate, signs of trouble presented themselves: a crumbling fence here, a cottage in grave need of a new roof there, a field pooled with rainwater.

Much to his annoyance during his tour, the estate's land agent, a Mr. Robert Hunt, had been nowhere to be found. Edward had therefore left a note at the man's dwelling, requesting that he call at Highfield Park immediately. However, it was now four o'clock of the following day, and there was still no sign of him, leaving Edward shut up in his study, growing increasingly irate. To pass the time while waiting, he had pulled out the estate's account books, and the more he perused them, the more his body tensed.

Whenever Hunt decided to show up, he would have much to answer for.

A row of particularly concerning figures jumped out at him, and Edward threw aside the rent roll he had been studying and lowered his head to the cool walnut surface of his desk. He wondered momentarily how much the desk would fetch at auction but quickly cast the idea aside. He could sell every stick of furniture in the house, and still, it wouldn't be enough to even make a dent in what he owed.

A sudden shuffling noise caused him to look up and, at long last, in strode his very disheveled-looking land agent.

"Ah, Mr. Hunt," he said bitingly, "so kind of you to spare me a moment of your valuable time."

The man stumbled forward and gave a clumsy bow. "Terribly sorry to have kept you waiting, my lord. Pressing estate business prevented me from coming until now."

"Indeed." Edward appraised him with a frosty stare. Hunt must have been hired as land agent by the former earl at some point during the last six years, for aside from a brief meeting at his father's funeral, Edward didn't know him. However, now that Hunt stood close at the other side of the desk, the unmistakable scent of liquor radiated off him, and Edward took an immediate and immense dislike to the man.

"Well then, Mr. Hunt," he said, "since you are so devoted to your position and make matters of the estate your topmost priority, perhaps you can explain this." He picked up the rent roll once more and shoved it in the land agent's direction. "Why are so many tenants behind on their rents? Furthermore, why are there so many vacancies? For it was clear to me as I rode about the estate that a number of the cottages sat empty."

"We have not been favored with good yields over the past several years," Hunt answered, his words slightly slurred. "During such times, the promise of factory jobs enticed many former tenants to London, and those who remained have had trouble making payments. It's been a difficult time, to be sure, but all we need is a stretch of agreeable weather, and you'll soon see profits coming in as they used to."

"On the contrary," said Edward, his voice venomous, "I believe it will take far more than fair weather to remedy the situation. For if that was the only cause of trouble, then what is the meaning of this?" This time he tossed several more account books in Hunt's direction and began tearing through pages. "I noticed many things about the estate that looked in want of repair, but I see no records of recent repairs in any of these books. Why, some of these pages are hardly legible!"

Hunt winced at the sound of Edward's raised voice. Judging by the way he smelled, he no doubt had a splitting headache. "I assure you, my lord, I have everything under control," he muttered.

"Do you?" Edward snarled in return. "For it appears as though your duty to manage the estate comes second to your fondness for passing hours in the alehouse."

"My lord," Hunt said, "I would never—"

At that unlucky moment, a loud hiccup escaped him, amplifying the sour stench that surrounded him. Edward's stony expression caused the protest to die on his lips.

"My father never took much interest in estate business," Edward said, fighting to keep his voice calm and even. "He may have never opened an account book in his life. Therefore, he was willing to tolerate such incompetence. I, on the other hand, am not." He reached for the bell on his desk to give it a shake and was relieved to see Higgins, who must have been lurking nearby, step into the room within seconds. "I appreciate your time, Mr. Hunt. Regretfully, I must inform you that your services are no longer required here, and I will ask you to leave the estate immediately. Higgins, please see Mr. Hunt out."

"Yes, my lord," answered Higgins as he stepped forward, eying the unfortunate Mr. Hunt with distaste.

"Lord Ashton!" cried Hunt. "Surely you cannot be serious."

Edward leaped from his chair and turned toward the window, unwilling to look at the offensive man any longer. "Quite serious. You may go now. I bid you good day."

Hunt's clumsy footsteps thumped against the floor as he made his retreat, accompanied by the sound of Higgins's steady gait. Edward had just let his shoulders slump when Hunt's wavery voice called out to him from the hallway. "Very well, my lord. However, you may be dismayed to learn that the funds to repair a crumbling estate do not fall from the sky."

"Get out!" yelled Edward without turning around, although he immediately regretted raising his voice in such a manner. He had always found his father's bouts of ill-temper distasteful and had therefore made an effort throughout his life not to shout and rave in anger. However, he wanted nothing more at this moment than to scream so loudly the whole county would hear. Why did it appear as though the world was conspiring against him? Moreover, why did life in England seem to bring him nothing but misfortune?

As he had many times over the past two weeks, Edward imagined himself swiftly departing the country, leaving all his troubles behind as if they were nothing more than a terrible nightmare. After all, he had done so once before. However, at that time, he had merely been Viscount Camden, a man with a courtesy title and few responsibilities. Now, he was the Earl of Ashton and owner of the estate. While that in itself did not give him any undeniable sense of obligation, he kept coming back to the one responsibility he did not feel he could rightly shirk: his sister.

During his time on the Continent, in those rare moments when he had spared a thought for Catherine, it had been easy to picture her growing up to resemble their mother—a golden-haired beauty so vain and selfish that her loveliness extended no deeper than the surface. However, from the brief time he had been reacquainted with her, he could see that nothing was farther from the truth. He thought of how devotedly she had sat at their father's bedside in his final days, thinking nothing of how little attention he had paid her when his health still permitted him his usual entertainments. He also thought, more regretfully, of how enthusiastically his sister had welcomed him home, holding no grudge or ill will for the years he had neglected her. Indeed, Catherine had proven herself to be the picture of kindness and graciousness.

He supposed his low opinion had been quite unfair. After all, their mother had only lived long enough after Catherine's birth to express her disappointment at not bearing another son and therefore had no hand in her daughter's upbringing. Likewise, the former earl's inattention to her had perhaps been a blessing in disguise, for she had in no way been influenced by his selfishness and overindulgence. Through some fortunate happenstance, her solitary upbringing at Highfield Park, during which she had been surrounded almost exclusively by nursemaids and other servants, had turned her into a young lady opposite from her parents in every way.

He also supposed he should be quite glad of this fact, and he was, mostly. However, he couldn't help but think how much easier it would be to leave her behind without a care were she the shallow, conniving creature their mother had been. Instead, Catherine's gentleness made him worry for her. He could see how unprepared she was to be thrown into the unforgiving world of the ton, and being left with no funds or close relations would make her especially vulnerable.

He frowned as he remembered her tear-stained face as he had told her, just after their father's funeral, that she was to return with Lord and Lady Bathurst to London and accompany them to their estate in Devonshire. Ignoring Catherine's pleas to let her stay at home and not send her back to the company of mere acquaintances had made him feel like the worst kind of fiend. But what else could he have done? Though she didn't yet realize, there was very little left for her at Highfield Park. Unless he took drastic action, the house would soon sit empty while he either fled the country or stayed and faced a life of penury.

He stared out his study window, taking in the brilliant greenness of the perfectly manicured lawn and the sparkling blue of the lake that glimmered underneath the rays of the afternoon sun. In the distance, he could just make out the forms of sheep as they grazed near a copse of oak trees. The scene was picture perfect, giving no indication of anything amiss, yet if he could only see a ways farther toward the tenant farms, the signs of trouble would undoubtedly still be there.

Between his years spent away at school, in London, and on the Continent, Edward had passed relatively little time at Highfield Park, but he felt sure the estate had once been profitable. Certainly, his family had always lived as though money were not of the slightest concern. Likewise, while the land agent's negligence and his father's indifference had sent things into a downward spiral of late, with proper management, surely the estate could thrive again.

However, the odious Mr. Hunt's words still rang through his mind: *You may be dismayed to learn that the funds to repair a crumbling estate do not fall from the sky.* Therein lay the heart of the matter—if he were to have a hope of repairing the damage that had been done and of saving his sister from poverty and shame, he would need a viable way of getting the funds to do so.

He felt as if he were hovering on the edge of a precipice, coming dangerously close to falling off entirely. Yet, he had never truly forgotten his final conversation with his father and the solution the former earl had devised. There was a helping hand reaching out for him if only he would consent to take it. And as loath as he was to take it, what other options remained to him?

He spun away from the window and rushed from his study before he could think on the matter anymore. As he reached the entrance hall, he came upon Higgins standing near the doorway with a satisfied smirk on his face.

"Mr. Hunt has been escorted from the property, my lord. He should trouble you no more."

"I'm glad to hear it," replied Edward, although his current state of mind couldn't really be described as joyful. "I suppose I shall have to advertise for a new land agent directly." He mentally added that task to the long list of things requiring his attention. "First, though, I am going out."

"Very good, my lord." Higgins offered him a small bow. "Will you still be dining at home this evening?"

"Yes, I believe so. I shan't be long." Edward took in a deep breath, then blew it out heavily. He had come to a decision, and though every inch of him was filled with trepidation, he couldn't afford to allow himself to be dissuaded. "I am just going to pay a quick call. At Hinshaw House."

Chapter 3

Eliza Wright knew she had been banished to Lancashire during the Season as punishment. Nevertheless, as she lay sprawled out in the grass, delighting in the warmth of the late July sunshine that hit her face, there was truly no place on earth she would have rather been. Anticipating the heat of the day, she had paid her calls early that morning, dropping off a calamint decoction for young Peter Wilson's cough and an alkanet ointment for Mrs. Smith's scalded hand. Now, there was nothing pressing left for her to do. And while she rarely headed outdoors without her pencil and notebook in hand, in case she happened upon some plant or flower worth remarking, today she had brought only a novel to occupy her.

She opened the cover of her book and allowed herself to become absorbed in its pages, only vaguely aware of the blackbirds' song above her. But before long, a low distant rumble broke her concentration, and she pushed herself into a sitting position so she could better see where the noise was coming from. She shielded her eyes from the sun and could just make out a coach hurrying down the road toward her current residence of Riverton Hall.

What on earth was a coach doing here? With her uncle, aunt, and cousin still in London, visitors had been a scarce occurrence of late. She stared a moment longer as the coach drew closer, and its glistening green paint and red-spoked wheels came clearer into view. Surely it couldn't be …

"Papa," she exclaimed aloud. She tilted her head at the unexpected sight, as meanwhile, a pit formed in her stomach. What possible cause could he have to visit? Although business frequently brought him north to Liverpool, it was rare for him to venture on to Riverton Hall, especially because he and her uncle Havelock bore no great affection for one another. Of course, the only Havelock presently at home was her mother's eldest sibling, Augusta, but still, that didn't seem like enticement enough for her father to pay a purely social call. No, there had to be a reason for which he wished to see her.

Eliza jumped to her feet and hastily brushed bits of stray grass off her skirts. "Blast," she muttered at the sight of a spot where dirt had stained the white muslin. Augusta would have her head for that after she finished chastising her for being in the sun without a bonnet. Of more pressing concern, though, was getting back to the house in time to greet her father. Thomas Wright wasn't known for his patience and wouldn't take kindly to being kept waiting.

Even in her haste, a momentary pang of sadness hit her, as it always did, as she crossed this familiar stretch of field. She wasn't far from the dower house, the home she and her mother had shared for many years. This spot drew memories of previous summers when they had picnicked together. But though the temptation arose to sit in the grass and weep, she quickly pushed the memory aside, forcing herself to focus only on running as quickly as she could.

When she reached the front of the main house, flushed and breathless, no one was in sight except for the groom who had come to attend to the horses. She hadn't been quite quick enough, then, to arrive ahead of her father. Still, she took one final moment to straighten her wind-blown hair and smooth her skirts before entering through the front door.

She sucked in her breath, unsure of what sort of temper she might find her father in. However, when she set eyes on him, still standing in the entrance hall, he bestowed upon her a broad smile.

"Eliza, my dear. Out enjoying the day, were you?"

"Yes, Papa," she said, curtseying prettily while hoping he didn't notice the dirt stain on her skirts. Fortunately, Augusta was nowhere to be seen. "I'm sorry I wasn't here upon your arrival. I was unaware of your intention to visit."

"Think nothing of it," her father replied, clasping her hand in a gesture of affection. "Only, pray, take me to the drawing room, and call for some refreshments."

"Of course." Eliza hastily murmured instructions to a nearby housemaid and ushered her father down the corridor and into the drawing room. On Augusta's insistence, the curtains were drawn tightly shut each afternoon to protect her complexion from the bright summer sun, making the room unbearably dark and stuffy. However, if her father took any notice, he made no mention of it as he settled himself into an armchair.

His contentment was a positive sign, but still, she couldn't shake the prickly sensation that left her on edge. Although she and her father had spent little time in each other's company overall, she knew him well enough to realize that he did not visit for the mere enjoyment of it. Likewise, his extreme displeasure with her when they had last seen each other three months prior made her wonder at the affability he now showed.

"Did business matters bring you north?" she asked, determined to ascertain the motivation behind his visit. "I seem to recall from your last letter that you planned to settle at your new home in Kent for the remainder of the year. I trust all is to your liking there?"

Her father smiled at her anew, flashing his gleaming, wolfish teeth. "Why, I came to see you, my dear. And since you're so full of inquiries, yes, I like Kent very much. I've made a brief departure from Hinshaw House to bring you excellent news."

Eliza peered at him, trying not to let her bewilderment show. Her father, while charming when he wanted to be, usually kept himself highly composed. His current animation, almost an overexcitement, was therefore puzzling.

"You are to return to Kent with me," he announced. "You've spent quite enough time shut away here."

"Very well, if you wish it," she said carefully. Why did this news bring him such exhilaration?

"Capital," he remarked, looking exceedingly pleased. "We'll depart on the morrow. I'm most anxious for you to meet our neighbor, the new Earl of Ashton."

He said the name with a flourish, clearly expecting her to be impressed. However, her head spun far too much to give him his desired reaction. "But why—" she began, but before she could say any more, the maid shuffled in with the tea tray.

"At last," her father interrupted, reaching for a biscuit as soon as the tray was set before them. "I'm positively famished and parched. Eliza, will you pour?"

She lifted the teapot and did her best to keep her hand steady as she poured the steaming liquid into two cups. Her mind still raced as she tried to discern the meaning of the situation. "Sugar?" she asked, although the word came out as little more than a squeak.

"No, it's fine as it is." He took a long swallow and settled back in his chair, eyeing her approvingly.

Eliza sipped from her own cup, not because she truly wanted tea, but because she couldn't manage sitting in quiet stillness now that her father had suddenly stopped talking and left her in suspense. She set down her cup before immediately picking it up and drinking again until she could stand it no more. "Do go on," she urged.

Her father gave a low chuckle. "I thought mention of an earl might interest you. And even better, he very much wishes to meet you, too."

"Me?" She couldn't believe her ears. "Why would he wish to meet me?"

"Because, my dear," he answered, delight radiating through the words, "I have good reason to believe he wants to make you his wife."

Eliza froze in her seat, although she felt the slight movement of her mouth dropping open. Her father couldn't have shocked her more if, while sitting before her, he suddenly sprouted a second head. She remained speechless for a minute before abruptly blurting out, "What in the world can you mean?" She was being impolite, but she was also far beyond caring. "Why would an earl, whom I've never met, never even heard of for that matter, wish to marry me? Does he not realize I'm a merchant's daughter who is shrouded in scandal?"

Her father's pale eyes glinted with craftiness. "This particular earl is in a situation where an appropriate dowry would entice him to forgive any sin."

Her heart sank in her chest. "You mean to sell me to the earl, then?"

"How dramatic you are!" her father scoffed. "You should be on your knees, thanking me for concocting such an arrangement. For I believe the arrangement will suit you both very well."

"I don't understand." She could barely choke out the words. "How did all this come about?"

"I became well acquainted with the former earl, the current Ashton's father, in London earlier this year. He was exceedingly fond of spending his days at Crawford's, the gaming hell where I, too, enjoy passing time. Unfortunately, luck never appeared to be on his side, which especially distressed him as his health started to fail. He was quite concerned about what would become of his son. It seems the boy rushed off to the Continent in grief after the death of his first wife. The old earl was troubled to think of what would await him when he returned to England to assume the earldom. Luckily for him, he had a friend such as I, someone willing and able to help him devise a solution to this most grievous of problems."

Eliza couldn't suppress her gasp. "Do you mean to say you've spent your leisure time bankrupting a dying earl?"

"I've done nothing of the sort!" cried her father, suddenly indignant. "It was not I who made wagers with him. I've never been a heavy gambler, you know. I have no desire to leave the making or losing of my fortune to chance. That I choose to frequent establishments that offer such entertainments, for the purposes of forming new associations, perhaps lending a helping hand with the understanding that I'll then be owed in return ... Well, that's another matter entirely."

Eliza could barely reach for her teacup without shaking as another dreadful realization dawned on her. "Your sudden desire to rusticate in Kent," she said, taking a large mouthful of tea to help ease the unbearable dryness in her throat. "I presume this was the cause?"

Her father gave her a bitter smirk. "As I said, my dear, I leave very little to chance. If there's one thing I've learned, it's that success does not come by simply sitting back and wishing for it."

"And the current earl is aware of, and content with, this whole arrangement?" she asked in a whisper.

Her father nodded. "Now that he has returned to Kent, he did me the honor of paying a call. And as I said, he is most anxious to meet you."

She stared at him for a moment longer before crossing her arms and shaking her head. "No. I will not marry him."

She probably looked and sounded like a petulant child, but it was of no matter to her at present.

"Do my ears deceive me?" Her father's tone turned vicious. "Perhaps you do not fully appreciate the situation. In case you have forgotten the mess of things you made in London, let me remind you that you are currently shunned by polite society. Were you to become a countess, and a very wealthy one, thanks to the dowry you would bring to the marriage, I'm sure the ton could find a way to forgive you. In fact, they would practically beat down your door for the chance to become acquainted with you."

"Indeed," remarked Eliza, her voice turning cold. "Am I to understand, then, that in making this arrangement, you thought only of my success and happiness?"

"Impudent chit!" her father snapped. "Of course I think of your success, and in turn, I consider my own. You couldn't possibly comprehend such a thing. You have spent your entire life in company with the Havelocks, and as such, you are considered a lady of good breeding. When people regard you, they are willing to overlook what they view as an unfortunate mistake on your mother's part. I, on the other hand, could outrank all the ton in wealth and prosperity, yet still be regarded as nothing more than a Liverpool butcher's son. If, however, I become the father of a countess, the grandfather to the future Earl of Ashton, I feel that will change."

"Your plan is very clever indeed," said Eliza sullenly. "Only, I have no interest in elevating myself to the top of the ton, just as I have no desire to marry."

Her father's expression darkened, his eyes flaring, and she braced herself for his imminent shouting. However, the low voice he used instead, steely and menacing, was far worse. "It's all very well for you to say such things, but what do you imagine you will do instead? Spend the rest of your life in the country, traipsing about the fields and concocting your little tonics? Let me make something very plain. You will not do so at my expense. If you refuse me in this, I will have no further association with you."

She could only stare at her father as if he'd slapped her. Taking advantage of her stunned silence, he continued. "I suppose the Havelocks might consent to keep taking you in, even without the allowance I provide you. However, they have certainly proven themselves to be no great friends of yours. And even if they should be so kind, where would that leave you in the end? Why, you would be fit for nothing more than to take Augusta's place as the crotchety old spinster of Riverton Hall!"

Eliza turned her eyes to the floor, unwilling to let her father see how much he had wounded her. She had meant her words most adamantly—she did not wish to wed. Maybe, if she truly had to, she could endure a marriage where only a vague camaraderie existed between her and her husband, as seemed to be the case with Uncle James and Aunt Frances. However, she had seen how her parents' marriage, and subsequent estrangement, had brought her mother nothing but sorrow. How could she risk having such a fate befall her as well?

However, she now realized what a fool she'd been. Every so often, of course, doubts about the future had wiggled their way into her thoughts, but she had promptly cast them aside, opting instead for mindless naivety. And in that naivety, she *had* pictured herself inhabiting the same countryside where she and her mother had always lived, continuing with her study of herbs, and distributing her medicines to the village residents she had come to know and care for. As for the details of how that arrangement would work, given her mother's death, her father's ambition, and her family's displeasure with her, she had done her best to put that out of her head altogether.

Her father was right, though. If she remained unwed and received no allowance from him, she would spend the rest of her life at the Havelocks' mercy, which would be a hard fate indeed. Perhaps she would become an unwanted companion to any future children of her cousin Louisa, just as her aunt Augusta had become a companion to her. She would still have her gardens, her fields, and her neighbors, but would that alone be enough to sustain her for a lifetime? For she was forced to face another terrible realization. Her mother, the one source of unconditional love in her life, was dead and gone, never to return. And if she remained at Riverton Hall, though surrounded by her mother's kin, she would never experience that love again.

"Oh, come now," said her father, breaking her dismal train of thought. "Don't be so morose. Surely you can see reason here. This union with Ashton would be very much to your benefit. You would become a countess, Eliza. A countess! And while you say you care nothing for society, think of what other advantages the position might hold for you. Your *dear* cousin Louisa wouldn't dare cross you again." He spat out the name as if it were poison. "And as for a man like Walker, why, he wouldn't be fit to wipe mud from your shoe."

Eliza sank into her chair as a weighty sense of fatigue washed over her. The position would have surely earned her aunt Augusta's reproach. She wanted nothing more than to flee to her bedroom. However, her father still gazed at her eagerly, reminding her that she needed to see this conversation through to its end.

"Is Lord Ashton aware of what transpired at the Havelocks' ball?" she asked, forcing herself to adjust her posture and meet her father's eyes once more. "For it's very important to me, if we are to meet, that he knows the truth of the matter."

Her father pursed his lips. "Really, that ridiculous scandal warrants no further mention. But, as it worries you, you will be pleased to know that I discussed the absurdity of the matter with the former earl and assured him that it in no way reflects your true character. He was not troubled by it, and his son is in no position to be either. All you need do is meet him, say a few pretty words to him, and I'm sure he'll find no fault in you at all."

Eliza sighed, hating the feeling of defeat that had overtaken her. Yet it seemed her path forward had been decided, and at present, there was little else to do but accept it.

"I suppose," she said, "that you will have to excuse me now, for I must prepare for the journey to Kent."

"I knew you would come to your senses." Having gotten what he wanted, her father's voice became cheerful once more. "Now, make haste, for we'll leave tomorrow at first light. You must find Augusta and tell her the news as she will need to accompany us."

"Augusta? Are you sure her presence is necessary?"

"Quite sure," he was quick to reply, "for I will allow no suggestion of impropriety to come near you again, and no one could possibly accuse you of anything untoward with that old dragon standing over your shoulder at every turn. She can return here to Riverton as soon as you're wed if that provides any extra incentive for you."

"Indeed," mumbled Eliza as the gloom surrounding her intensified. "But must we really leave in such a hurry? Aunt Augusta will do no end of complaining at the sudden upset."

Her father's mouth turned upward in a sly grin. "That we must, for Lord Ashton has accepted an invitation to dine with us on Saturday."

"You cannot mean this Saturday," she exclaimed. "That's only six days away."

"All the more reason to make haste."

She jumped from her seat, and with that, her father pulled himself upward as well. He stretched his shoulders and peered around the sultry, darkened room as if noticing his surroundings for the first time. "Lord, Eliza," he muttered, "this house is like a crypt and hotter than Hades besides. Why you would even consider staying here over what I've offered you, I surely do not know."

Eliza didn't even trouble herself to answer as she walked swiftly across the room. However, when she reached the doorway, she spun around to face him one more time and let her words come out in a tumble. "I'm going to my room to see that my things are packed and will ensure Aunt Augusta does the same. The housekeeper, Mrs. Fletcher, will see you to a guest room. I doubt Uncle George would be pleased to welcome you to his home, but because he isn't here, I suppose we shan't let that bother us. Dinner will be served at seven."

She then hurried away and ran up the stairs as quickly as she could without making enough noise to disturb Augusta, who was likely still in the midst of her afternoon repose. She didn't stop until she was in the safety of her bedroom, the closed door providing a temporary barrier against intrusions from the outside world.

She would soon do as she had said and summon her maid to begin packing and rouse Augusta to tell her what was transpiring. First, though, she needed to take a minute, just one quiet moment alone, to see if she could stop her uncontrollable trembling.

Chapter 4

Hinshaw House was no match for Highfield Park in either size or opulence. But as Edward stood within its sunlit entrance hall early on a Saturday evening, dressed in his stiff black evening coat and crisp black cravat, he felt it to be much more intimidating. The butler, Price, had greeted him most cordially and was now offering to escort him to the drawing room. Despite the outward pleasantness of the scene, Edward found himself in utter disbelief that he had dared come at all.

He supposed he was very foolish for having such apprehension. After all, his previous visit here, during which he had introduced himself to Thomas Wright, had gone as well as could be expected, with Wright showing nothing but affability and good humor. The fact that Edward would never trust the man's character as his father had done was of little consequence, for what he could trust, after their brief meeting, was that Wright was still very much interested in the arrangement made with the former earl. However, Miss Wright had surprisingly still been in Lancashire during his initial call, and knowing that she was now inside the house, awaiting their first meeting, left Edward tangled up in knots.

He wordlessly followed Price down the corridor as thoughts of Miss Wright filled his head. Would she be cunning? Coquettish? Brash? Vapid? Perhaps it was unfair of him to judge her so harshly, but since all he knew of her was her involvement in scandal and her subsequent willingness to wed a stranger for a title, it was difficult to form a favorable opinion. In fact, by the time he neared the drawing room, he had decided he wouldn't like her at all.

There was no time to dwell on this, though, for the butler announced his name, and suddenly, he found himself standing in the drawing room with Thomas Wright approaching him enthusiastically.

"Good evening, Lord Ashton," Wright greeted with a bow. "Delighted to see you again." He continued speaking, asking after Edward's health or something to that effect, but while Edward must have managed an acceptable reply, his attention had turned to the two figures rising from the settee at the opposite side of the room. Wright turned his head, following Edward's gaze with a smirk. "Ah, yes. Please, allow me to make introductions."

The two figures approached them, giving Edward his first unobstructed view of Wright's infamous daughter. Wright began by gesturing to the thin, dour-looking older woman who now stood at his side. "My sister-in-law, Miss Augusta Havelock." He then smiled broadly and pointed at the young woman trailing just behind Miss Havelock. "And allow me to introduce my daughter, Elizabeth."

So, this was Miss Wright. As she stepped up and curtseyed before him, all he could think was how different she was from what he'd expected. For some reason, he'd been picturing a traditional English beauty, pale-haired and pale-eyed, just like—No, he didn't even want to let himself remember the other lady's name.

However, Miss Wright had dark auburn hair, and the way her large green eyes tilted slightly at the corners almost reminded him of a cat. The light green silk of her dress complemented her eyes perfectly, and he couldn't help but notice the way the fabric hugged her curves to perfection. Perhaps she wouldn't be considered a traditional beauty, but she was striking—alluring.

He tried his best to ignore that fact and gave her and her aunt a stiff bow, hoping the direction of his thoughts didn't show in his expression.

"It's a pleasure to make your acquaintance, Lord Ashton," Miss Wright said, her voice soft and polite.

"Likewise," he replied blandly, wanting nothing more than to shake off this odd attraction to her. She adjusted her position slightly so that she now stood in the direct path of a window, and the rays of evening sun shining through it created highlights in her hair that blazed like fiery copper. He hated that he had noticed.

"Please excuse me a moment," Wright said, snapping him out of his trance. Bloody hell, had he been staring? Wright sauntered to the doorway. "I must make a quick Inquiry regarding dinner."

Before departing, Wright gave the briefest glance to Augusta, who immediately said, "And you will forgive me, my lord, if I return to my seat in the corner. My legs tire easily. Eliza, you may remain here by the window and entertain our guest."

Mr. Wright and Miss Havelock were certainly not subtle in their intentions, but this didn't seem at all worrying to

Miss Wright, who smiled at Edward and said, "I hear you are newly returned to England, my lord."

"Yes," he answered, still too perturbed to give her more than a one-word answer.

She looked at him with just a hint of sadness. "Allow me to offer my sincerest condolences on the loss of your father."

"Thank you."

She must have sensed he did not wish to discuss the matter further, for she turned back to her initial topic of conversation. "I believe Papa said that before your return, you'd spent a great deal of time in Italy?"

"Florence," came his curt reply.

Still not dissuaded, she said, "I imagine it's very beautiful there, especially if one has an interest in architecture or art."

"Indeed." He was being unspeakably rude in his brevity, but the last thing he wanted was for her to begin asking questions that pried into his past.

Clearly, his behavior affected her, for the serene expression on her face turned slightly dejected as if she were afraid she had somehow displeased him. Feeling an obligation to redeem himself at least a little, he asked, "Have you traveled yourself, Miss Wright?"

"Sadly, I have not." She brightened once more upon his effort to converse with her. "Papa has often traveled to India over the years, but I never had the opportunity to accompany him. Instead, my mother and I always stayed at our home in Lancashire. I believe I'd enjoy traveling someday, though, especially now that there's no longer such turmoil on the Continent."

He owed her a reply, but once again, his fear that this would then encourage her to ask about more of his own experiences abroad prevented him from doing so. Fortunately, they only stood together in silence for a moment before Wright re-entered the room, followed directly by Price, who announced that dinner was ready.

Although he was not particularly hungry, Edward eagerly made his way to the dining room and took his seat at the table, glad to bring the stilted conversation in the drawing room to an end. Of course, the reprieve was short-lived, for Miss Wright had unsurprisingly been seated at his side for dinner. Furthermore, while both Mr. Wright and Miss Havelock exchanged pleasantries with him as they all started in on bowls of turtle soup, they soon became engaged in conversation with each other, leaving him and Miss Wright to converse once more.

He took his time helping himself to the numerous dishes before him and seeing that Miss Wright had a selection of everything she desired. With that task complete, he was then left to come up with another way to fill the silence.

"I understand you are newly arrived to Hinshaw House, Miss Wright," he said, turning to her in between bites of roasted beef. "What are your initial impressions of Kent?"

"Oh, I like it very much." Her voice sounded so glad that he couldn't doubt her sincerity. "Hinshaw House has a wonderful cherry orchard, and the herb garden is so—"

Miss Havelock gave her a barely perceptible scowl, and Eliza abruptly stopped mid-sentence, continuing with only, "Yes, I like it very much."

"I'm pleased to hear it," he muttered, directing his attention back to his plate.

"Lord Ashton," said Miss Havelock, turning to him with what was likely supposed to be a smile, but on her pinched face looked more like a grimace, "are you pleased to be back in England?"

Edward wondered how he could possibly answer that question with honesty. Tell them that he had returned only out of a sense of obligation, one that he now regretted? Tell them that every day he imagined how satisfying it would be to simply leave once more? Since he couldn't possibly state anything close to the truth, he returned to giving a one-word answer. "Yes."

Miss Wright, who was already well aware of his aversion to the subject, set her mouth in a straight line. Miss Havelock, on the other hand, had seemingly not picked up on his discomfort, for she said, "Travel is all well and good, I suppose, but I've always said there is no place better to be than standing on English soil. I'm partial to Lancashire, having lived there all my life, but I hear your home at Highfield Park is one of the finest in the country."

He suppressed a sigh. Highfield Park, extensively renovated and expanded within the last century to become a sprawling neoclassical behemoth, *was* perhaps among the best houses to all outward appearances. However, it was impossible for him to forget the irresponsible Mr. Hunt and the crumbling farms that made up the estate. He wondered if Mr. Wright was aware of that aspect of his troubles. Clearly, Miss Havelock was not, and he certainly had no intention of discussing the subject over dinner. Therefore, he plastered what he hoped was a pleasant expression on his face and simply said, "Thank you, Miss Havelock."

He took the opportunity during the next moment of silence to peer at these near-strangers sitting around him: Augusta Havelock, who even in her attempts at being cordial had an air of unpleasantness; Thomas Wright, whose respectable, appealing exterior seemed to mask a far more dangerous interior; and Eliza Wright, the woman he had already decided not to like but whose striking features still caught him off guard. He wondered what it would be like to have these people as his kin and associate with them for the rest of his life.

Not wanting to ponder the matter any further, he changed the subject with the first thing that came into his head. "I understand you made your debut this year, Miss Wright. Did you enjoy all the entertainments London had to offer?"

He realized immediately that, given what he knew of how Miss Wright's first Season had ended, his question was in poor taste. But while Miss Havelock's face darkened, Miss Wright looked him squarely in the eye and said, "London is very thrilling, to be sure. I must confess, though, that I far prefer life in the country."

"Oh, come now," Thomas Wright interjected. He turned his attention toward Edward, smiling placatingly.

"Eliza enjoys traipsing about in her gardens, but I assure you, she is just as suited to spending time at any of London's finest events and establishments. Is that not correct, Eliza?"

"Quite," she replied, although any hint of enthusiasm was gone from her voice.

The four of them spent the remainder of the meal exchanging mindless comments, and while Edward had initially been eager to escape from the drawing room and start dinner, he was even more relieved when, their dessert plates empty, Miss Havelock said, "Eliza, shall we retire to the drawing room for coffee?"

Miss Wright leaped to her feet, nearly tipping her chair in her haste. She threw out her hand to steady it, her cheeks flushing scarlet. Could she possibly share his discomfort with the whole situation? She was certainly not behaving like a lady intent on ensnaring an earl.

His eyes followed her as she exited the room, her hair glowing beneath the candlelight and her green skirts swishing behind her. Once again, he reminded himself that he did not care for her at all.

The ladies gone, Wright approached him with a bottle of port. Edward gratefully accepted a glass, settling back in his chair and letting the rich, sweet taste distract him from all else.

Wright reclined in his chair as well, appearing relaxed and contented. After a moment of companionable silence, he fixed his gaze upon Edward. "I hope you have enjoyed your evening thus far, my lord. Was everything to your liking?"

The ambiguity of the question gave him pause. Was Wright referring to the food or his daughter? Edward took a long drink of port before answering, "The meal was most enjoyable. In fact, I cannot recall an occasion where I've had food any better." The compliment was sincere, for it was obvious that no expense had been spared with the numerous dishes served, and Wright clearly employed a cook of great skill.

Wright appeared flattered, although a question still lingered in his eyes. Edward, however, was disinclined to say anything regarding the matter of Miss Wright. He didn't know what Wright expected. That the new Lord Ashton would be so taken with his daughter, or so desperate for funds, that he would request permission for her hand right then and there? Edward was indeed desperate, but he still had not reached the point of being that unbelievably rash.

After waiting another minute but receiving no further reply, Wright asked, "Shall we rejoin the ladies in the drawing room? I would normally linger here a little longer, but I'm sure you'll find my daughter's company far more pleasant than my own."

"By all means." Edward managed to deliver the words with a tone of indifference despite the odd feeling that had risen within him. As he moved to accompany Wright out of the dining room, his palms turned clammy. Perhaps this outlandish situation had finally driven him to the brink of madness.

The ladies had clearly not expected the gentlemen to enter so soon, for Miss Havelock seemed to be nodding off over her embroidery hoop, and Miss Wright was curled up on a settee with her nose in a book, her brow furrowed as she studied the pages before her.

Wright cleared his throat, causing Miss Havelock to snap her head up with a start and Miss Wright to throw her feet back on the floor and toss her book aside. Edward just caught the title before she shoved it under a pillow: *A Curious Herbal*.

"Good evening again," Wright said, strolling in and relaxing into an armchair near Miss Havelock. "As you can see, we were eager to rejoin you." He peered at Edward, where he still lingered near the doorway, before rapidly turning to his daughter. "My dear," he said, gesturing toward the pianoforte that stood in one corner, "won't you favor us with a song?"

The look on Miss Wright's face turned to one of sheer dread. "I couldn't possibly," she stammered. "I'm sure my skills are far inferior to those to which Lord Ashton is accustomed. I have not had nearly enough practice, and—"

"Really, Eliza," cut in her father, "you are far too modest. You have received only the finest instruction, and I'm certain your abilities are more than adequate. Please, do us the honor of sharing your talents with us." The words were pleasant enough, but a certain hardness had crept into his tone.

"Indeed, Miss Wright, I would be delighted to hear you play." Edward didn't want her feeling inferior on his account, but more importantly, entertainment that would temporarily excuse him from making conversation sounded just the thing.

His words were enough to make her rise from her seat and shuffle toward the pianoforte, but based on how miserable she looked while doing so, he wondered if he had been wrong in his encouragement.

Seeing that Miss Havelock and Mr. Wright were settled on the opposite end of the room, Edward opted to take a seat on the settee nearest the pianoforte and watched carefully as Miss Wright rifled through several songbooks before deciding on a suitable piece and placing it on the instrument before her. But as she did so, his mind suddenly wandered to another drawing room, to a London dinner party much larger than this one, on an evening seven years prior.

"Lady Julia, won't you give us the pleasure of a song?"

"Oh, yes, Lady Julia, your musical talents are beyond comparison."

"Very well, if you wish it," she said, flashing her demure smile. "I just learned a new ballad to perform for you all for this very occasion. But I shall require someone to assist me in turning the pages of my music."

"I would be pleased to be of service," offered Lord Palmer, puffing himself up to try to appear taller than he really was.

"No, allow me," insisted Sir George as he pushed himself to the front of the group of admirers who had gathered around her at the pianoforte.

"Hmm ..." she murmured, tilting her head coquettishly and drumming her fingers against her chin as she eyed the gentlemen before her. "I think ... I think Lord Camden may assist me."

Edward shoved the memory aside, instead forcing himself to focus on Miss Wright's performance as she began her song. He recognized the music right away as a Beethoven sonata, although it quickly became apparent that her interpretation of the piece had little in common with Mr. Beethoven's. Her fingers, although slender, stumbled heavily over the keys, resulting in music that was disjointed and scattered with wrong notes. Edward shifted uncomfortably and glanced across the room in Thomas Wright's direction. He was whispering angrily to Miss Havelock, and Edward could only imagine what he was saying.

He didn't know what it was about the whole scene that compelled him to do so, but he found himself walking toward the pianoforte and stopping directly behind Miss Wright's shoulder, his desire to sit alone and without conversation gone. Keeping his voice low, he asked, "Would you like me to turn the pages for you, Miss Wright?"

She didn't turn to glance at him, instead maintaining her concentration on the notes in front of her, but it almost looked like she was choking back a laugh. "Am I to take that to mean you are enjoying the performance so much you wish me to play on?"

"To be sure, Miss Wright," he said dryly, "I don't believe I have yet experienced nearly enough of your charms."

"I assure you, Lord Ashton, I have no illusions that my playing is charming, and you needn't imply anything to the contrary," she answered with piqued bluntness. She gave a half-hearted sigh. "Sadly, I cannot claim musicality as one of my talents."

"Do you not play another instrument? Or sing?" Those seemed suitable enough questions for polite drawing room conversation.

"Only when I wish to inflict misery on those around me."

"I suppose I should be grateful, then, that Beethoven's sonatas are not accompanied by lyrics." He smiled in spite of himself. He could think of very few people willing to openly admit anything was lacking in their accomplishments. Quite the opposite, actually. His mind again wandered to that long-ago evening as he had stood beside that other pianoforte turning pages and considering himself the most fortunate of men.

"You are perfection in all things, Lady Julia," he whispered close to her ear, just loud enough so she could hear him above the enthusiastic applause she had garnered at the completion of her song.

She turned her face upward to him, her expression coy, her eyelashes fluttering. "I do try, Lord Camden."

Edward once more tried to stifle the memory, irritated at its repeated intrusion on his thoughts. He had since learned that perfection was overrated, and furthermore, a falsehood. The fact that Miss Wright made no claim to it was somewhat … refreshing.

Still keeping her eyes on the music as her song plodded on, she said, "Tell me, does my papa appear very displeased?"

Edward once more looked in Wright's direction, where the man sat facing ahead in stony-faced silence, his lips pinched together in a tight line. "Either that or his coffee cup has been filled with vinegar."

At this, Miss Wright giggled openly, the sound bright and airy, filled with musicality even if she claimed her singing voice was not. "Oh, dear. I knew this was likely to upset him, and I suppose I should take care not to let him see me laugh. You see, Papa hired a music instructor for me earlier in the year, hoping I would improve upon my skills. However, I fear I have not been the most diligent of students."

"You do not care for music?" he inquired as he stepped forward to turn the page of her songbook.

"I like it well enough, when the performer has a shred of talent," she replied, starting in on what was fortunately the final page of notes in the sonata. "My preference, though, is for spending time outdoors."

"Do you enjoy gardening, then?" He remembered the title of the book she had been reading, along with her comments about preferring the country.

"Of a sort. I have a particular interest in medicinal plants."

"An unusual pastime amongst ladies of the ton," he remarked casually.

"Yes, well, I have never made the claim of being 'usual,'" she shot back, just as she brought her song to an ungraceful end.

He would have liked to question her further on her remark, but as the pianoforte now sat silent, there was nothing left but to politely applaud her performance. Across the room, Mr. Wright and Miss Havelock both appeared pained to be doing the same.

"Would you care for another song?" asked Miss Wright, keeping her voice low so that it was only within his hearing. She arched an eyebrow. "Perhaps with lyrics this time?"

"Alas, the hour grows late, and I think I must take my leave," he replied loudly enough to be heard across the room. At this, Wright's face darkened even further, his expression still making it look like he had been sucking lemons. It was clear he thought that his daughter's efforts to charm an earl had failed, and he didn't seem the type to take kindly to failure.

Edward suddenly found himself wondering if Wright was kind to his daughter. And in his attempts to orchestrate his daughter's aristocratic marriage, did he think at all of her happiness, or was his only consideration what he might serve to gain from the union? The thought of Miss Wright being ill-treated caused Edward's fists to involuntarily clench. Their meeting had led him to believe she was somewhat unconventional, but nothing in her behavior had suggested vulgarity or artifice. In fact, he found himself wishing they could speak further so that he could learn more of her and her situation. Perhaps they could even come to an understanding.

With that in mind, after paying his compliments to his host, Edward turned to her where she still sat at her pianoforte and asked, "May I call on you tomorrow, Miss Wright?"

A slight flush, barely detectable in the candlelight, crossed her cheeks. "Yes, of course."

Out of the corner of his eye, Edward noticed Mr. Wright's face brighten considerably. At the very least, he may have spared Miss Wright her father's wrath. "I'll come tomorrow at three o'clock then. I bid you all a good night," he said, offering a bow.

He rode home more quickly than he should have. He had barely walked out the door of Hinshaw House before wanting to slap himself over his sentimentality toward Miss Wright. He hardly knew her, yet he had allowed himself to make up fanciful stories regarding her good nature and innocence. In truth, she was embroiled in a scandal surrounding her lack of virtue, and scandal didn't arise from nowhere.

He forced himself to think of her no more, instead focusing on the steady stream of night air that hit his face as he galloped through the black countryside. Only when he was back at Highfield Park and safely seated in his library, a glass of brandy in hand, did he try to make sense of his jumbled thoughts.

That odd, uncomfortable sensation from earlier simmered within him once more, but it didn't need to. It still wasn't too late to forget the whole thing and return to Italy at once. Catherine might suffer a little on account of that decision, but would it really be so bad? Perhaps the Bathursts would allow her to remain with them out of respect for the friendship their families had once shared. Or if not them, then another family of the old earl's acquaintance. She was attractive enough that some besotted young gentlemen might forgive her lack of dowry.

Yet as hardened as Edward had become, he knew he could never do such a thing. Whatever his aversion to his title, his parents, and society in general, Catherine was blameless in it all. She deserved to live as more than just a poverty-stricken charity case. No, what he needed was a large sum of money, and quickly. Unfortunately, he had come up with no other way to obtain such a thing than through marriage.

However, while the last thing he ever dreamed he'd do was return to England and remarry, perhaps the whole situation didn't need to be entirely distasteful. Marriage to Miss Wright would be a business transaction, a mutually beneficial arrangement in which he received the funds he required, and she received a title that would allow her re-entry into society. Nothing more. After they put in a few appearances together to demonstrate the validity of their marriage, they need not even see each other again. He could go back to his rented rooms in Florence and resume his unencumbered life there. Once he saw to Catherine's dowry, he would allow Miss Wright to use the rest of her money as she saw fit, whether that involved the upkeep of Highfield Park or not. And whether Miss Wright chose to use her newfound status of countess to flaunt herself at the ton's most exclusive events or to simply stay in the country plucking herbs from her physic garden, it would be of no consequence to him.

He told himself this as he stumbled upstairs and into bed, brandy burning in his throat. But the thoughts that filled his head as he drifted into a fitful sleep were of Eliza Wright sitting at her pianoforte, accompanied by the sound of her musical laugh.

Chapter 5

It was after midnight, and though her new bed was soft and comfortable and her room pleasantly cool due to the breeze drifting through the open window, Eliza found that sleep eluded her. She wanted nothing more than to rest, so she could rise early in the morning and continue her exploration of the grounds surrounding Hinshaw House while still arriving back fresh-faced in the drawing room to greet Lord Ashton in the afternoon. However, try as she might, she couldn't stop the evening's events from running over and over in her mind.

On the one hand, dinner with Lord Ashton had been disastrous, as she had known it would be. She didn't know the first thing about entertaining an earl, and in forcing them together, her father had highly overestimated her abilities to flirt and charm. Furthermore, why would she want to? Perhaps, after all her years in Lancashire spent mainly in the company of her mother, she was inadept at flowery conversation. But Lord Ashton, with his curtness and seeming antipathy to the whole event, had been no better. From the time of their introduction, it had been clear that he took no enjoyment in her company, and while he was an earl and a guest to whom she had been obliged to show politeness, she had felt little warmth for him in return.

But then, during her humiliation at the pianoforte, when she had felt certain his disdain for her only grew, he had approached, and turned the pages of her music for her, and spoken to her without any hint of contempt. From the corner of her eye, she had even detected what looked like his smile, almost. Most importantly, he had asked to see her again, much to her father's satisfaction.

But what could she make of a continued association, and possibly even marriage, with a man capable of such brusqueness? The thought of spending the rest of her life with someone who treated her with cold detachment, knowing he tolerated her only for her wealth, was a miserable one indeed.

Yet as she lay tossing and turning, descending into melancholy, something new occurred to her. Her father had told her that Lord Ashton departed for the Continent upon the death of his first wife and that the cause of his return to England was the death of his father. Could it be that his behavior, his aloofness, stemmed from grief? And given time, could the pain of his grief fade, and his aloofness along with it? The idea made her soften to him a little.

And then, there was the matter of Lord Ashton's person: his tall, lean form, his dark golden hair, his piercing blue eyes that reminded her of the ocean on a cloudless day ... He was nothing like the stodgy, uninspiring earl she had pictured before their meeting. On the contrary, he was rather ... handsome.

"It's of no significance," she whispered to herself as she stared up at the ceiling, trying to shake his image from her head. But she couldn't stop imagining herself back on the bench of the pianoforte with Lord Ashton behind her, leaning toward her to turn the page of her songbook, filling her nose with the scent of port and sandalwood and the out-doors, sending just the tiniest wisp of his breath to the back of her neck …

These thoughts continued to fill her head as she sat in the drawing room the following afternoon until an unex-pected clatter drew her back to the present and set her pulse racing. She instantly sat up taller, anticipating Lord Ashton's approach. But instead of intensifying, the noise disappeared, and as she peered around the room, she realized it had only been the sound of Augusta's embroidery hoop dropping to the floor. Augusta, blissfully free of any feeling of anxiety, had fallen fast asleep in her chair.

"Aunt," she said softly. "Aunt, wake up."

Augusta's head remained turned down against her chest as she inhaled and exhaled.

The small clock on the mantle showed nearly three o'clock, and Eliza rose from her seat to throw open the room's curtains. Surely the sudden burst of light would rouse her aunt. However, Augusta, who was in the habit of retiring to her room at this time of day, still didn't stir. Eliza briefly debated if she should shake her aunt awake, but do-ing so would feel rather like prodding a bated badger. She instead returned to her seat at the escritoire by the window. She would deal with the task of waking Augusta when she was certain of Lord Ashton's approach.

She picked up her quill and turned her attention back to her notebook, where she had idly been scribbling away, although it was difficult to concentrate on the task. What a tangled ball of nerves she had become!

Once again, a slight noise caught her attention, and she chastised herself for being so anxious. This time, though, the sound did not disappear but instead got louder until there could be no doubt that the steady thumping signified footsteps.

"Augusta," she hissed, leaning across the escritoire to bring herself closer to her aunt, "you must wake up. Augusta!"

The footsteps sounded outside the door now, and she hastened to sit back gracefully in her chair. However, as she pushed herself off the escritoire, her arm brushed against the inkwell, and suddenly, the contents of the open jar were splattered across her lap.

"Damn and blast!" she cried, jumping up and then looking down in horror at the black splotches staining her sprigged muslin dress.

A small shuffling noise came from the doorway. Either that, or she was in the midst of an increasingly horrifying dream. Her body didn't want to move, and when she finally forced her gaze upward, she encountered the exact thing she most dreaded: Price standing there with Lord Ashton just behind him, both men staring at her with bemusement.

"Lord Ashton to see you, miss," announced Price before hastily backing away from the drawing room. Much to his credit, he had uttered the words blandly enough to conceal that anything was amiss.

As for Lord Ashton, he turned his face to the floor as he bowed to her, but that didn't conceal him biting his lip and making a quiet choking noise. It seemed she had shocked the earl so badly she had made him ill. Her cheeks flamed, and she was about to issue a profuse apology when the twist of Lord Ashton's mouth brought her to a new realization. He wasn't ill. Why, he was laughing at her!

Eliza sank into a curtsey with all the dignity she could muster. "Good afternoon, my lord." She looked him directly in the eye, daring him to say something of her current predicament.

On the contrary, Lord Ashton composed himself quickly. "Good afternoon, Miss Wright," he said without a trace of mirth. "I trust you are well today."

"Quite," she answered with a detachment in her voice that could match his own. She was torn between excusing herself so she could rush upstairs and change or simply ordering tea and carrying on as though nothing had happened when an unexpected snorting noise in the corner caught the attention of them both.

Augusta had slept through the whole incident, and her mouth now hung wide open, each breath she took coming out as a noisy snore.

Eliza hadn't thought her humiliation could get any worse, but apparently, she'd been wrong. She needed to escape this awful drawing room at once. "Lord Ashton, would you care to take a stroll about the gardens?" she asked without thinking.

He nodded, his expression perfectly neutral. "As you wish, Miss Wright."

Through some small mercy, she had left a shawl on the back of her chair, and she hastily used it to cover herself as she rushed out of the room with Lord Ashton at her heels. Perhaps she had been too forward in suggesting an unchaperoned meeting outdoors, but she would have sooner flung herself through an upstairs window than wake Augusta at this point.

Being outside in the sunshine, surrounded by fresh air that held the light scent of the roses lining the garden path, lifted her spirits considerably. After taking a few calming breaths, she turned to Lord Ashton and said, "The weather has been very fine since my arrival." It was an inane topic of conversation, but it was the best she could muster at present.

"Indeed," he replied distractedly. It seemed he was once more the reserved stranger he had been at their introduction.

She didn't press him any further, instead contenting herself to walk in silence. After a minute, though, he stopped abruptly and faced her, saying, "May we speak plainly with each other, Miss Wright?"

"By all means." She watched him keenly, willing him to continue.

"We could utter countless fanciful words to one another, engage in some semblance of courtship, but frankly, I do not see the point. We both know the truth of our circumstances, and I see no reason to pretend otherwise."

Maybe the polite reaction would have been to smile and agree, but she couldn't let such a statement stand without questioning it. "I think," she said, "that you had best explain the circumstances to me, so I can be certain that my understanding of them is equivalent to yours."

He blinked rapidly and cleared his throat. "I'm sure you are aware of the arrangement our fathers made for us to wed. And while I confess that the last thing I ever wanted to do upon returning to England was marry, upon careful consideration, I have begun to see the benefits of the arrangement."

"Lord Ashton, you have the soul of a poet," Eliza exclaimed. "If you make such passionate declarations to every young lady of your acquaintance, it's a wonder they are not all worshipping at your feet!"

He scowled at her and began walking along the footpath once more. "We agreed to speak plainly, and I have done so. I wouldn't want to form a relationship based on pretenses. Therefore, in case your father has not fully apprised you of the situation, let me be very clear. My estate requires repairs, my sister requires a dowry, and on account of my father's gambling debts, I have the funds for neither. Marriage to you will remedy that. I assume you do not require me to explain how the union will be to your advantage in return."

She had joined Lord Ashton when he resumed walking, but upon hearing this speech, she halted in her tracks. Her face burned again, but this time her mortification was accompanied by a sensation that made her veins feel like they were filled with fire, and her ears started to pound.

Noticing she was no longer keeping pace with him, Lord Ashton stopped and regarded her questioningly. Eliza didn't pause to consider her words; she simply let them pour out, blistering and irate. "Yes, I can imagine how you believe the union would be advantageous to me—the naïve country girl with the lowborn father. A girl so inept, so untoward, that the ladies of the ton whisper behind their fans when she enters the room, should be weeping in gratitude that you would condescend to make her your countess. Well, you requested honesty, and now I shall speak plainly with you. I don't give two figs for a title! On the contrary, I would gladly remain on my own as a simple country girl. Regrettably, that option has not been presented to me."

"I will not force you into a marriage you are clearly so averse to," he said, looking both startled and affronted.

"How very kind of you," she spat. "Alas, my father has made our marriage a condition of his continued association with me. Should I no longer receive his patronage, the best I could hope is that my uncle James would continue to tolerate my presence in his home out of a sense of duty to his late sister, my mother, for he and his family would certainly not consider me a welcome addition. From there, I'm afraid there would be nothing left for me but to become a bitter, tiresome old woman, much like my aunt Augusta. And that, Lord Ashton, is a fate I dread even more than marriage to you!"

With that, she turned on her heels, intending to storm back to the house in an indignant huff. Unfortunately, her foot caught on a loose rock, and she felt herself pitching forward until a powerful arm took hold of her slender one. The force with which Lord Ashton grabbed her to prevent her fall caused her to spin toward him, and she found herself pressed against him in a most inappropriate way.

She should have pulled herself away at once, but something about the novel sensation, the feel of her body against another that was rigid as iron yet radiated intense warmth, had her rooted in place. His breathing was heavy, almost as heavy as her own, and when she dared to look up into his face, his vivid blue eyes blazed even more penetratingly than usual. Once more, she felt a burning flush spread across her face, but this time she was unsure whether it was due to embarrassment, or anger, or something else entirely. He held her gaze, and as they continued to stand with their bodies pushed together, it seemed almost as though a magnet within him were pulling her face upward to his. They were so close now, the tips of their noses nearly touching, and his lips were mere inches away.

Abruptly, Lord Ashton stepped away from her, dropping her arm as if it had scorched him. "My apologies," he said quietly, taking an additional step backward. "I hope you have not been hurt."

"I'm quite all right," she uttered, wishing she could melt into a puddle and sink into the earth beneath her feet. "Thank you for your assistance. Now, I must bid you good day." She walked away from him, the only thing stopping her from sprinting across the lawn being her fear of appearing even more ridiculous.

"Miss Wright?"

In response to Lord Ashton's call, she turned, forcing herself to look at him where he still stood farther down the garden path.

"I propose we wed by special license. I see no sense in waiting for the banns to be read when my mourning period will prevent us from having any type of large celebration. Additionally, I would prefer not to draw a great deal of attention to myself at present, and I think it possible you feel the same."

Eliza first thought to ask him if he had taken leave of his senses. Did he truly still seek to marry her after all she had said? Next, her whole body tensed as she considered the possibility of being wed within the week. The plan was preposterous, absurd, and doomed to inflict unhappiness on them both. But if she rejected it, what would she do instead? And as far as the wedding date, what difference would advancing it by a few weeks make in the span of a lifetime?

She should have told him how nonsensical he was, that a union between them was an impossibility. Instead, all she said was, "Very well."

For a man whose marriage proposal had just been accepted, Lord Ashton looked decidedly indifferent. "I will speak to your father," he said, "and call on you again when all the arrangements have been made."

This was her final chance to tell him that she had been too hasty in her reply, that she couldn't accept his proposal and would choose to face the consequences of her refusal as they came. But she didn't. She simply nodded.

She didn't dare approach Lord Ashton again. She didn't even want to walk back to the house with him. "We shall meet again soon, then," she said, slowly moving in the direction opposite him. "Once again, I bid you good day." She stopped only to give him a swift curtsey and then quickened her pace as she made her retreat down the garden path. Much to her relief, this time, she didn't stumble.

Chapter 6

Beneath the trees in the orchard at Hinshaw House, ripened cherries littered the ground. Eliza lay in the grass among them, not at all concerned by the crimson stains that covered her finest white silk dress. She closed her eyes and deeply inhaled the fragrant air, basking in the rays of sun that shone down between the leaves above her.

A sudden shadow blocked the light, and when she opened her eyes, Lord Ashton was standing at her feet, his golden hair tumbling across his forehead and his stiff black coat nowhere in sight. He smiled at her in a way he had never done before. "Let me pick some for you, Miss Wright." He extended his arm to reach one of the highest tree branches and then knelt beside her with a fistful of cherries.

Eliza gratefully accepted one of the cherries he held out to her and popped it in her mouth, the tart juice bursting around her tongue as she took a bite. "Delicious," she murmured languidly. "You should try one."

He peered down at his hand and cast the cherries he held aside. Then, he slowly stretched out beside her, allowing his body to skim against hers. He brought his face nearer and nearer, until ever so gently, he placed his mouth on top of hers, running the tip of his tongue over the cherry juice that lingered on her lips. "Yes," he agreed, his words a heated whisper. "Delicious."

Eliza awoke with a start, feeling so feverish that she wondered if she had become ill. She looked around, disoriented until she realized that she was in her bedroom at Hinshaw House for the last time with dusk falling. How odd that she had fallen asleep at such an early hour, still fully dressed and on top of her counterpane. After close to a week of near-sleepless nights, it seemed overtiredness had finally caught up to her.

An insistent knocking at her door roused her from her stupor. "Eliza? Eliza, are you there? Open the door at once."

The peevish voice belonged, unmistakably, to her aunt Augusta, and it occurred to her that Augusta's knocking was what had awoken her from her dream. She jumped up, thankful for the pitcher of water on her washstand, and hastily splashed some onto her face, though it did little to cool her. The weather had turned unpleasantly sultry, to the point where even nightfall brought little reprieve, and it felt like the inescapable heat had penetrated to her core.

She ran to the door and opened it to admit Augusta, trying her best to appear composed. "Good evening, Aunt."

"Lud, Eliza, you look a fright," said Augusta, wasting no time on pleasantries as she pushed her way into the room and sat in the small armchair across from the bed. "I didn't realize you would already be abed at this hour."

"I must have fallen asleep inadvertently," she replied, reaching up to smooth her tousled hair. It was unlike Augusta to come to her bedroom, especially for idle chatter, so she eyed her aunt warily as she took her seat at the foot of the bed.

"Ah, well, I suppose that is for the best," Augusta conceded. "You will want to look fresh-faced for your wedding in the morning."

"Yes," said Eliza, although she had been trying to put the whole matter out of her mind. She feared that if she dwelled on it too long, she might combust.

"It is on account of your impending status as a married woman that I have come to speak with you."

Eliza stared at her aunt wordlessly. What could Augusta, a spinster, possibly have to tell her on the topic of marriage?

"Specifically, it is regarding your wedding night."

This turn of the conversation would have horrified Eliza had it not been so humorous. As a young child, she had assumed Augusta remained unmarried because gentlemen were too frightened to come near her, and even as a grown woman, she still thought there might be some truth to her childhood belief. The idea that Augusta would now explain to her the private doings of a husband and wife ... She tried her best to keep her mouth pinched in a straight line, but a giggle rose in her throat and burst out before she could stop it.

"Wipe that smirk off your face at once, gel!" snapped Augusta, instantly affronted. "You may think it very funny that I would presume to speak of such things, but there is no one else here to do so, and one does not reach my stage of life, married or not, without knowing a thing or two of how the world works."

"My apologies," mumbled Eliza, trying to look contrite while still on the verge of bursting into laughter.

"Perhaps you think you already know what transpires between a husband and wife on account of the filth you read—"

"Filth?" Eliza interrupted. "Surely you are not referring to the medical texts I peruse."

"Filth," repeated Augusta, glaring at her with beady eyes. "So, let me say this. As a wife, you will have certain duties to perform. In performing these duties, it is imperative you remember to do as your husband bids you, and even though it may be unpleasant, it is something to be endured.

"Above all," she continued, "remember that you are not some bawdy house trollop but a countess, and it is therefore never your place to show enthusiasm. It is merely your place to endure. You have already garnered an accusation of impropriety, so you had best not give Lord Ashton cause to believe the accusation is true. Do you understand?"

Any prior feeling of humor Eliza possessed was now gone. This speech had filled her with so many questions, but none that she dared to ask. Instead, she simply nodded to Augusta. "Indeed."

It wasn't until Augusta had bid her good night and left her in peace that she tried to make sense of her aunt's words. Had Augusta been correct in all she said? If so, she couldn't imagine having too much difficulty showing indifference to Lord Ashton, as he had certainly shown indifference to her. Yet she couldn't forget the sensation of his heart racing as she had stood pressed against him in the garden. Could it have possibly signified something more? Her mind flashed back to her dream, of his body lying next to hers and the ephemeral sensation of his lips on her lips, and she felt a deep flush creep over her anew.

She called her maid, Sarah, to help her dress for bed, hoping she could fall back to sleep and forget the whole matter, but once again, her night was restless. When sleep did finally claim her, just as the first glimmers of dawn became visible outside her window, it seemed like no time at all before Sarah was back again to rouse her and help her dress for the wedding.

Her exhaustion was so great that her wedding day passed by in a blur. She vaguely remembered donning her new lace-trimmed satin gown, obtained with particular expediency from a London dressmaker, and having a wreath of rosebuds fixed within her hair. She recalled entering Hinshaw House's drawing room for the ceremony, where the only guest present, aside from her father and Augusta, was Lord Ashton's solemn-faced sister, Lady Catherine. She remembered very little of standing beside Lord Ashton and saying her vows, but apparently, she had done so satisfactorily, for the vicar had pronounced them man and wife. She had almost no recollection of their time in the dining room, where her father had arranged for an elaborate wedding breakfast, and while she certainly must have eaten and made conversation throughout the lengthy affair, she didn't remember the specifics.

Now, as she sat beside Lord Ashton in his phaeton while they rode home to Highfield Park, it was all she could do to keep her eyes open. Unsurprisingly, Lord Ashton didn't attempt conversation, and for once, she was grateful for the silence.

It wasn't until they turned up a drive lined with massive oaks, and she caught the first glimpse of her new home, that she was startled to alertness. To say Highfield Park was one of England's finest estates was certainly no exaggeration. She could barely suppress a gasp as she beheld the house's extensive pale stone façade, stretching wider than any she had ever seen and adorned in the center with a colossal six-columned portico. Was she truly the lady of such a place? The idea was both surreal and overwhelming.

"Allow me to welcome you to Highfield Park." Lord Ashton glanced at her, seeming to notice her amazement.

"It's … breathtaking." Her throat suddenly went dry, making it difficult to say anything else. A line of servants stood at the bottom of the massive front steps, and she straightened herself up, hoping to make a favorable first impression.

Lord Ashton pulled the phaeton to a stop and jumped down, and Eliza gratefully took his proffered hand as she, too, disembarked.

"Higgins, Mrs. Parker." He motioned to the older man and woman at the front of the line. "Allow me to present the new Countess of Ashton. Lady Ashton, these are Highfield Park's long-serving butler and housekeeper."

"Welcome, my lady," Mrs. Parker said amiably, just as Higgins bowed down to the best of his ability. "We are most pleased to serve you."

"Thank you," Eliza said. Their welcome warmed her to them at once, although it sounded so strange to hear herself called by her new title. "I am delighted to meet you." She gave a small smile, and despite her weariness, she did her best to offer a few kind words to each additional member of the household staff as introductions were made down the line. At least none of them seemed to disdain their scandalous new mistress openly.

"Let me show you inside," said Lord Ashton as soon as she had finished, offering his arm. She accepted with hesitancy, her skin turning hot as she attempted to force away the memory of their encounter in the garden. Fortunately, the thick wool of his coat and the silk of her glove offered a barrier against intimate contact as they ascended the stone steps.

With its stately marble columns and soaring ceiling, the entrance hall was just as awe-inspiring as the house's exterior, but she lacked the energy to absorb it in full detail. Lord Ashton shot her a look of concern. "I'm sure Mrs. Parker has much she wishes to show you, but given the morning's excitement, perhaps you would prefer to rest and save your tour of the house for tomorrow."

Her first instinct was to protest and insist she merely needed to freshen up, and then she would be happy to see to business about the house. After all, she usually kept herself far too busy to retire in the middle of the day. However, she was so bone-weary and overwhelmed that she simply nodded. "Thank you. A repose would be very nice."

They still stood arm in arm, and he peered at her in an almost tender way, inching slightly closer as if he wished to say something. But then, he just as quickly pulled away, causing her arm to drop, and left her standing alone.

"Mrs. Parker will show you to your room," he said, already making his way down the corridor. "I'll see you at dinner, Miss Wright. That is, Lady Ashton," he corrected himself.

"You may call me Eliza," she said quietly to his back.

"Good afternoon, Lady Ashton," he repeated, not even turning around, and with that, he was gone.

Misery sucked the strength from her limbs, and she thought she might indulge her urge to sink to the marble floor of the entrance hall until Mrs. Parker approached her with another kind smile. "If you'd like to follow me, my lady."

They made their way up the stairs at a leisurely pace, then turned up and down corridors until Mrs. Parker finally opened one of the numerous paneled doors. "Here we are, my lady. Shall I summon your maid?"

"No, thank you." While some assistance in removing her gown would have been helpful, it paled in comparison to her desire to simply be alone. She hurried to seat herself at the dressing table, eager to remove the pins from her elaborate coiffure. "I have everything I need at present," she said, turning back to Mrs. Parker, where she stood hesitantly in the doorway. "I'm most grateful for your assistance."

"Of course, my lady," replied the housekeeper, her eyes so filled with compassion that Eliza could feel the sting of tears in her own. "If you do require anything else, you need only ring for it." She turned away, gently pulling the door closed behind her, and for the first time that day, Eliza was truly alone.

With her hair now unpinned and hanging in loose waves down her back, she kicked off her satin slippers and pulled herself onto the bed, not caring about how she crumpled her dress. The counterpane and bed curtains had an elaborate pink floral pattern, trimmed with gold thread, and though it was not entirely to her taste, she stared at it, desperate for even a menial distraction.

However, this quickly led way to a most unwanted thought. Had this room once belonged to Lord Ashton's first wife? And if so, had she "endured" his attentions here? The idea of settling herself amongst another woman's things, in another woman's bed, caused her skin to prickle. While she knew very little of his former wife, it especially troubled her to think that whoever she was, she almost certainly was above a scandal-ridden merchant's daughter whom he was obligated to marry for financial gain. Would Lord Ashton ever be able to look at her, his new wife, without recognizing her inferiority?

She wasn't usually prone to bouts of dejection and self-doubt, and now that she was a countess, she had every reason to feel more confident than ever before. Instead, she felt lower than she had in her entire life.

Fortunately, her fatigue soon outgrew even her strongest anxieties, and though she lay atop what was presumably another lady's counterpane in the middle of the afternoon, she dropped into a deep and dreamless sleep.

Chapter 7

With the nuptials over and his new wife brought over the threshold of Highfield Park, Edward made a hasty retreat to the sanctuary of his study. There he remained for the entirety of the afternoon. Upon hearing the news that Lady Ashton was still resting, he gladly instructed for dinner in the dining room to be canceled, instead requesting that a tray be brought to her room while he took one in his study. He justified this by saying that many urgent matters pertaining to the estate required his attention, and he simply couldn't put them off any longer. In truth, a pamphlet on crop rotation had lain open on his desk for hours now, but he hadn't read past the first couple sentences.

Darkness was beginning to fall, and with every passing minute, the question of how to proceed with the remainder of the evening weighed heavier on his mind. His new wife lay alone upstairs, and if they were to be husband and wife in more than just name, he would need to go to her and consummate the marriage.

He downed the contents of his brandy snifter and snatched up the decanter to replenish it. He had spent the past week insisting to himself that he didn't care for his new countess, but that didn't prevent her fiery hair and emerald eyes from filling his dreams. Having her stumble into him in the garden and press her soft curves against him, looking up at him with a face containing lips practically begging to be kissed, had only made his desire burn hotter. She had been so angry that day, so passionate, and he wondered what it would be like to feel that passion beneath him, alongside him, astride him …

This predicament was all his own bloody fault. He had remained celibate for far too long. During his first few years on the Continent, there was a period when he had pursued women the same way he pursued drink and dice games: with abandon. But while he had initially longed for the distraction brought by those fleeting moments of pleasure, after a time, the sheer emptiness of it all grew tiresome. Further motivated by his fear of becoming as depraved as his father, he abruptly stopped his pursuits.

Too abruptly, it now seemed.

In any case, nothing about the former Miss Wright seemed passionate today. On the contrary, she had gone about the day with an air of despondency about her. On the day of his half-hearted marriage proposal, she had yelled at him about not caring to be his countess, words he had assumed came only from her fury. But could it be their union *was* truly unwanted on her part?

It really shouldn't have mattered. He himself had been adamantly opposed to the marriage and had frequently insisted he didn't care for her, so if she disliked him in turn, then what of it? Except, some ridiculous part of him deeply wanted her favor.

With the brandy decanter now empty and little else in the study left to divert him, he decided he would approach her bedroom for the purposes of enquiring after her wellbeing. As for what happened after that, it remained to be seen.

On account of the day's stifling heat, he wore only his shirtsleeves, and he briefly debated if he should don the coat he had tossed onto an armchair and refasten his cravat. Ultimately, he opted to forgo that one formality and hurried upstairs before he overthought the matter any further.

His footsteps slowed as he approached the countess's room, and all at once, the decanter of brandy he had consumed went straight to his head, making it swirl. Surely, this signaled that it had all been a mistake and that it would be best for him to turn back toward his room and save his inquiries for the breakfast room the next morning.

But then, the door opened, and out came his wife's lady's maid. "Good evening, m'lord," she said as she dropped into a quick curtsey before scurrying away. Assuming he would wish to enter, she had not fully closed the door behind her, and it seemed he now had no choice but to do so.

He took a steadying breath and stepped into a room he hadn't entered for many years. The new Lady Ashton sat at her dressing table wearing only her thin lawn nightgown, her hair twisted into a loose braid that nearly reached her waist.

"Good evening, Lady Ashton," he said, his pulse quickening. He diverted his gaze so that he looked in her direction without looking directly at her. "Are you well?"

"Very well, thank you." The shadows beneath her eyes were no longer so prominent, but an element of strain still lingered. "I'm not usually one to sleep the afternoon away. I shall be very glad to become better acquainted with the house tomorrow."

"It's quite all right," he assured her, puzzled by how subdued she was compared to the Miss Wright he met little more than a week before. "Is this room to your liking?"

"Yes, thank you."

She was quick to reply, but as Edward peered at her against the backdrop of the gaudy pink floral pattern that covered the upholstery, coverlet, and curtains, he couldn't help but notice that it didn't suit her. "You are welcome to make changes to the décor as you see fit," he said. "As it has been some twenty years since my mother last decorated the room, you may find it in need of refreshing."

It was an inane subject to discuss at present, but the words caused her to visibly relax, at least a little. "As you have no objection, perhaps I will. Thank you."

He still lingered near the doorway, unsure of what to say or do next. The excess of brandy now churned in his stomach, and he stood there feeling sick and ridiculous and as awkward as a schoolboy awaiting his first encounter with a woman.

He sensed his wife's green eyes fixate on him, and when he met her gaze in return, she motioned to the settee at the foot of the bed. "Would you care to sit?"

He accepted the invitation, if for no other reason than to get off his feet while he waited for his head to stop spinning. She eyed him hesitantly, but after a minute, she made her way to the settee and seated herself on its edge, careful that no part of her touched him. She did lean toward him a little, though, enveloping him in the calming scent of rosewater.

"My lord?"

The degree of formality that existed between them was absurd. Surely, now that they were wed, he should ask her to call him Edward, just as she had requested that he call her Eliza. It was only the smallest of intimacies. However, while his eager body showed clear signs of a desire for physical intimacy with her, his mind was staunchly made up that any closeness they shared could go no farther than the physical. Therefore, he only looked at her, saying nothing.

"My lord," she repeated, taking his silence as an invitation to continue, "I know very little of marriage, but I do want to be a satisfactory wife to you." She cast her eyes downward and began playing with an errant strand of hair that had slipped free from her braid. "I understand you've been married before …"

"Yes." After what had clearly been a trying day for her, she deserved the opportunity to speak her mind, but he didn't have it in him this evening to discuss the details of his first marriage. In fact, he was unsure if he ever would. "I would prefer not to speak of it," he said, his head pounding and his stomach coiling anew.

"It's merely that …" She gave a small sigh. "I understand you heard of my involvement in a scandal, and—"

"Lady Ashton," he cut in, not wanting to hear any more, "I think it best we both put the past behind us and instead direct our attention to the present."

He could already imagine what she had been going to say. It was something he had previously suspected, based on his mistrust of Wright and how the man seemed to spin the truth to work to his advantage. The scandal concerning Eliza Wright's intimate involvement with another man was more than a mere fabrication. He didn't need her to speak the words aloud to confirm his suspicions.

It was of no matter either way. Her virtue, or lack thereof, would change nothing regarding the circumstances of their marriage. Only ... his chest clenched tight as he imagined the man, servant or not, who had been involved in the scandal with her. The tension only grew as he pictured men who would come later, after he returned to Florence and left his wife to her own devices. He gritted his teeth and curled his hands into fists, his entire body now so rigid that it felt like it could snap. He didn't want these other men to have her. *He* wanted to have her. All of a sudden, he needed to have her, as if his very existence depended on it.

He allowed his fingertips to sweep over the flawless alabaster of her face as he reached to gently push the loose strand of hair she played with behind her ear. The touch made her shiver, a reaction that sent heat coursing through him. He shifted nearer to her as he gave her face a light nudge upward to his, and her eyelids fluttered closed. With that, he traversed the final few inches between them and brushed his lips against hers, savoring their soft fullness. He kept his caresses gentle, enjoying the way she returned them with a sort of uncertain sweetness, but when she reached a tentative hand up to the back of his neck and began running her fingers through his hair, he suddenly needed more.

He pressed his mouth more urgently to hers, running his tongue against her lips until he coaxed them open and could plunder inside her mouth. She was still at first, her hands dropping to her lap, but he flicked his tongue over hers repeatedly, and soon she was meeting him with insistent strokes.

He brought his hand to the side of her neck, relishing the feel of her silky skin, and swept his fingers downward, so they skimmed the tips of her breasts through the thin barrier of her nightgown. She moved toward his touch ever so slightly, and carefully, he pulled his mouth away from hers so it could travel the same path as his hand. He pressed hot kisses into her neck, letting his teeth graze the sensitive skin, and continued down until his mouth connected with a pert nipple. Her breath came in quiet pants, and when he peered up at her, her eyes were closed, and her lips slightly parted in a look of pure pleasure. The image sent a jolt of desire straight to his groin, and he closed his mouth around her and began to suckle.

A low moan escaped her, intensifying his yearning, but the sound seemed to startle her, and she bit down hard on her lip. She flinched and pulled away a little, and a drop of blood settled on her lip where her teeth had left their mark.

"Are you all right?" he asked through heavy breaths.

"Yes." She nodded but then frowned. "I mean, no. I mean, I don't know what to do. I don't know what you expect of me!"

He looked at her in bewilderment. "I don't understand. I thought you had …"

"I mean, I believe I *know* certain things," she rushed to say, "but I don't know—" Her expression quickly changed to one of shock. "Wait. You thought … You thought the rumors about me to be true? Despite assurances to the contrary? Despite telling me, mere moments ago, that you had no need to hear what I wished to say on the subject?"

He needed only to look at the deep hurt in her eyes to recognize how wrong he'd been in his assumption. He could mistrust her motives all he wanted, but, based on her reaction, it seemed highly unlikely there was any truth to the accusations of her scandalous behavior. The realization rendered him speechless, and the racing of his heart slowed to a dull throb. Why had he been so stupid to allude to his belief out loud?

She scrambled off the settee and stood in front of him with her arms crossed. "I find myself growing tired." Her voice was cold, and the pain in her eyes was now mixed with anger. "I think you had best leave now."

He clumsily arose from the settee and stumbled a few steps away from her. He knew he should apologize at once. He should beg her forgiveness for suggesting something so maladroit. He should admit the error of his belief and promise not to pay heed to rumors any longer. He should explain that while trust did not come easy to him, he would do his best to have faith in her going forward.

But he said none of these things. He rushed to the bedroom door, uttering only, "Good night, Lady Ashton."

Just that morning, he had reluctantly ordered his things to be moved to the earl's bedroom, separated from the countess's by a single connecting door. However, this was not where he headed. Instead, he burst out the door that opened to the corridor and didn't stop walking until he reached his former bedroom. After slamming the door closed behind him, he hurried over to the desk in the corner and tugged open the drawer. He rummaged through the contents, letting old papers and books tumble to the floor until he finally laid his hands on the copper-framed miniature resting at the bottom. He held it close to his face, running his finger over the brilliant white-blond hair and the lifelike innocent blue eyes. An aching, seething burn spread through him as he was flooded by memories both old and new. Before giving it another moment's thought, he threw the miniature across the room, the painted ivory hitting the floor with a satisfying crack.

Through some stroke of luck, the partially filled brandy decanter had not yet been removed from the bedside table, and with shaking hands, he poured the amber liquid into the accompanying snifter. He tipped it to his mouth and took a long swallow, then promptly cast up his accounts into the nearby washbasin.

He slumped into the closest armchair, shutting his eyes with a heavy sigh. He was an idiot. A damned, stupid, bloody idiot. He had always known this marriage was a terrible idea, and he had managed to start it off in the worst way possible. Why he had thought it a good idea to approach the countess's bedroom on this night, and how he would even begin to remedy the damage from doing so, he hadn't the faintest clue.

But perhaps he didn't need to. After all, his plans hadn't changed. He still had every intention of returning to

Florence just as soon as the Season began anew, after he put in a few appearances with the new Countess of Ashton. Why, his ridiculous yearning aside, there was really no need to even consummate the marriage. And if they were to remain together for only a short time, while they were not even truly married, then perhaps his behavior made no difference at all.

But deep down, he knew it did.

Chapter 8

As tempting as it was to spend her second day at High-field Park shut in her bedroom, sleeping her troubles away, Eliza refused to let herself succumb to misery. There-fore, she turned down the offer of a breakfast tray and instead had Sarah help her dress early so she could take her meal downstairs.

Her resolve weakened as she approached the breakfast room, her hurt and ire from the previous evening simmering dangerously close to the surface as she thought of coming face to face with Lord Ashton again. She hated that he had been so quick to believe the worst of her. But … perhaps some of the blame lay with her as well. She had tried to heed Augusta's words regarding her wedding night, even though they were of questionable veracity. However, when Lord Ashton had approached her in her bedroom, she had leaned into him without even thinking, and caressed him, and tasted him, and moaned beneath his touch. She had been too eager, and in turn, he had assumed the rumors of her to be true. But although she might not have behaved with as much passivity as a proper countess, it didn't make his judg-ment hurt any less.

Yet what good would holding a grudge do? If she were to have any semblance of happiness, she would have to find a way of getting on with him. With that in mind, she entered the breakfast room determined to treat Lord Ashton with at least polite detachment while she did her best to forget what had transpired between them on their wedding night.

Surprisingly, the person sitting at the table was not Lord Ashton but rather his sister, looking especially somber in her dress of black crepe.

"Lady Catherine," she exclaimed, "I was unaware you were here." As tired as she had been the previous day, she felt certain Lord Ashton had told her that his sister intended to journey to London directly after the wedding breakfast and then travel on to a friend's estate in Devonshire.

"I hope you are not displeased." Catherine turned her face down to stare at her plate, her cheeks flushing. "I developed a headache during the wedding breakfast, so my brother said I could return to Highfield Park and postpone my journey until today. Your father was kind enough to send me home in his coach shortly after you and Edward left. Nevertheless, I'm very sorry for my intrusion here today."

"Not at all. This is your home, after all, Lady Catherine."

"Please, address me simply as Catherine," she said softly, daring to meet Eliza's eyes for just a second before turning her face away again.

"Of course. I hope you will call me Eliza in return." She offered her new sister-in-law a reassuring smile as she headed to the sideboard to take a plate. As she helped herself to brioche and coddled eggs, she slid a few discreet glances in Catherine's direction. Upon meeting the girl the day before, her first impression was that she shared her brother's aloofness. However, now that she had the opportunity to observe her more closely, she wondered if the issue could be simply that Catherine was exceedingly shy. On top of that, something in the slight redness of her eyes and the tense line of her mouth suggested that perhaps she concealed inner distress.

Hoping she was not overstepping, upon seating herself at the table and receiving a cup of chocolate from a footman, Eliza asked, "Catherine, are you quite well? Does your headache still plague you?"

"No, I'm very well, thank you," she answered without conviction.

Eliza suppressed a sigh. It seemed making conversation with Catherine would be equally as difficult as making conversation with her brother. Yet she was determined not to give up just yet. "I'm sorry we have not yet had the opportunity to become better acquainted." She eyed Catherine carefully. "You see, I have no siblings of my own but always thought it would be very nice to have a sister."

"I wish I did not have to leave," muttered Catherine, slumping in her seat in a way that misaligned with her usual straightlaced mannerisms.

It appeared that Eliza drew close to the root of the problem. "Are you apprehensive about your journey to Devonshire?"

Catherine shot her a worried look, and suddenly her words came rushing out. "I do not want to go! Lavinia Bathurst has been a friend to me, and Lord and Lady Bathurst are kind enough, but no one understands. They look forward to balls, musicales, and soirees as though there is nothing better on earth, whereas I positively despise these events. I know I must force myself to grow used to such things in preparation for my debut next year, but as soon as I enter the company of strangers, I find myself fumbling and speechless and wishing I could just disappear. Being at Highfield Park, away from it all, is the greatest sort of reprieve."

She seemed on the verge of tears, and Eliza's heart wrenched to watch her. "I think we are not so different, you and I." She lowered her voice as if sharing a secret. "During my Season, I did no shortage of fumbling, and consequently wishing I could make my escape to the country."

She hesitated to continue, realizing that she had, in fact, gotten her wish of returning to the country early. Did Catherine know anything of the circumstances surrounding her failed first Season? It was certainly not an appropriate subject to introduce in polite company, especially if that company included a seventeen-year-old girl. However, Catherine showed no sign of disdain; in fact, the assurances appeared to have brightened her a little.

"I understand your brother's desire to see you prepared for your entrance into society," Eliza said. "With that said, because you are in mourning and unable to avail of certain entertainments for the time being, I see no reason you couldn't remain at Highfield Park."

Catherine looked surprised. "But you are the new mistress of the house. Surely you do not want me underfoot as you settle in."

"Not at all," she exclaimed. "As I said before, this is your home, much more than it is mine, and I would welcome the presence of my new sister as I adjust to my surroundings here. I shall speak to your brother about it."

As if on cue, footsteps echoed in the hallway, and in walked Lord Ashton. Despite her irritation with him, her traitorous heart gave its usual little lurch as he came into view. But while he could surely never be anything less than handsome, a second glance revealed him to be far from in prime condition this morning. His pallor looked downright sickly, dark circles shadowed his eyes, and his golden hair fell in unruly waves across his forehead. Even his cravat was tied in disheveled knots and bunched untidily into his waistcoat.

"Good morning," she said, remembering the strong taste of brandy the night before as her tongue had circled his. Too much brandy, it would seem.

"Good morning, Lady Ashton, Catherine," he replied dully as he settled into the chair at the head of the table.

She gestured to the silver teapot in the middle of the table. "Tea?"

At his nod, she picked it up to pour, purposefully knocking the pot against the side of its tray with a clang. His resulting wince gave her a petty feeling of satisfaction.

But it would be of no benefit to keep antagonizing him. She had an important matter to discuss and would waste no time. "Lord Ashton, after you have breakfasted, might we have a moment to converse, just us two?"

Catherine hurriedly set aside her cup of chocolate and pushed out her chair. "You can speak alone right now if you like. I'm nearly finished here and should really go upstairs and see that my things are packed—"

"Please, do not rush away on my account," Eliza said. "I just recalled there's something I must fetch from my bedroom. I'll go up directly to retrieve it, and when I return, perhaps we may then speak, my lord."

"As you wish," he answered, although it was unclear if he was truly paying attention. His focus had turned to the sideboard, where he was eying the food with a grimace.

She took her time heading up to her bedroom and rummaging through the one trunk that remained in the corner, the one she had insisted on unpacking herself. Once she found what she needed, she clasped the item tightly in her palm and sauntered back to the breakfast room. By that time, Catherine had gone and her dishes were cleared away, leaving only Lord Ashton sitting at the table with an untouched plate of food before him.

Wordlessly, she walked over to him and loosened her grip on the vial she held, dropping it in his lap with more force than she intended.

"Borage seed oil," she said in response to his questioning look. "I suggest you take a spoonful and wash it down with a cup of strong tea to help with your … malaise."

He looked back and forth between her and the vial before eventually unscrewing the lid and doing as she had instructed. With the oil washed down, he regarded her wryly. "Are you trying to poison me, Lady Ashton?"

"Surprisingly, no." She sat back down and poured her own cup of tea, careful not to bang any dishes this time. "For reasons unbeknownst to me, I have a desire to help rid you of your self-inflicted misery. With that in mind, let me advise that, while you may not feel like it, it would be to your benefit to eat something."

He at least had the decency to look shamefaced. "I sincerely thank you."

She could hardly make sense of these dueling desires of hers. On the one hand, she wished to cause him discomfort as revenge for what he had said to her during their wedding night, while on the other, she wanted to ease his suffering. Ultimately, it seemed her latter wish was coming true, for after taking a few more mouthfuls of tea and munching on a strip of bacon, Lord Ashton appeared slightly more alert and not nearly as wan.

It was as good a time as any to have her discussion with him. "Might I speak with you now?"

He nodded. "Does this, perchance, have to do with my sister?"

"As a matter of fact, it does," she said, raising a questioning brow. How could he have known?

"I do apologize. Catherine was detained from returning to London yesterday, but as you heard her say, she has only to see that her things are packed and will be on her way. She has an invitation to stay with friends for the remainder of the year and will trouble you no further."

"Trouble me?" Eliza couldn't believe what she was hearing. "But Lord Ashton, I wish for her to stay."

Now he was the one who looked perplexed. "I would have thought that, as a new bride and countess, you would not want anyone else in the house right now. It is yours to reign over, after all."

"That is just as Catherine said, but I assure you, it is also quite untrue. She is my sister now, and I would never want to displace her from her home. As a matter of fact, I would welcome her company."

Lord Ashton pressed his fingers to his temples as if trying to clear his head.

"If you're concerned about having her well-prepared for her debut next Season, we could hire her a governess," she added. "I'm sure she would benefit from both the instruction and the extra companionship. I would gladly take on the task of finding one if you like."

"I don't know …" His expression stayed hesitant.

"Please," she begged. "Catherine has indicated a desire to stay here, and as she is in mourning, I think it especially important that she resides where she feels most comfortable. I understand all too well the hurt that comes with losing a parent, and if there's any small gesture I can make to help ease her pain, I will gladly do so." She had to stop talking then so she could swallow the lump that had risen in her throat.

"I'm not sure why Catherine is so pained by the death of a man who took little interest in her. Nonetheless, she seems to feel the loss deeply." His tone was bitter, but as she continued to sit silently, still not trusting herself to speak, the steely look in his eyes softened.

"I'm sorry you had to experience loss of your own," he said. "Were you very young when you lost your mother?"

She shook her head. "It was not even two years ago. Consumption."

"I did not realize it was that recent. Again, I'm very sorry," he said quietly.

She nodded her thanks and looked away, desperately wanting the wave of grief to pass so she didn't have to worry about crying before Lord Ashton at the breakfast table.

She could feel his gaze upon her as he said, "Catherine will remain here with us if you are certain that is what you want."

"Thank you!" A smile broke out on her face, and without thinking, she reached over to clasp his hand. "Truly, thank you."

Whatever had possessed her to act with such familiarity, she hadn't the faintest idea. But rather than looking affronted, Lord Ashton placed his other hand on top of hers. "You are the one deserving of thanks. I appreciate your concern for my sister. And … for me."

The uncomfortable heat was rising in her again. "Think nothing of it," she mumbled, straightening herself up in her chair and pulling her hands into her lap. "May I tell Catherine now? She should be made aware at once that there is no longer any need for her to ready herself for a journey."

"Of course. And once you are through, I know Mrs. Parker is most eager to give you a tour of the house."

"I would welcome one. Will you join us, too?" she asked.

Apprehension clouded his face once more. "No. That is, I must ride out to meet with Mr. Locke, my new land agent. We're expecting laborers this morning to assist in the hops garden, and I want to be there when they arrive. After that, I have several other matters to attend to, and I anticipate being gone most of the day. In any case, the house and gardens are yours to do with as you please, and I'm sure you will have much to occupy you."

"Indeed." It was just as well; she didn't care to see more of him anyway. Did she? She leaped from her seat to exit the room before the sinking feeling in her stomach had a chance to intensify.

"Eliza? That is, Lady Ashton?"

His call caused her to turn back to face him just as she reached the doorway. "Yes?"

His blue eyes regarded her with such intensity that it seemed he would see right through her. As she stared back, she could almost detect a hint of remorse. She waited, eying him coolly as he began drumming his fingers against the table. She would wait all day if that's what it took.

But Lord Ashton got up from the table himself, no longer meeting her gaze. "I should be on my way now as well. Have a pleasant day."

He moved to exit the room with much greater speed than he had entered it. But she refused to let him rush away from her again. Just as he reached the doorway where she stood, she spun on her heels, slamming her foot on top of his as she brought it back down.

"I'm terribly sorry," she said in response to his grunt of surprise, although her voice sounded far from contrite. "Please forgive my clumsiness. Good day."

And she hastened down the corridor and up the stairs before they had the opportunity to injure each other any further.

Chapter 9

Eliza had much to occupy her during her first week at Highfield Park. Mrs. Parker helped familiarize her with the house and even assisted in unpacking her final trunk filled with medicines in the stillroom. She and Catherine walked about the gardens and rode out together so Catherine could show her the land about the estate. On a few afternoons, Catherine was even patient enough to sit upon a picnic blanket as Eliza stopped and sketched some of the flowers she came across in the fields. During a rainy day, she took a trip to Rochester to select new fabric for her bedroom, and on Catherine's insistence, she chose new drapery fabric for the main drawing room as well. Then, there was the task of interviewing potential governesses for Catherine, something she did with great care in the hopes of ensuring her sister-in-law's happiness.

It was all nearly enough to distract her from the fact that she saw very little of Lord Ashton. He stayed from home all day, and while she could hear him rustling about in his connecting bedroom at night, he never tried entering her room again. While tossing about in bed, if she turned her mind to the tasks she needed to complete the following day, she could almost set aside her riled thoughts and forget the relentless throb in the pit of her stomach. Almost.

However, on the first day of her second week as Lady Ashton, during which Catherine was occupied with welcoming her new governess, Miss Martin, and Lord Ashton had ridden off somewhere with his land agent in the hopes of acquiring a new flock of sheep, Eliza found herself in want of something to do. She could have discussed the week's menus with Mrs. Parker, or strolled through the gardens on her own, or even taken a novel and settled herself beneath a tree for the afternoon. Yet on this day, none of these ideas were enough to hold her interest.

Wanting the distraction of something new, she instead decided to take a walk into the village, a place she had not yet ventured. It was a journey of several miles, but the day was sunny and pleasant, and she enjoyed sauntering down the road and getting her first view of the rows of thatched-roof cottages. Then, arriving at the village High Street, she peered at all the shopfronts, wondering where she should begin when a commotion by the open door of the haberdashery shop caught her attention.

She ventured a little closer, not caring to interfere but also wanting to ensure that nothing was direly amiss. A woman's choked, pleading voice reached her.

"Please. 'Tis only a bit of ribbon, and as you can plainly see, I have the money for it right here."

"The nerve of you," a much harsher woman's voice replied. "You should be ashamed to show your face in here."

"Please," the plaintive voice repeated, and Eliza could now see that it came from a woman who stood near the shop's doorway. "'Tis meant for Jenny, for her birthday. I'll buy it and be on my way, and you need see no more of me."

"This is what comes of having a mother like you," snapped the other woman, seemingly the shopkeeper, who was standing by the edge of the counter with her arms crossed and her mouth turned down in a scowl. "You refused to turn her over to the respectable members of her family, and now, you and she both must suffer the consequences. Now, get out before I have you thrown out."

The woman who stood near the doorway gave a little sob as she flung the ribbon onto the counter and turned to hurry out of the shop, brushing past Eliza on her way out as though she didn't even notice her there. With the woman facing forward, it became apparent that her belly was swelled hugely with child.

After watching the woman rush down the street, Eliza took a few tentative steps into the haberdashery.

The shopkeeper watched the woman's retreat as well, with her face pressed to the window. "Shameless trollop," she muttered, not seeming to notice that anyone had entered the shop.

Eliza cleared her throat as she glanced around at the colorful fabrics, ribbons, and lace that filled the shop. "Is something amiss?"

"Indeed, it is," answered the shopkeeper, still not turning from the window, "when the likes of Alice Turner thinks to come parading in here, showing off her condition as if she hadn't a care in the world."

"I'm not sure I understand." The woman, Alice, was obviously near the time of her delivery, but why would that in itself cause such offense?

"Why, Alice has been widowed for a year. I thought everyone knew …" The shopkeeper trailed off as she turned around to face Eliza, and she gave a small start at seeing an unfamiliar face. "But I don't believe we're known to one another." She eyed her, looking up and down from her flower-trimmed bonnet to her intricately trimmed walking dress to her smart new half-boots, and her face took on an expression of shock and horror. "Surely it can't be ... Surely you're not ... the new Countess of Ashton?"

"The very one," she said, smiling to show she had taken no offense.

The shopkeeper was still visibly flustered and sank into an awkward curtsey. "I *am* sorry, m'lady. I should have been paying better attention, should have given you a proper welcome—"

"Not at all," she cut in, unnerved to find her presence could cause such a fuss. "Might you tell me your name?"

"Fanny Turner, m'lady." The shopkeeper reddened. "I'm sorry to say that woman of ill repute and I share a name on account of a former family connection, but I promise you, my husband and I have cut all ties with her."

"It is of no consequence," Eliza assured her. She gazed down at the pale pink ribbon where it had been flung on the counter and lifted it between her fingers. "I just noticed how pretty this is. I believe I shall buy it." Wanting to appease the shopkeeper, she also grabbed several ribbons that hung on a line in the window next to her, not pausing to consider their color. "These, too."

"Very good, m'lady." Fanny Turner now looked exceedingly pleased that the new Countess of Ashton had seen fit to patronize her shop. "And I do hope you won't let that unpleasant scene from earlier prevent you from making future visits here."

"On the contrary," said Eliza as she reached into her reticule and handed over the coins she owed, "now that I'm beginning to settle at Highfield Park, I hope to make many more visits to the village, including your lovely shop."

The shopkeeper beamed with pride. "I'm so glad to hear it. A very good day to you, m'lady."

"Good day." Eliza exited the haberdashery as quickly as she could without appearing rude. She glanced up and down the street, but none of the people walking along it looked familiar. After a moment's debate, she headed back in the direction she had come, toward the little cottages.

Upon turning the corner, she caught sight of the very person she wished to see. Alice Turner was facing away from her once more, but she was no longer running. Instead, she took slow, heavy steps, almost like a waddle, and her hands gripped her lower back.

"Mrs. Turner?" she called out hesitantly.

The woman stopped, brushing her hands to her face before slowly turning around. Her puffy, red eyes held a look of confusion.

"Mrs. Turner," repeated Eliza, momentarily neglecting all sense of decorum to run toward her. "We are not yet acquainted, but I was hoping to introduce myself. My name is Eliza. That is, Elizabeth Adderley, the new wife of the Earl of Ashton, and—"

"Lady Ashton!" Just like Fanny Turner's had, Alice Turner's mouth dropped open. She immediately tried to bend herself into a curtsey.

"No, please," said Eliza, placing a hand on the woman's arm to still her. She reached into her pocket and withdrew the pink ribbon, holding it forward. "I merely wanted to give you this."

Somehow, the look of deep shock on Alice Turner's face intensified. "But why ..." She tentatively reached for the ribbon, no longer able to speak.

"I did not mean to eavesdrop," said Eliza, "but as I neared the shop, I couldn't help but hear that you wished to purchase this ribbon as a gift. As it seemed you had some difficulty, I wanted, as your new neighbor, to assist you."

Alice Turner's eyes welled with fresh tears. "I meant to buy it as a present for my girl. She turns ten tomorrow, and she wished for nothing more than a pink ribbon for her hair. 'Twas the least I could do for her, and ... Oh, m'lady, how can I ever thank you!"

Despite the tears, she broke into a smile, and Eliza found herself smiling as well. "Please, think nothing of it. Would it be all right if I walked with you a while, Mrs. Turner?"

"Call me Alice, m'lady," she said, wiping her eyes again. "And yes, of course you might, but are you sure? Fanny Turner, from the haberdashery, loves nothing more than to gossip, so I imagine she told you something of my situation."

"She may have made some comment," said Eliza, beginning to stroll at a leisurely pace so that Alice could easily keep up. "However, it is irrelevant to me."

"Are you certain, m'lady?" Alice started walking alongside her, but her smile had been replaced with a worried frown.

"Quite certain. I pay very little heed to gossip."

They continued walking down the street until Alice turned toward the small limestone cottage at the end of a row, tidy enough but with a roof that looked sorely in need of repair.

"This is home, m'lady," she said, breathing heavily and putting her hands to her back once more as they reached the front door. "You're most welcome to come in if you like."

"Thank you, but I will not take up any more of your time."

Alice gave her head a little shake. "Of course. It wouldn't do for the lady of the estate to be seen in the home of someone like me. 'Twas foolish of me to suggest it."

"Not at all," Eliza rushed to assure her. "I merely do not want to impose on you at a time when, forgive my forwardness, you are visibly tired. Does your back trouble you often?"

"Day and night." She sighed wearily. "I'm at a loss for what to do. I never had these troubles when I was big with Jenny."

"Would you allow me to call on you tomorrow? I could bring you something that might help."

"Of course, m'lady, but you needn't inconvenience yourself." Alice leaned against the doorway, peering down at her feet.

"It is no inconvenience, truly." Eliza smiled at her. "In fact, I insist. I'll bid you good day for now, but I shall come again tomorrow morning if that would suit you."

"It will, m'lady. Good day. And thank you."

Alice still appeared bewildered, although as they waved goodbye to one another, Eliza thought she could detect a hint of joy reemerge on her face.

She walked home, all the while pondering how best to assist Alice with her struggles. While she longed to discuss the matter with another, she decided to keep the details of her time in the village to herself for the time being, unsure of how Lord Ashton or Catherine would react.

The following morning, Lord Ashton was off attending to some sort of farm-related business as usual, and Catherine was once more occupied with her governess, making it easy for Eliza to slip away without explanation. This time, she left Highfield Park and wandered down the road to the village carrying a large basket.

The weather was fine once more, and she made good time arriving back at the door of Alice's little cottage. Alice answered her knock quickly, her eyes widening at the sight of the basket. Behind her stood a young girl who shared the same hazel eyes and sandy brown hair as Alice, looking equally in awe.

"Good day to you both," Eliza greeted them as she stepped inside. "I'm happy to see you again, Alice." She turned her gaze to the girl. "And is this your daughter, Jenny?"

"Yes, and I'm very pleased to meet you, m'lady," the girl said, offering a curtsey.

Eliza smiled to see the pink ribbon tied at the bottom of her braid. "I'm pleased to meet you as well," she replied, "especially on the occasion of your tenth birthday." She reached into the basket to fetch the bag of lemon drops within and held it out to Jenny. "A small token to mark the occasion."

Jenny's face lit up in delight as she accepted the gift. "Oh, thank you, m'lady." She wasted no time in popping a bright yellow candy into her mouth.

"Yes, thank you," Alice echoed. Jenny's happiness seemed to have rubbed off on her, and her drawn expression from the previous day was replaced with a look of joy. "Would you care to join us today for a cup of tea?"

"Yes, do," said Jenny, bouncing over to the hearth with her mouth full of lemon drops. "I'll prepare it, and you can sit right here." She motioned to one of the rickety chairs surrounding a weathered oak table.

"That would be lovely, thank you," said Eliza, carrying the basket with her as she took the offered seat. A glance around revealed to her how small and dark the cottage was; only one room with a bed in one corner and the hearth in the other. On account of the continuing warm weather, the temperature inside was comfortable, but with the stone walls and defective roof, it surely grew unpleasant in wet or colder weather. She would have to speak to Lord Ashton about it, especially since it wouldn't be long before a newborn baby came to live in the cottage, and the summer heat gave way to an autumn chill.

She reached into the basket once more to withdraw another bundle and placed it on the table. "And because we are celebrating a birthday, perhaps we could have this to accompany our tea." She pulled off the cloth, revealing a cake laden with candied fruit. "My sister-in-law, Lady Catherine, assures me that our cook's ginger cake is beyond comparison."

Jenny's elated grin grew even larger. "How lovely! Thank you, m'lady, for your kindness."

The three of them spent the better part of an hour sitting around the table with cups of tea and slices of cake, Jenny chatting eagerly the whole time, until Alice said, "Why, you'll talk Lady Ashton's ear off!" She cast her daughter a fond look. "You'd best take yourself outside for a time and run off some of those fidgets."

While she had seemed to enjoy taking tea with a countess, Jenny went outside without complaint, saying she wished to pick some wildflowers. With the cottage now quiet, Eliza turned her attention to Alice.

"I've brought a poultice for your back," she said, turning to the basket at her feet to retrieve it. "Also, some valerian, to be taken as a tisane at night to help you sleep."

"I can't begin to thank you for all you've done," said Alice as she accepted the items Eliza handed her. "I don't know any other who would have offered us such kindness. Ever since news of my situation spread around the village, no one has wanted to come near me, and Jenny in turn." Her tone turned hard. "You being new here, I suppose you haven't yet heard all the gossip about me. You will, though, in time, and then you, too, will be a stranger to this house."

Eliza shook her head. "As I said yesterday, I have no interest in gossip. My wish is to befriend you, not judge you."

Alice looked unconvinced. "I think I'd better tell you the details of the matter, and you can see then if you still feel the same."

"You are under no obligation to tell me anything," Eliza insisted. "You can say as much or as little as you wish."

"Although everyone now says I played him false, I *did* love John Turner and was faithful to him every day of our marriage." Alice gazed out the window, seemingly lost in thought. "When he died suddenly of fever, Jenny and I were offered a place in his father's home. And I should have contented myself with that, with seeing to the upkeep of the home and the bakery he owns. But though I had John's family, and of course, Jenny, the loneliness was unbearable. Then, one day, the militia came through with all these gallant-looking men …"

She stopped to choke down a sob. "I was such a fool. Jenny was born nearly nine months to the day after I wed, and then, for so many years, there came no others until I thought I could get with child no more. And I thought he cared for me—would take me with him. But he was gone as quickly as he came, never to be heard from again."

"I'm sorry," Eliza said softly, although that hardly seemed sufficient.

"I should have left as soon as I found out I was with child," Alice said, still not looking at her. "I could have gone to London, tried to find some sort of work there. But in those early days, the babe made me so sick that I could hardly rise from bed each morning. By the time the sickness eased, my belly had swelled, and word of my condition spread around the village faster than the plague. No one knew exactly how it had happened, but they knew enough to judge me as the worst kind of harlot. Needless to say, John's father wanted nothing more to do with me. And as for Jenny ..." Her voice had been growing increasingly weary, and she paused to take a deep breath. "Yesterday, when Fanny Turner told you of me, did she say how her husband and John were brothers? And how she thinks I should turn Jenny over to her, to help spare her from my disgrace? She's right, I suppose. But somehow, I just can't bear the thought of being separated from my girl."

"Of course you cannot." Eliza's thoughts of her own mother arose with a painful stab. "I can see the great affection you have for one another."

Alice looked grim. "There may come the day when I have no other choice. I moved into this cottage four months ago, and already, I'm sorely behind with my rent. When I can no longer afford to stay here, I don't know what I can do but take the babe with me to London and seek employment there. If we end up in the poorhouse, at least I'll know Jenny is looked after here."

"No," Eliza said firmly. "That is a fate too terrible to mention. Please, try not to worry over it right now. I will stand as your friend and do everything in my power to help you. Your only concern at present should be to keep yourself well in preparation for the baby's arrival. Once the little one is safely born, then we can ponder what to do going forward."

Alice looked like she was about to protest, but Eliza quickly said, "Please, trust me when I assure you that we will find a way to make things right again. I should be going, but do take the time to try the remedies I've brought you and see if you can find some relief from your discomfort. If you like, I could call again tomorrow to see how you have fared."

"I couldn't ask that of you, m'lady." Alice shook her head in dismay. "I fear I've already taken far too much of your time."

"Not at all," Eliza insisted. "I have a particular interest in medicine, you see, so allowing me to see to your wellbeing is not an imposition in the slightest."

Alice managed a small smile. "I don't know what to say but to thank you again. It was a fortunate day indeed when the earl brought you home as his countess."

Eliza pondered this comment during her journey back to Highfield Park. She doubted Lord Ashton would agree with it. He no longer even wanted to come near her.

But while her relationship with Lord Ashton was sorely lacking, her visit with Alice had brought a feeling of fulfillment. She worried for Alice and Jenny, of course, but seeing the joy her small gestures of kindness had given them brought her a glimmer of happiness of her own. After all, following her mother's death, her closeness with the villagers of Riverton and her ability to help them with her medicines had been the only thing that gave her a sense of purpose. If, as Lady Ashton, she could now do something to help the residents of the estate village, perhaps that sense of purpose would return.

It would never take the place of a loving, devoted relationship, but if she really set her mind to it, maybe it would somehow be enough. Right now, it was all she had.

Chapter 10

Edward had every reason to leave the dinner table feeling fully satisfied. On account of his increase in funds and what he assumed to be Lady Ashton's menu planning, the meals served had increased in quality, and after a day spent mainly outdoors, the food had tasted especially good.

More importantly, his time spent with Locke, the new land agent, had proven highly productive over the past few days. They had procured a flock of Romneys to take the place of the troublesome Merinos. The weather had been fine enough to make progress with the harvest, and Locke had convinced him of the merits of a threshing machine, which was due to arrive the following week. They had also begun discussing plans to dig a drainage ditch in the south field, which Locke was certain would increase yields the following year. It was a fine start to remedying some of the many problems plaguing the estate.

Even more importantly, Catherine was in far better spirits than he'd seen since his return. He had initially found it hard to believe that a girl of her position would prefer being shut up alone in the country over being surrounded by friends and entertainments, but a quiet life at Highfield Park clearly agreed with her, and she and her new governess seemed to be getting on well. He would be remiss, though, in attributing her contentment to only those two factors. From what he had observed, much of her happiness came from the presence of her new sister-in-law. From the day

Lady Ashton had begged for her to stay, Catherine had taken an immediate liking to her, chatting with ease and even referring to her as "Eliza, dear."

Therein lay the problem, the reason he had fled to his study instead of remaining at the table to enjoy a leisurely glass of after-dinner port. His own relationship with his wife was on as shaky ground as ever, with every passing day making it all the more difficult to mend. So much so that immersing himself in estate business, business he had sworn to his father he didn't even care about, seemed the far easier task.

He picked up a list from his desk detailing the many repairs required for the tenant cottages and slumped in his chair to mull it over. But try as he might to concentrate, a piece of information Locke had imparted during their afternoon meeting kept turning over in his head.

A gentle knock at the door brought him back to the present, and he called out for the person to enter, grateful for the interruption.

As it turned out, the person was his wife, the very one who drove him to such distraction. While they always exchanged a few polite words as they sat at opposite ends of the dinner table, this was the first time she had approached him since the day after their wedding, and he tried to keep his expression neutral so his feeling of pleasant surprise would remain undetected.

"I'm sorry to disturb you, my lord," she said as she approached his desk, "but I was hoping we might converse before retiring for the night."

"Yes, of course," he said, motioning to the chair opposite him for her to sit. It was high time they had a conversation, just the two of them. He should have privately approached her days ago, but that was of no matter now. She had made the first overture, but he could take this opportunity to speak his piece as well, for there were words he needed to say and that she deserved to hear.

"It is of a matter pertaining to the estate," she clarified once she was seated.

The estate? He blinked several times, absorbing this unexpected information. And here he had sat thinking she wished to speak of something more personal. He crumpled the list he still held and threw it back onto his desk. "Blast the estate! I'm tired of always thinking of the estate. By rights, I should leave it to crumble and return to the Continent at once, just as I told my father I would do."

The countess's eyes widened. "What a horrible thing to say. Hundreds of people depend on you for their livelihood, and you think you could simply ignore that and leave them all destitute?"

For a moment, it looked like she might shower him with wrath, but instead her expression calmed. "I know you do not truly mean it, though, for I have seen how tirelessly you've been working to ensure the estate is set right again."

Her eyes glittered defiantly, daring him to contradict her, but he said nothing. "And so," she went on, "an additional problem with the estate, regarding a tenant, has come to my attention, and I humbly request your assistance in remedying it. Are you familiar with Mrs. Alice Turner?"

"As a matter of fact, yes," he replied, although he offered no further information.

"And are you aware of her situation? Of her widowhood, and of her … condition?"

"Funnily," he said, "it was brought to my attention only today."

"And do you agree we must help her?" She stared at him imploringly. "Please say you do. She has informed me that she has great difficulty with making rent, so we can start by at least relieving her of that burden. She has nowhere else to go right now, having had former friends and relations turn their back on her. If someone does not step in to see that she and her daughter are cared for, I don't know what will become of them."

"I think, in light of the circumstances, we could forgive her what she owes for the time being."

"Oh, thank you," she exclaimed, her face lighting up. "I have noticed as well that Alice's roof is in need of repair, and with autumn soon upon us—"

"I will send Locke to Alice's cottage to make a list of necessary repairs and see that they are performed at once," he assured her. "But for the time being, perhaps you would like to know how Alice Turner's name became familiar to me today."

"Yes, if you have an inclination to tell me."

"It seems," he said, "that earlier today, you were seen entering Alice Turner's cottage carrying a large basket. Within hours, word of the new mistress showing favor to

Alice had spread throughout the village, at least far enough to reach Locke's ears by the time of our afternoon meeting."

Her face clouded over. "I hope they do not think less of me for it. I will gladly bring baskets and visit with them all in time. However, of the few I have met so far, Alice's need is greatest, and it is on her and her daughter that I have chosen to focus my attention at present. I certainly hope *you* do not think less of me for it."

"I do not," he said. On the contrary, it seemed she held a low opinion of him if she thought he would be angry with her for helping one of his tenants. Then again, what had he done to show her he was anything more than cold and un-feeling? "In your short time here, you have proven yourself to be generous and selfless, which are admirable qualities indeed. But do you never stop to think of your own reputa-tion? Many ladies of the ton, of my acquaintance at least, would shrink from associating themselves with such dis-grace."

"Countess or not, I will always seek to help where I am able, regardless of the circumstances. In a way, Alice's situ-ation made me want to assist her all the more. For while my life is quite simple in comparison, I *do* understand what it's like to be the subject of a scandal, and to feel as if the world has turned against you as a result."

From the moment he had first heard tell of Eliza Wright, he had spent so much time doubting her, assuming she had ulterior motives and was prone to deception. But as he peered into her striking, earnest face, he had no cause to question her sincerity. It was true she had made some sort of slipup in London, the details of which remained a mystery to him. However, knowing what he knew now, he couldn't imagine her purposely doing anything with ill intent.

As he continued looking at her, the words he had thought to say when she first entered the study returned to him.

Say it, prodded a small voice inside his head.

But then again, why should he? He had made an error in judgement, to be sure, but any man would have done so when knowingly wedding a woman embroiled in scandal.

Say it. The voice was more insistent now, but still he remained silent. He was an earl, so the fault always lay with others, not with him, or so his father had led him to believe.

Say it!

"Lady Ashton," he uttered before he could torment himself any longer, "I feel I must apologize."

"Apologize?"

"Our marriage has gotten off to a bad start, I'm afraid, and the blame rests on me. On the night of our wedding, I confess to having over-imbibed, but that is no excuse. I was wrong to make presumptions about you, and I hope you can forgive my unfitting behavior."

She was so lovely, the way her dress almost glimmered and her hair shone with a crimson tinge beneath the candle-light. And with his words, a half-smile crossed her lips.

"I appreciate and accept your apology. As the state of matrimony is new to me, I have much to learn and improve upon as well. If you are not already aware of it, perhaps I had best explain the nature of my scandal so there are no longer questions in your mind."

"No," he rushed to say. "You are not obligated to give me an explanation. Please, let us dwell on bygone events no longer. I wish only to think of you here, now."

"If you are certain." She shifted in her seat, looking like there was much she still thought to say.

"I am." The words came out as a hoarse whisper that failed to convey his adamance. Surely, though, she must see that digging too deeply into events of the past, either hers or his, was not the key to their happiness. If they were to have a hope of getting on, they would have to focus on each other as they existed in the present.

She made no additional comment on the subject, only sat there and continued to regard him with her alluring emerald eyes. And as he gazed at her in return, he wanted so much for all to be well between them. For with the burden of the apology he owed removed from his shoulders, what remained was desire.

Suddenly, even the desk between them presented too great a distance, and he sprang from his chair and hastened to her side. He reached to take her silk-gloved hand, and as she returned his grasp, he gently pulled her upward to stand before him. Still, too much distance remained, and he pulled her in closer until her body pressed tightly enough against his that he could feel the steady drumming of her heartbeat.

"Eliza," he murmured into her hair, inhaling her sweet floral scent as the silky strands brushed against his cheek.

She turned her face upward so their eyes locked, and her heart pounded more vigorously against him. "Edward."

Coming from her mouth, his name sounded like the sweetest song, one he wanted to hear over and over. How would it sound if she uttered it as a breathy cry of pleasure beneath him? The thought made him harden, but if she noticed the rigidness pressing against her thigh, she didn't shy away.

He placed his lips over hers, too needy to be delicate, and let his tongue trace circles in her mouth as he drank in her enthralling taste. All the while, he stroked the soft skin at the back of her neck and then dragged his fingers downward to her lower back and the swell of her bottom, relishing the feel of her supple curves. How he yearned to feel her caress him in return, and to hear her moan with pleasure from his touch once more.

But this time, something was different. Lady Ashton—Eliza—was perfectly still. Perhaps the intensity was all too much. With great difficulty, he lightened the pressure of his lips and touch and waited until she relaxed into him. Then, feeling her soften, he caressed her once more, bringing his hand between them until it skimmed the sensitive place between her legs.

She inhaled sharply, biting her lip just like last time, and the next thing he knew, she was struggling in his arms and shoving him away.

"I believe I will retire now," she said, her voice breathless and wavering. She hastily straightened her crumpled dress and backed away from him, looking much like a cornered animal. "Good night, Lord Ashton." Then, she darted out of the study without another word, leaving him alone and bewildered.

After the unfortunate events of his wedding night, he had been trying to keep his consumption of brandy to a minimum, but right now the temptation was too great to resist. He poured himself a generous glass from the nearby decanter and sank back into his desk chair to consume it as he waited for the fiery sensation within him to abate.

He had thought that he and his wife had reached an understanding. That with her characteristic kindheartedness, she had seen fit to forgive the ways in which he had wronged her. Fool that he was, he had even thought that she returned his desire and their union could become more than just a marriage in name.

Apparently, he had been very, very wrong. And surprisingly, he cared very, very deeply. It was all well and good to ride to London in the pursuit of pleasure, or to contemplate his return to Florence and the mistress he could seek to fill his bed there, but that was no longer what he wanted. The only thing that would satisfy this intolerable ache was Eliza, and he had succeeded in driving her away.

It all pointed to a truth he had come to accept long ago: He wasn't meant for marriage. The fact that this particular marriage was born of circumstances not of his or his wife's choosing only served to complicate matters. But maybe ... maybe, given enough time, they could come to an accord, to a certain level of comfort with one another.

Then again, maybe not. For he knew all too well that some wounds cut so deep, they were beyond repair.

Chapter 11

"Eliza? Did you hear me?"

A glance at Catherine's puzzled face across the breakfast table told Eliza she had been daydreaming, an annoyingly frequent occurrence over the past few days.

"I apologize," she said, focusing her attention back on Catherine. "Could you repeat the question?"

"I asked if you thought Alice could use any of the items from our nursery. As it has been ten years since Jenny was born, I thought she might be in want of a few things. I could take you up to the nursery to have a look around if you like."

"That's very kind of you." Eliza smiled at her sister-in-law, touched by her thoughtfulness. Through conversations they had shared over the past couple weeks, she had gotten the impression that neither of Catherine's parents had been much inclined to perform charitable deeds. Yet when she had made a passing comment about Alice over dinner the previous evening, Catherine had asked questions and then expressed an immediate desire to help however she could.

Therefore, when both of their breakfast plates were cleared, she allowed Catherine to lead her up the stairs and through winding corridors until they reached the nursery. Mrs. Parker had shown it to her briefly during her arrival tour, but this was her first opportunity to spend any length of time in it. The room was positioned to receive the morning sun, and with light streaming in the windows and hitting the pale blue walls, it looked bright and cheerful. All sorts of playthings lined the walls, and in the center of the room stood an intricately carved oak cradle. Eliza smirked as she imagined the solemn-faced Lord Ashton as a young child, toddling about this room in leading strings.

Seeing her expression, Catherine smiled as well. "I always rather liked it here." She walked over to the trunk that stood at the foot of the little bed in one corner and knelt to open the lid. "Perhaps Alice could use some of these. They will require airing but should otherwise do nicely."

Eliza joined her to sort through the piles of blankets, caps, and gowns. "There certainly is a lot here. I'm sure Alice will be grateful for whatever we offer, for it will spare her the need for constant laundering."

"You will likely have need of these items yourself someday, of course," said Catherine, adding a tiny linen gown to the pile they had started, "but I think we have more than enough to spare."

Eliza nodded in agreement, trying to conceal her discomfiture from Catherine's harmless comment. Catherine, in her innocence, had no idea of what had passed between her brother and his new wife, and Eliza would have sooner died than admit her shame, especially to Lord Ashton's sister.

How could she even begin to utter the words that something was wrong with her, or that the mere thought of Lord Ashton's touch heated her to the core and left her so she couldn't think straight? And that because she seemed incapable of sitting still and behaving as a proper lady should when it came to intimate matters, she was unsure how she would ever successfully share a bed with her husband.

"Shall we go down now? It's rather hot in here." Eliza hoped the words provided an adequate explanation for the flush spreading over her cheeks.

"Yes, I suppose. Miss Martin has arranged for a dance instructor to come today, and I imagine he will be arriving soon." She wrinkled her nose in distaste, but then her expression brightened. "You could join us. I imagine you have already acquired such skills, but it would be so much better with you there."

"Thank you, but I should prepare these things to bring to Alice straight away." As much as she didn't want to disappoint Catherine, Eliza didn't feel up to the task of twirling about the floor while having every move criticized.

Catherine smiled resignedly. "Very well. I certainly cannot fault you for your refusal. The lesson is sure to be tedious."

Eliza gave her a sympathetic grin in return as she picked up the large pile of baby items and moved to exit the nursery. But just as she reached the doorway, Catherine's gentle voice called out to her. "Eliza, dear?"

She turned to face her sister-in-law where she still stood by the sturdy oak cradle. "Yes?"

Catherine took a deep breath, hesitating for a moment. "I thought I might speak with you while we are up here alone without interruption. I hope you will not think what I mean to say too forward."

"Please, just say it," Eliza urged her. "Let us speak openly with one another as true sisters."

She peered at Catherine, eager for her to continue, but Catherine turned to the bookshelf that lined one of the walls, running her fingers over the leatherbound spines.

"I do not know my brother well," she finally said, keeping her focus on the bookshelf. "By the time I was born, he was already away at Eton. Then, he went on to Oxford, and then came his courtship and marriage, followed by all his years on the Continent. There were times, though, in those earlier days, when he would come home for a holiday. And during those times, he never neglected to come up here to the nursery to see how I was getting on." She paused with a small smile as her fingertips reached the end of the row of books. "He was an excellent reader. He always did all the voices for me."

Eliza's previous image of Lord Ashton in leading strings turned to one of him as a youth, sitting beside his sister on her little bed with a book spread across his lap, both of them golden-haired and laughing as he read the words aloud. Maybe he had been different in those days, with no hint of the hardness that now clouded his ocean blue eyes.

"But I'm rambling," said Catherine, turning around to look at Eliza once more. "My point is, I know Edward may seem distant at times. He tries to escape his troubles, I think, and I cannot blame him, not after all that passed with his first marriage."

The temptation to question Catherine further on this statement and learn more about the past that Lord Ashton was so determined to keep from discussing with her was great.

"But it is not my place to discuss such things," Catherine added before Eliza could say a word, "and here I am, rambling again. What I mean to say is, it is my honest belief that although he does not always show it, Edward cares deeply for those close to him and has a desire to do right by them. That includes you, his wife."

Eliza's first reaction was to tell Catherine how wrong she was. Of course Lord Ashton didn't care for her. She was an unwanted wife, tolerated only for her wealth. She was surely no match for the proper lady he had previously wed and loved.

But then she recalled her initial belief after meeting him, which related to what Catherine had just said: His coldness came from grief. It did not define who he was at his core.

It was easy enough to think of examples of the caring he showed to others. His willingness to terminate Alice's rent payments without a second thought, his hard work repairing the estate despite claiming he cared nothing for it, his desire to see his sister happy and provided for.

And when she really thought on it, she could recall small glimmers of warmth he had shown her as well. His slight smile at the pianoforte, the sincerity in his voice when he had thanked her for the remedy she offered him, and again, when he had apologized for his misbeliefs about her. And then, there was the way he had held her, somehow hard yet gentle at the same time. His fingers had traced over her as if she were some deity to be revered, awakening sensations in her she hadn't known existed.

The difficulty lay in reconciling this facet of him with the aloof stranger who spent much of his time avoiding her. Which side was the true him, the one with whom she would spend the rest of her life? And did she even possess the ability to make him happy either way?

These thoughts kept her on edge long after she and Catherine left the nursery and parted ways. She tried to put them out of her mind as she walked toward Alice's cottage that afternoon, but she couldn't shake her persistent sense of discomposure. Maybe it had something to do with the weather. It had turned unpleasantly muggy once more, to the point that her dress clung to her like an uncomfortable second skin, and the air seemed almost too heavy to breathe. Thick clouds billowed off in the distance, suggesting the possibility of rain, and she hoped they would float in her direction and provide a welcome reprieve.

She had nearly reached the familiar row of cottages when her foot twisted beneath her, and she found herself toppling forward. Instinctively, she threw out her arms to catch her balance, and she was lucky enough to steady herself and avoid crashing to the ground. She looked down to see a loose rock on the road, which had surely been the cause of her stumble. It was just like what had happened on the garden path at Hinshaw House, except that time, Lord Ashton had been there to catch her, pulling her against his chest and then—

No. She couldn't afford to think of such things at present.

It suddenly occurred to her that her hand was smarting, and when she peered at the damage, she realized that, upon pitching forward, she must have driven her hand into a loose piece in the wicker basket she carried.

"Blast," she muttered, for although the pain was not severe, she had torn a hole right through her glove. She supposed it was a fitting match to her hem, which was now spotted with dirt on account of her stumble.

By the time she reached Alice's cottage, she felt overheated and bedraggled, and she could tell by Alice's surprised face when she answered the door that those feelings were reflected in her appearance.

"Come in, m'lady," urged Alice, ushering her inside. "Sit down, and I'll fetch you a cup of tea."

"I'll sit for a moment," said Eliza, heading for the rickety wooden chair where she had sat and visited with Alice and Jenny several times now. "But please, you needn't trouble yourself with any refreshments.

"'Tis no trouble," Alice assured her. "I already have the water at a boil. Jenny's out playing in the meadow, but I'd be most pleased if you'd stay and take tea with me, if you're willing. I'm not nearly so weary as I was, on account of your remedies, I daresay."

"Very well. Thank you." Eliza mumbled the words and then sat silently, trying to regain her composure, until Alice placed a steaming cup before her.

"Why, your glove," exclaimed Alice, peering down at the ripped cotton. "Did some misfortune befall you?"

"It is nothing," answered Eliza quickly. "I seem to be always getting myself into some scrape or another. Clumsiness, I suppose." She tried to smile, but her mouth didn't want to turn fully upward.

"Allow me to mend it for you. I might not get it looking new again, but I can at least have it looking better for your journey home."

Eliza was about to protest, but Alice insisted. "Please, m'lady. You've shown me no end of kindness. It's high time I repaid you in some small way."

"If you insist. Where are your sewing things? I'll fetch them," she offered now that Alice was already seated.

Alice pointed to a trunk at the foot of the bed, and Eliza went to it, opening the lid with a creak. A basket of needles and thread sat on top, but as she pulled it out, she noticed it had been resting on an intricately embroidered white linen table runner. Beside it lay a folded pink apron of cotton voile, embroidered with delicate blue flowers. The beauty of the items provided a stark contrast to the drab interior of Alice's cottage.

"How lovely," she commented. "Alice, did you make all this?"

"A long time ago." Alice smiled dimly. "I don't have much use for such things now."

"You have great skill," Eliza said as she set the sewing basket on the table before Alice and handed her the torn glove.

"At one time, I fancied I could become a seamstress. But then I got swept off my feet by John Turner, and then came Jenny, and all the while I was needed to help mind the Turners' bakery." Alice gave a short sigh as she ran her needle in and out through the glove. "But never mind my grousing. Are you sure you're quite well, m'lady?"

"Yes, quite," said Eliza, although the words pinched in her throat. Suddenly realizing she had not yet revealed the reason for her visit, she picked up the basket she had set at her feet and pushed it across the table. "Here, this is for you. Well, for the new baby. Items from our nursery, sent to you by Lady Catherine."

Alice dropped her sewing to rummage through the knitted blankets and tiny gowns and caps. Her eyebrows lifted in wonder, and she quickly pushed the items back into the basket as if she had just been caught touching something she shouldn't have. "Surely my child can't be wearing clothing from the home of the earl!"

"I see no reason why not." Eliza gently nudged the basket closer to her. "A baby is a baby, after all, and it is my understanding that they go through gowns with remarkable speed."

Alice still appeared uncertain. "But you might have need of these things yourself before long."

And there it was, the same seemingly harmless comment that Catherine had made, yet it caused Eliza's cheeks to burn and her stomach to twist into knots. She wanted to smile and nod, while assuring Alice that plenty of baby items remained at Highfield Park for her own use, but she couldn't even bring herself to look up from her cup of tea.

"I fear I've been taking too much of your time," said Alice, noticing her discomfort. "Here you've been to visit me three days in a row now, and for that I can't thank you enough. But you're a new bride with a new home. Surely you'd much rather spend time with your husband, the earl."

Eliza took a deep breath, trying to steady herself. It would be beyond humiliating to explain what a mess her brief marriage had become. But what was the alternative? Would she forever be on tenterhooks whenever Lord Ashton came into her presence, feeling an uncomfortable heat burn through her core while at the same time recalling Augusta's words about behaving as a proper lady in the marriage bed?

Then, she looked at Alice, whose hazel eyes brimmed with kindness and concern. Alice wasn't a highborn lady, but she had once been married, so she must know something of the subject. In any case, who else was she to speak with about such matters? She longed more than anything for her mother's advice, but her mother was gone, and there was no one left she could trust.

But maybe she could trust Alice. It seemed unlikely that Alice would judge her or gossip about her. They occupied two very different stations in life, but here in this cottage, they were friends.

Finally, she allowed her frustration to burst to the surface. "There are things about marriage I cannot comprehend!"

Her outburst clearly surprised Alice, until a sudden look of understanding spread across her face. "If there are any questions I can answer, you need only ask, m'lady."

"When a husband and wife are alone together …" She paused, feeling her face flush once more as she searched for the appropriate words. "Is what occurs ever meant to bring pleasure to the wife?"

With the question out, Eliza now wanted to crawl under the table. Fortunately, Alice remained unphased. "Why, I should say so," she replied, "if the husband has any sort of skill."

The memory of Lord Ashton's mouth pressing against her sprang to the forefront, but she quickly pushed it aside. The answer was reassuring, but it still did not get to the heart of the matter. She summoned up the courage to speak once more. "And do you think that is true even if the wife is, for instance, a countess?"

Alice looked thoughtful. "I can't rightly say, being only a farmer's daughter and baker's wife myself. But when it comes to feelings that arise from the marriage act, I can't see that making a difference."

The confusion she had felt ever since Augusta's speech the night before her wedding was finally starting to lift, although one final question remained. "And if a wife experiences pleasure, would that be pleasing to the husband in turn? Whether the husband was a baker or, say, an earl?"

"No matter his station in life, I think he would have to have rocks in his head not to appreciate an eager woman in his bed," said Alice bluntly.

Hearing the words spoken aloud made it all seem so obvious. Rather than embarrassed, she now felt incredibly naive for all her former trepidation.

"Thank you," she said, clasping Alice's hand as she rose from her seat. "Your words have been most informative. I should really be on my way now."

"Of course," said Alice, handing her the now-mended glove. "I'm always here for a chat. But won't you stay a little longer?" She cast a worried glance out the window. "The clouds have moved in, and it looks like rain."

The clouds did indeed appear dark and threatening, but Eliza couldn't risk lingering and losing her resolve. "I'll walk quickly and be back at Highfield Park in no time. I'm sure I can escape the worst of the rain. Please pass on my regards to Jenny, and I'll return to see you again soon."

"Don't feel you have to come rushing back right away. I'll understand if you're occupied at home for a time." Alice flashed her a knowing smile, and for the first time that afternoon, she was able to offer a genuine smile in return.

A weight had been lifted from her shoulders, allowing her to depart the cottage with far greater lightness than when she had arrived. As she traversed the road, tiny shreds of doubt began to creep back into her thoughts, for the possibility still existed that, when it came to intimate matters regarding the peerage, Augusta had been correct all along not Alice. Yet if she allowed her actions to continue to be influenced by Augusta's words, she feared she might go mad.

No, she would go forward believing what Alice had told her, hoping it was the key to closing the agonizing distance that had sprung up between her and Lord Ashton.

In any case, she would soon find out.

Chapter 12

Reaping corn was backbreaking work, but Edward found the monotonous task strangely calming. He stayed bent over with his scythe, his lower back throbbing after an extended period in that position, watching with satisfaction as, little by little, the stalks that would become profit for Highfield Park fell to the ground. He had been in the field for several hours now, but he still felt the curious eyes of the other laborers upon him as he worked. These men undoubtedly saw the new earl working away with a scythe and thought he had taken leave of his senses, but their opinions were of no consequence. When he toiled in the field, he could concentrate only on the sun's warmth against his face, the burning sensation in his limbs, and the next section of stalks that required cutting. All other thoughts left his head, and that was exactly as he wanted it.

He stayed this way, despite the stifling afternoon heat, until a low rumble caught his attention. He peered up to the sky, and much to his surprise, it had clouded over and now appeared threatening. How that had escaped his notice until now, he hadn't the faintest clue. A bright flash in the distance illuminated the sky, followed by another rumble.

He took a long swallow from the mug of ale beside him and pushed himself up to his full height, stretching out his cramped back.

"Pause what you're doing and see that this gets stooked before the rain," he announced to the reapers. "It looks like we are in for a storm, and it would do none of us good to be caught in the middle of it. You can take refuge in the barn until it passes, and I'll see that more ale is sent down."

The reapers mumbled their assent as he went to fetch his horse, Apollo, from where he grazed nearby. Fortunately, the thunder was still distant enough so as not to spook him, and they galloped back to the house at top speed, returning just as the first heavy drops of rain began to fall. Edward handed the reins to a waiting groom and dashed into the house and up the stairs to his bedroom.

The water in the washbasin had long turned tepid, but he splashed it over himself anyway, welcoming the cooling sensation it brought to his overheated skin. Once he had exchanged his dirt-stained clothes for clean ones and made himself presentable, he went back downstairs, thinking he would read over farm reports in his study until it was time to prepare for dinner.

Strains of music from the drawing room greeted him as he reached the bottom step. He immediately thought of Eliza banging away at the keys of her pianoforte as he stood behind her, just close enough to reach out and touch the skin at the back of her neck. The memory propelled him toward the drawing room, even though the notes that reached him were smooth and melodious, suggesting Eliza wasn't the current musician.

Sure enough, when he reached the drawing room, he was greeted with the sight of Catherine sitting at the pianoforte while Miss Martin lounged in a nearby armchair. Upon his entry, Catherine stopped playing and looked up hopefully from her music, but then her face fell.

"Oh. It's only you."

"That's a fine greeting for your only brother." He pursed his lips in mock indignance.

Catherine rolled her eyes. "I was hoping you were Eliza. She went to visit Alice Turner some time ago and still has not returned. Given the current weather, I'm concerned."

The rain had indeed grown much heavier, and a clap of thunder boomed as if to affirm Catherine's fears.

"I'm sure she cannot be far. I will go and ask if any of the servants have seen her." He kept his tone reassuring, but an annoying twinge of worry accompanied him as he left the room.

They were probably both overreacting. After all, Eliza was known for her enjoyment of spending time outdoors. Could she possibly be foolish enough to stop and sketch plants amidst a thunderstorm? Nevertheless, upon learning from Higgins that no one had laid eyes upon Lady Ashton since her departure for the village earlier that afternoon, he felt the knot in his stomach tighten.

He rushed to the entrance hall and opened the front door to peer out, his view of the drive obstructed by the pouring rain. He paused only a moment before making his way outside and down the stone steps, receiving an instant drenching as soon as he left the shelter of the portico. He looked left and right, eager to spot some sign of movement, but the grounds were empty. It was foolhardy to be out here, especially without any sort of protection from the elements, but he found himself incapable of retreating to the safety of the house as though nothing were amiss. Instead, he put a hand to his brow to shelter his eyes from the rain and continued up the drive, only partially aware of the deafening crack of thunder from above.

Finally, he saw her, running down the far end of the drive toward him. As Eliza came closer, it became clear that she, too, had received a thorough drenching. Her soaked straw bonnet was a deflated lump atop her head, and strands of auburn hair that had fallen from their pins were plastered against her face. The rain had turned the airy white fabric of her dress semitransparent, and her skirts clung to her so tightly as to leave no curve to the imagination.

After letting out a breath he hadn't even realized he'd been holding, he ran to meet her, wanting to ensure that the figure rushing toward him wasn't just a figment conjured up by the driving rain. Their paths soon crossed, and he reached for her hand, grateful when his fingers met with a warmth masked by a saturated cotton glove. He could have taken her in his arms right there. Instead, he tightened his grip on her hand and started pulling her back toward the house.

"What in God's name are you doing out here?" The sharpness in his tone made him inwardly cringe.

"I was visiting Alice and thought I would have enough time to return home before the rain started," she said, breathless after her prolonged period of running. "It seems I was wrong."

He gritted his teeth and made no reply as he continued marching with her back up the drive, not stopping until they climbed the stone steps at the front of the house.

Once they reached the shelter of the portico, Eliza stopped and wrenched her hand free. "What were you doing outdoors, then, if a bit of rain makes you so cross?"

"What do you think I was doing?" he snapped, eying her defiantly arched eyebrows with a scowl. "I was looking for you."

Her face, heavily dotted with raindrops that became tiny rivers running down her cheeks, turned incredulous. "Looking for me? But why?"

"Damn it," he shouted, his exasperation boiling over, "I was worried about you!"

Eliza froze, fixing her emerald eyes upon him. The only part of her that still moved was her chest, rising and falling with each heavy breath. Until suddenly, she launched herself at him and pressed her mouth to his, her hands grabbing fistfuls of his dripping hair.

His shock lasted only a split second before turning into an intensity that matched her own. He deepened the kiss, swirling his tongue against hers as he savored her intoxicating heat. All the while, he pulled at the ribbon under her chin until her limp bonnet fell to the ground, and he ran his fingers through the silken locks underneath.

She made a little sound at the back of her throat and pulled away to look up at him with huge eyes, as if in disbelief over what she had set in motion. His body felt as though it were screaming in protest at her withdrawal, and he pulled her back to him, claiming her mouth once more. Mercifully, she made no objection. Instead, she cast off her gloves and strengthened her grip on him, pushing herself into him even more tightly.

He desperately wanted more yet feared that this moment of perfect, unencumbered closeness would vanish if he broke the embrace. Thus, they stayed pressed together at the top of the stone steps until beneath the thin fabric of her dress and her sodden velvet spencer, Eliza began to shiver.

"Come," he breathed into her ear, moving slightly to join hands with her. Then, he pushed open the front door to be greeted by the sight of an astonished Higgins.

"Why, Lord Ashton, Lady Ashton," he exclaimed, staring at the two drenched figures before him.

"Lady Ashton and I are going to our rooms and will not be down for dinner this evening," Edward said before the butler had a chance to fuss. "We do not wish to be disturbed. If we require anything, we shall ring for it."

"Very good, my lord," answered Higgins. At least, that's what Edward thought Higgins had said. By that time, he and Eliza were already halfway up the stairs. He kept her hand in his, leading her quickly down corridors until he reached her bedroom door, and they both stumbled into the room. He nudged the door shut and pressed her alongside it, joining his mouth to hers once more. His arousal pushed achingly against her, and he broke the kiss to tug open the buttons of her spencer and pull it off, desperate to rid her of all these extraneous layers of clothing.

Her fingers began fumbling with the knots of his cravat until it came undone and fluttered to the floor, and she turned to unbutton his coat and waistcoat with clumsy urgency. He shrugged off the garments, and she brought her attention to his shirt, pulling it from the waistband of his trousers and reaching beneath it to run her hand from his navel upward to his chest. The feel of her fingertips against his bare skin sent fire coursing through him, and he inhaled sharply at the sudden burst of sensation.

With that, Eliza dropped her hand and looked away from him, squirming against his weight. "Easy," he soothed, easing off her a little but placing a finger under her chin so she would look up at him again. "You have nothing to be afraid of." He would do anything she asked of him, anything she needed, but if she were to run away from him again, he wasn't sure how he would bear it.

"Did I do something wrong?" she asked, her voice strained.

Edward stared at her in disbelief. "Of course not." He leaned in, planting gentle kisses against her throat, right at the spot where her pulse throbbed rapidly. "You are exquisite. Ideal. Why would you think otherwise?"

She reddened from the roots of her hair to the swell of her breasts, where they peeked out of her dress. "Because," she said, barely above a whisper, "I was led to believe that when it comes to intimacy, proper ladies do not show passion."

He gave a choking laugh, although it was a sound of incredulity, not mirth. "Who in blazes gave you such a preposterous idea?"

"My aunt Augusta, on the night before our wedding," she mumbled, turning her eyes to the floor.

"Your aunt Augusta?" This was growing increasingly more absurd. "Do you mean to say you have allowed yourself to be influenced by the ramblings of an unpleasant spinster?"

"I'm sure you must think me very foolish," she said, furrowing her brow and pouting.

"Oh, indubitably." He pressed his lips to the indignant crease between her eyes and stroked the back of her neck until she softened beneath him. "In fact, I mean to show you just how wrong you have been."

He spun around with her in his arms and strode across the room, not stopping until they stood before the fireplace. A maid must have come in to light it upon the change in the weather, for flames danced in the grate, providing much-needed warmth and casting a soft glow around the room darkened by the black thunderclouds. He dashed behind her and set to work unfastening her dress and petticoat, pushing them from her shoulders until they fell to the floor. She took a step away from the pile of garments, kicking off her shoes in the process, and he leaned in to circle his tongue around her earlobe as he began unlacing her stays. She gave a small shiver.

"You see," he murmured into her ear, "I value your pleasure above all else." Her stays dropped to the floor as well, leaving her standing in only her shift and stockings. He brought his hands forward until they ran over her breasts and reached the hardened buds of her nipples. He circled them with his fingertips and gave each one a soft pinch through the fabric, causing her to let out a guttural, needy sound.

"I want to hear you moan with desire," he said, grazing the soft skin of her earlobe with his teeth. As if on cue, she let out another throaty cry. "I want you to lie beneath me and call out my name in yearning. I want to make you feel things you have never even dreamed of." He moved a hand up to loosen the ribbon at the neckline of her shift, and at last, that final concealing bit of clothing fell away. "For giving you pleasure," he uttered, absorbing the fire from her exposed skin, "would bring me indescribable pleasure in return."

He turned her to face him, pausing a moment to appreciate her unclothed beauty before steering her toward the edge of the bed. She gave another inpatient tug at his shirt as he coaxed her back on to the counterpane, and he happily obliged, pulling the garment over his head and then moving on to take off his boots and trousers. Her eyes widened, staring at his bare form in wonder until her lips curled into a seductive smile, and she reached out for him to join her.

He lowered himself to lie beside her, his every nerve ending throbbing with need as his skin brushed against hers. He had to fight the urge to sink deep inside her at once and put a swift end to his aching torment. But no, he would never allow himself to act on that impulse, not when prolonging the experience would make it so much better for them both. Especially for Eliza, who deserved to know just how much pleasure a countess could receive.

He dropped a featherlight kiss to her lips, resisting when her mouth tried to pull him in more tightly. Instead, he trailed kisses down her neck and collarbone and kept going until he reached a taut, rosy nipple, finally taking it into his mouth without the interference of a fabric barrier. She panted heavily as his tongue swirled around the exposed flesh, and he placed a hand between her legs, running his fingers through the soft curls until her thighs instinctively opened. Low sounds emerged from deep in her throat until his finger connected with her sensitive peak, causing her to let out a high-pitched whimper. He continued running his finger over her with languid circles, feeling her press into him as her muscles began to tense. Then, he brought his other hand to her entrance, letting a finger invade the wet heat.

"Please," she moaned, her body thrashing against the mattress.

He circled her peak harder and faster, and when her eyes screwed shut and her palms pressed into the pillow, he added a second finger to the one already inside her, stroking her. She shattered around him, crying out a garbled version of his name, and suddenly he could wait no more. He climbed atop her, bracing himself with his arms as he positioned himself at her entrance.

"This might hurt for just a moment," he started to say, but she was already urging him toward her.

"I want you," she whispered.

He gave a gentle thrust and eased himself forward until he was buried deep inside her, absorbing her lingering shudders. She gasped, this time a sound of discomfort, and he leaned in to place his mouth over hers, wishing he could instantly dissolve her pain. As difficult as it was, he kept his body still as he kissed her, giving her time to adjust to his intrusion. She wiggled a little before propelling her hips up to meet him, sending a jolt of desire through him and causing her eyes to widen in awe.

"Please," she begged again, and he knew she was ready.

He began to move, trying to go slow at first, but the irresistible sensation of her tight warmth compelled him to quicken the pace. Her quiet moans increased in intensity, and soon she was arching her hips to meet him with each stroke, urging him to go deeper. He complied, and her body started to quiver and tighten before she exploded beneath him with a loud cry. It was enough to trigger his own climax, and he heard himself make an unintelligible sound as waves of ecstasy washed over him.

Exhausted, he rolled to the side, keeping his eyes on Eliza's serene face. After they had spent a few minutes lying together in silence, he asked, "Are you all right, sweetheart?" He ran a hand through her disheveled hair.

"Yes." She smiled. "Better than all right. That was wonderful."

"I wholeheartedly agree." He almost smiled in return, but then a thought struck him, and he pulled himself to a sitting position. Their lovemaking over, he was now unsure how to proceed. He had known many women on the Continent, but they had all left his bed as quickly as they entered it, for he always insisted upon sleeping alone. And then there had been Julia, whose words still lingered in his mind.

"Of course you cannot spend the night in my bed, insatiable man. Why, you are apt to keep me awake all night. Retire to your own room and dream of me, and on the morrow, once we have settled ourselves in Brighton, perhaps you may come to me again."

He hated how well he remembered such things and angrily tried to push the memory from his mind, turning his attention back to the beautiful woman before him. However, his elation was beginning to dissolve, leaving only shreds of doubt.

"Would you like to get up for dinner?" he asked, the words sounding awkward and ridiculous. "I think we're too late to ready ourselves for a meal in the dining room, but I could request a tray for you."

She shook her head. "I just received all the sustenance I require at present." Her sated smile lingered another moment, but as she watched him sitting silently at the edge of the bed, it turned into a frown. "I'm rather tired, actually, and think I will rest. Will you not join me?"

He hesitated, eying the nearby door that connected their rooms. Then he turned back to Eliza, who still lay naked on the counterpane, warm and welcoming, although just a hint of worry had crept into her gleaming green eyes.

"Yes," he said, extending a tentative hand out to pull down the counterpane so he could slip between the sheets, although he remained sitting.

Eliza wriggled into the sheets herself, lying on her side to face him. No sooner had she placed her head back on the pillow than her eyelids began to droop.

"It seems that for the second time since my arrival here, I'm abed long before nightfall," she said, stifling a yawn. "Most uncharacteristic of me, I continue to assure you, although perhaps you no longer believe me."

That did elicit a smile from him, at least a small one. "I might suspect there was something wrong with my performance if you were not at least a little tired. Sleep, and do not trouble yourself in the least."

Her eyes drifted closed, and soon her breathing became quiet and even. Certain she was asleep, he lowered himself to lie alongside her, lightly encircling her in his arms.

This house, this country, and this marriage were all things he had so adamantly sworn he wanted no part of. But as he peered at his wife's peaceful face, he experienced a sense of contentment, of fulfillment, that had escaped him for so long, and he knew that in this moment, there was nowhere else he would rather be.

That was a frightening realization indeed.

Chapter 13

Eliza woke to the sound of birds chirping outside her window as rays of early morning sunshine streamed in. It appeared the previous day's storm was long gone, giving way to calm brightness.

The storm. The memory of being caught outside in the rain, and all that had transpired as a result, came rushing back to her. It almost seemed like a dream, although the slight soreness between her legs provided proof that the evening's events had, in fact, been real.

She turned her head, and sure enough, there was Edward sprawled out beside her, still fast asleep. How wonderful he looked with his golden locks spilling onto his forehead and his face holding none of the strain or doubt that often appeared during the day. The sheets covered them both, but she could now picture the perfectly sculpted form that lay underneath. A smile crossed her lips as she remembered waking up to him late the previous night and how she had studied him carefully as he dressed before going downstairs to fetch refreshments. Then, they had sat by the dying fire drinking wine and nibbling on biscuits and grapes until she helped him remove his clothing, and he took her once more, this time with slow, careful strokes.

The memory stirred up an ache deep within her core, and she nuzzled into him, craving the sensation of his warm body next to hers. Her slight movement caused him to stir, and he blinked a few times as if trying to get his bearings before fixing his eyes on her with a look of recognition.

"Good morning," she whispered, bringing her hand up so she could trace her fingertips over the sprinkling of hair on his chest.

"Good morning," he said in a voice still thick with sleep, gazing at her as if he didn't quite believe she was real.

His hardness nudged against her thigh, and she pushed herself against him more insistently, her desire deepening.

But suddenly, he sat upright and pulled himself from the bed, hastening to the fireside to retrieve his discarded pile of clothing. Her heart sank at the sight, causing her strong sense of yearning to vanish as quickly as a candle flame beneath a snuffer. Why was he always running from her? She had been so sure that things would now be different after all they had shared the previous night. But as she watched him hurriedly throw on his shirt, she began to fear that nothing had really changed after all.

"Are you in a hurry to be somewhere, my lord?" she asked, trying to keep her tone disinterested and her face expressionless. She couldn't stand the thought of him seeing his ability to hurt her.

"Estate business to attend to," he muttered as he fastened his fall front.

"I see." She knew she was failing miserably at hiding her discontent. So, this was how things were to be, then. He would share her bed at night while remaining as aloof as ever during the day. She bit her lip as irritation began to simmer within her.

He rushed over to the door that connected their rooms, placing his hand on the knob, but instead of turning it, he spun back to look at her. "Eliza?"

At least he had not reverted to the formality of calling her "Lady Ashton," for that would have likely sent her ire spiraling out of control. She gave a slight nod as encouragement for him to continue.

"I should ride out after breakfast to ensure the storm caused no significant damage, but perhaps we might spend the afternoon together if you are agreeable to the idea. I'm sure you have already journeyed about the estate, but I thought I might show you some of it myself, and it's fine weather for a picnic."

Her initial thought was to insist she was otherwise occupied for the day, for that was the soundest way to protect herself from additional hurt. But as she peered across the room at his face, so cautious, yet containing the tiniest trace of hopefulness, something within her softened. He had made an overture, and given her underlying desire that they grow closer to one another, it wouldn't benefit her to refuse it.

With that in mind, she said, "Yes, I would be agreeable."

***

The bright afternoon sunshine helped to elevate Eliza's mood further. She took in deep breaths of the fragrant air, made crisper after the heavy rain, as she strolled the grounds with her husband at her side. It seemed to have a positive effect on Edward as well, for as he strode through the lush grass, swinging a picnic basket at his side, he looked carefree in a way she wasn't used to seeing.

He led her around the lake, toward the far side where there stood a soaring stone rotunda. She and Catherine had ridden past it once before, but this was the first time she had walked up to it and truly taken in its beauty. Heavy, ornate columns supported the domed roof, and the center of the structure was adorned with a marble statue of Aphrodite. He guided her up the steps and spread a thick blanket just below the statue, where they both sat, close to each other but not quite touching. As usual, he spoke few words, but in the tranquility of the afternoon, she found the silence appealing rather than grating. She accepted a glass of the chilled champagne he retrieved from the picnic basket and stretched her legs out along the blanket, enjoying the gentle breeze that wafted toward her from the lake.

"This is lovely," she remarked, vaguely gesturing around to indicate her appreciation for the scenery, although part of her joy came from the fact that they were finally alone together of their own free will, without any sort of coercion.

"I agree." He lifted his head to gaze up at the statue, the sun turning his hair an even more brilliant shade of gold. "I haven't come here in many years. Apparently, my father arranged for the construction of this rotunda upon his engagement to my mother."

"How romantic." She turned her head to peer at the goddess of love that stared down at them.

He gave a sarcastic laugh. "Yes, it must appear that way. Truth be told, it amazes me that my father was able to turn his focus away from himself long enough to come up with such an idea. Although, I suppose having the means to perform such a grand gesture helped stoke his vanity. As for my mother, no doubt she experienced a boost in her own self-importance as a result, though any appreciation she felt was seemingly short-lived."

"It was not a love match, then?" she asked, surprised. She thought of the portrait of the former Lord and Lady Ashton that hung in the gallery, the one where the earl's thick hand rested upon his countess's delicate shoulder, and their faces appeared united in regarding the world with disdain. It was difficult to imagine that, beneath their expressions of confident pride, there existed such turmoil.

There it was again, his sarcastic laugh. "I think the only love that existed within that marriage was the love they both held for themselves. Fortunately for them, they quickly produced the necessary son and were then free to lead separate lives. However, the situation did lead to unfortunate questions surrounding Catherine's legitimacy when she came along thirteen years later.

"But it is of no matter to me one way or another. It does not change the fact that she's my sister," he added quickly upon noticing her look of shock. "Forgive me. I do not know why I'm even speaking of such things. I hope learning of the scandalous misdeeds of the ancient earldom you have married into has not shocked or disappointed you too badly."

She reached over to clasp his hand, grateful he had finally seen fit to share something with her beyond mere pleasantries. Dredging up old memories clearly did not come easy to him, but if they both kept their pasts locked away, she didn't see how they could ever truly know one another.

"Not at all," she assured him. "On the contrary, my own parents were involved in a rather scandalous and subsequently unhappy marriage. Therefore, I would never dream of casting judgment."

"The cotton merchant and the baronet's granddaughter. How did that unlikely pairing come about?" he asked.

"Mama did not often speak of it." Eliza took a moment to think back through the rare occasions when her mother had addressed the topic of her marriage. "But it seems my father came upon her in the park one day when her carriage had broken a wheel, and he offered his assistance. Her lineage was no doubt very enticing to a man who had pervasive intentions of elevating himself. On the other hand, she was attracted by his lack of title or position, for high society held very little appeal for her. How unfortunate that they did not discover the extent of their differing aspirations until after the union. In any case, my father soon took himself off to India, and while he provided her a home in Liverpool, she never cared much for city life. Luckily, her grandfather forgave her imprudent marriage enough to allow her the use of the dower house at Riverton Hall, and when the baronetcy passed to her cousin and then her brother, they were kind enough to let us stay on."

She took a deep breath, trying to push away the sting of the memories of all that had transpired since that time. "The fact that Papa's visits to Riverton were exceedingly rare suited everyone quite well. He provided for us financially, of course, but other than that, we saw very little of him. Unless he saw some way one of us could benefit him, as was recently the case."

Alluding to her father's scheme involving their marriage caused her to stare down into her lap and blush. "I'm very sorry that he involved you in his conniving," she said, just loud enough for Edward to hear. "And I'm also very sorry if the consequences have been disagreeable to you."

"No." He pulled her close to him, wrapping a protective arm around her shoulders. "You mustn't blame yourself for your father's actions, just as I try not to blame myself for the actions of mine. We both had the misfortune of being forced into situations not of our choosing by two unspeakably selfish fathers. Things being what they are, I suppose all that remains is for us to try to be better than they were."

He nuzzled his face into her hair and planted a soft kiss atop her head. "And do you truly think you are disagreeable to me?" He pulled her against him a little more tightly, causing her skin to tingle.

No, when they were alone together like this, with desire sparking within her that she now felt free to embrace instead of deny, she couldn't see anything disagreeable about the situation for either of them.

But that didn't erase all the times, including that very morning, when he had rushed away from her or avoided conversation as if he couldn't bear the idea of letting her get too close. Unspoken words remained between them, and until these words were out in the open, they would continue to drive a wedge. Based on the information Edward had just shared, it was hard to believe he was consumed by grief over his father's recent passing, which left another possibility. One she didn't want to ask about, yet, if they were truly to understand one another, she had to.

"Will you tell me about your first wife?"

His body immediately tensed, and he sat up straighter, pulling his head away from her. "Why would you wish to speak of that?"

"Because … because …" The words were on the tip of her tongue, but she couldn't quite bring herself to say them aloud. Doing so would only expose her fears: that his previous wife had been a perfect lady, his one true love, and that he was distant with her because she provided a constant reminder of how far he had fallen from his former state of bliss.

"I'm not entirely sure what you wish to know," said Edward, sparing her the need to fumble through an explanation. "I became engaged when I was still young and foolish and was wed only a very short time before my wife died. Do not ask me to say more about it than that. I've told you before, the past does not matter!"

At first, Eliza thought he was angry with her, but when she dared to look into his eyes, the darkness in them didn't seem to be the result of fury.

"Please," he murmured, his tone softening, "can we not concentrate on the present? For with you sitting before me, looking more tempting than Aphrodite herself, it is very difficult for me to consider anything else but you."

He reached for her again, tilting her chin up until their lips met, and now she was sure that what she saw in his eyes was pure longing. Her desire ignited as a result, and she clung to him, running her hands through the golden waves of his hair as they deepened the kiss. He stopped only long enough to push the picnic basket out of the way, their need for food currently irrelevant, before lowering her to the blanket. His lips traveled downward, stopping at the hollow at the base of her throat while his hand worked to push up her skirts. Once the billows of fabric rested near her waist, he nudged her thighs apart so he could kneel between them and prop up her knees. She gasped at the exposure, instinctively reaching out her hands to cover herself, but he returned them to her sides and lightly pinned them in place as he resumed his trail of kisses down to her chest.

"Do not hide yourself from me," he whispered, his lips now under the swell of her breast.

She wriggled, wishing she could tear off the layers of fabric that prevented his mouth from connecting with her skin.

"Do not deny me such an exquisite sight." He was moving lower now, pressing kisses across the flat surface of her belly. And then, he went lower still, past the place where her skirts lay bunched up and down to where her intimate flesh was completely bared.

"What are you doing?" she managed to choke out, watching in awe as his lips hovered just above the most sensitive spot between her legs.

"Shall I stop?" His hot breath tickled her skin as he uttered the words, setting every one of her nerve endings on fire.

"No." She gave her head a little shake, and he lowered his mouth to the place where she ached with longing.

"No," she repeated, the word coming out more like a moan. "No, don't stop."

Perhaps everything people said about her was true, that she was wicked and wanton and shameful. At this moment, she didn't care in the least. All that mattered were the sensations pouring through her as his tongue circled and stroked her, driving her higher and higher until she felt an overarching need to have him inside her.

"Please," she mumbled between cries, all sense of propriety gone, "come to me."

He bestowed one more kiss upon her before sliding himself upward, his arousal brushing temptingly against her thigh. She grasped his shoulders, digging in her fingernails to draw him closer, and he made short work of freeing himself from his trousers before entering her with a powerful thrust. His strokes came hard and fast, and she raised her hips to match his rhythm, each movement bringing her closer to the edge. And then she shattered, waves of pleasure rippling through her, and she felt him begin throbbing within her as he found his own release.

After they had lain side by side on the blanket for a long time, sated and content, perhaps she should have tried talking to him again. And if not at that moment, perhaps after dinner. The opportunity had certainly presented itself, for Catherine and Miss Martin had retired early, leaving them alone in the drawing room. But then they had found themselves on the same settee, and she had somehow ended up in his lap, and what followed had left little occasion for conversation.

She could have also tried again that night when he had knocked at her bedroom door, just as she was brushing out her hair in the dim candlelight, but before she had given it a moment's thought, he was behind her, kissing the back of her neck, and then she was in his arms, and they were in her bed once more.

Now, she lay in the dark, listening to Edward's steady breathing as she ran over all the things she should have said that day. They all seemed obvious now that he was asleep and she was left alone with her thoughts. It was different, though, during waking hours, when his very presence caused a strange tingle throughout her body. And whenever he approached her, bringing the promise of pleasure she hadn't even known existed, it was difficult to think of anything else at all.

Chapter 14

No matter what difficulties were going on around her, Eliza always found solace in gardening. Much to the head gardener's horror, she had seated herself on the ground of Highfield Park's greenhouse and was digging in an empty patch of dirt, readying the soil for the lavender seeds she had brought along in her pocket. Despite the gardener's entreaties to let him perform the task on her behalf, she insisted on doing it herself, for the feel of the damp soil beneath her fingertips and the accompanying earthy smell brought her a sense of calm she was hard-pressed to find elsewhere.

She had no real cause for complaint. Things between her and Edward were as good as could be expected. In fact, "good" did not even begin to do justice to the way she felt when they were alone together at night, or sometimes even during a stolen moment during the day, caught up in waves of passion.

However, while he had not rushed away from their intimacy since that first time two weeks prior, something about their union, the part beyond the physical, was not quite right. It was difficult to describe, exactly. Their interactions were pleasant enough, and while it seemed unlikely Edward would ever develop a tendency toward excessive chatter, he had been making more of an effort to converse, talking with her about things like their crops, or their tenants, or even the books she read on plants. However, she still sensed that certain topics of conversation were forbidden, and the weight of these lingered in the air between them, never allowing her to feel fully at ease.

She sighed loudly as she sprinkled the lavender seeds into the black dirt, trying to reabsorb herself fully in the task. But that unsettled feeling in the pit of her stomach wouldn't dissipate, and as she raised her head to give it a little shake, a swift movement outside the greenhouse caught her eye. Someone was rushing in her direction, and she quickly discerned from his gold-braided coat that it was a footman. The sight took her by surprise; while she was used to seeing footmen throughout the house, silently standing by doors as they waited to be of service, this man was fervently sprinting toward the greenhouse door.

She pushed herself off the ground and hurried to the door herself, apprehension beginning to prick at her.

"Lady Ashton," the footman called as soon as she exited the greenhouse and came into his view. He kept running until he stood before her, panting and breathless. "I beg your pardon, m'lady, but you have a young visitor."

"A visitor?" Eliza stared at him, wrinkling her forehead. She had received few callers since moving to Highfield Park, but nonetheless, she couldn't understand why the appearance of a visitor would cause such a commotion.

The footman returned her gaze uncertainly. "Jenny Turner, m'lady. She showed up at the kitchen door, causing such a fuss that no one knew quite what to do. But then, Lady Catherine came down and bade me fetch you right away."

Eliza's former pangs of apprehension swelled into a heavy coldness that seeped through her body. If Jenny had come to seek her out here at Highfield Park, what could that mean but something was wrong with Alice?

She took off toward the house without another word, crossing the grass with frantic strides, but on second thought, she paused long enough to call out to the footman.

"Charles," she said, hoping she had identified him by the proper name, "could you please go to the stables and see that my horse is made ready?"

The words, "Right away, m'lady," had barely left his mouth before she turned and resumed running, fear giving her a burst of speed.

She reached the kitchen door in record time and burst through it to discover the sight of Catherine sitting on a long wooden bench with her arms encircling a weeping Jenny. Although some of the tension left her face when she noticed Eliza in the doorway, Catherine still looked fearful.

"Eliza, thank goodness," she said as she gently stroked Jenny's hair. "Jenny has come to see you, although she has not yet been able to fully explain the reason why."

Eliza rushed over to kneel before the distraught girl. "Jenny?" she said, keeping her voice as composed as possible. "Please try to calm yourself so you can tell me what is the matter. Is something amiss with your mother?"

In confirmation of her worst fears, Jenny nodded. Eliza's heart sank as she reached out to brush away Jenny's tears. "Please, tell me what has happened."

"The baby's coming," exclaimed Jenny between deep, shuddering breaths. "I went to fetch the midwife, but she was already tied up with Mrs. Hill. Then, I tried to find Dr. Clark, but he wasn't at home, and no one I asked had seen him. So, then I went to the apothecary, and he said—" At this, she burst into tears anew. "He said he couldn't associate himself with the likes of us."

Eliza scrambled to her feet, biting back the curse on the apothecary that threatened to burst out.

"I didn't know who else to ask," Jenny wailed. "She's been having bad pains since before daybreak, and then I remembered the medicines you brought that made her feel better before, and I thought maybe you could help her again. Please say you can, m'lady. I had to leave her all alone, and she's been screaming like I've never heard, and I'm so afraid for her, and oh, please—" Her entire body shook with sobs, rendering her unable to continue speaking.

Eliza had already crossed the kitchen, ready to make her exit, but she turned back to look into Jenny's imploring eyes. "I promise to do everything I can to help your mother." She tried to force a reassuring smile to cross her lips. "I will go to her at once. For now, you must stay here with my sister, Lady Catherine, and I will return to fetch you just as soon as all is well with your mother again."

She stayed in the doorway only long enough to see Catherine's brief nod of assent to the plan before dashing down the corridor and into the stillroom. She flung open the medicine chest, pulling out tiny bottles and tossing them into the wicker basket she retrieved from a shelf, her hands shaking the entire time.

She had been to see new mothers after they had birthed their babies, of course, bringing along tonics to help them recover their strength. As for assisting at a birth in progress, the situation was completely foreign to her, something she had merely vague notions of from her reading. She only hoped there was something she could do to help. And that it wouldn't be too late.

She snatched up the full basket and ran back into the hallway, nearly crashing into Mrs. Parker in the process.

"Lady Ashton, you've returned," exclaimed the startled housekeeper. "I do apologize for all the commotion—"

"Never mind that," she cut in, politeness now beyond her. "Alice Turner is laboring with her child as we speak and is entirely alone. I must go to her at once."

Mrs. Parker's eyes widened in horror. "Surely you cannot—"

"Yes, I can," she interrupted once more, "but I will require assistance. Please send someone to find a midwife. Or a doctor. Or anybody who can help, and see that they head to Alice Turner's home right away."

"But my lady," Mrs. Parker began to protest, but Eliza had already turned away from her and began running down the corridor once more. She couldn't afford further delays, and she silently prayed her instructions would be heeded.

A small wave of relief washed over her as she approached the stables and noticed her horse, Luna, standing saddled and waiting. She uttered a hurried word of thanks to the nearby stable boy before launching herself upon the horse's back. Luna was a lively young mare, a wedding gift from her father, and as she took the reins and urged her onward, she was grateful for the sudden burst of speed. They galloped down the drive and onto the road, her heart pounding as intensely as Luna's thundering hooves.

They were fortunate to have the wind at their back, propelling them onward as they whizzed past familiar trees and fenceposts. She focused only on the road ahead, bringing her ever closer to the destination she so desperately needed to reach, when an approaching figure on horseback caught her attention. Her momentary hope that this was the doctor vanished as it occurred to her that the person was traveling in the opposite direction of the village. Besides, something about the black thoroughbred looked familiar, and although her eyes stung from the wind and the world rushed by in a blur, she soon made out that the rider was Edward.

For a split second, she was gripped by the temptation to pull Luna to a halt, flag Edward down, and sob in terror before him as she begged for his help. He was an earl; surely, he had the power to command people to do as he wanted as soon as he wanted it, to have his every whim met with the snap of his fingers. But the rational part of her realized that even an earl couldn't make a doctor appear out of thin air, and with Alice alone and potentially in danger, she hadn't a moment to spare. No, she had to keep going, but Edward was presumably on his way back to Highfield Park, where Catherine would apprise him of all that was transpiring, and from there, perhaps he could think of some way to help.

She and Luna raced on, the horse not once slowing her pace, although every minute felt more like an hour. An eternity later, she rode up to the front of Alice's cottage and wasted no time in jumping down from Luna's back and tying her to a fencepost. But as she stood before the front door, her frenzied limbs suddenly froze in place, and she could go no farther. What sort of scene would greet her within the cottage? What if there was nothing she could do? What if Alice was already beyond saving? And what of the baby?

She took a deep, grounding breath, allowing herself a few seconds to regain her composure and brace herself for what was to come. Then, she pushed open the door.

Her eyes instantly fell upon Alice, lying pale-faced and listless on the bed, her belly still swelled with child. But then, Alice's gaze turned to meet hers, and Eliza nearly wept with gratitude at the realization that the woman was still alive.

"M'lady," murmured Alice, the word barely audible as it escaped her dry, cracked lips. "Where's Jenny? And the midwife?"

"Please, do not worry." She hoped Alice lacked the awareness to detect how her voice wavered. "Lady Catherine is entertaining Jenny at Highfield Park, and a midwife will be here very soon, I think."

She dropped her basket beside the bed and hurried over to the hearth, glad to see a pot of water hanging above the dying flames. She reached to the nearby shelf for a cup, intending to fill it, when a high-pitched shriek from Alice made her jump and sent the cup clattering to the floor. She watched, unable to even blink, as Alice clutched her belly while continuing to make keening, almost animal noises, as a spasm of pain enveloped her. Ignoring the broken pieces on the floor, Eliza forced her trembling fingers to grab another and clumsily ladled water in it before dashing to the bedside.

Alice's eyes were scrunched closed, and Eliza reached for her hand to give it a light squeeze, although who knew if Alice was aware of anything beyond her consuming agony. She mumbled gentle words of comfort, doubtful they would do much but not certain what else to say. Her free hand rummaged through her basket, settling on a bottle of pennyroyal just as Alice's tense body became limp as the spasm abated.

"The babe won't come," she whispered as a couple of silent tears trickled out from her closed eyelids. "The pains started yesterday, but I could handle them well enough then. It wasn't until early this morning that they got so bad I couldn't help but cry out and wake Jenny. It feels they've lasted an eternity, but all for naught. I'm so tired …"

"Just try to rest a moment." Eliza brushed away the damp strands of hair that clung to Alice's face. She had mixed the pennyroyal tincture into the cup of water, and she pressed it to Alice's lips, relieved to see her take a few small sips. "This might help," she added, although no sooner had the words left her mouth than another spasm gripped Alice.

Eliza hurriedly put the cup to the side and grasped her hand. This time, Alice squeezed back so tightly that it felt like the bones in her fingers might shatter. It made little difference to her if the result was that it would help Alice be safely delivered of her child. But the pain came and went, leaving Alice a little more exhausted but no closer to having the baby in her arms.

Eliza held the cup to Alice's lips once more, all the while searching her brain for every fact she had ever read about childbearing. She knew the longer Alice labored while the child refused to come, the greater the danger to them both. But what more could she do to urge things along? Her ears stayed on high alert, listening for any outside sounds signifying the arrival of the doctor or midwife, but all was silent until another wave of pain caused Alice to scream in distress.

She offered her hand for clutching again while turning her attention back to her basket. With desperation, she resumed raking through the bottles, casting some to the floor with a clink, until the label on one brought her out of her panicked stupor and invoked the memory of a medical text she had recently read—ergot powder.

At the first sign of Alice's pain fading, she jumped up to fetch a spoon and hastened back to the bedside so she could fill it with the powder.

"I want you to take this," she said, keeping her voice surprisingly steady as she held the spoon to Alice's mouth, "followed by a little more of the tisane."

Thankfully, Alice made no protest. In fact, her fatigue had grown so great that she hardly seemed aware of what was happening. That, however, presented a problem for what Eliza wanted to occur next.

"Alice," she said, turning her tone more assertive, "I want you to try standing."

Alice's eyes flew open, and she gave her head a tiny shake. "I can't. Too tired."

"I know," said Eliza, peering at her with sympathy. Making such a request when Alice was already pushed to the brink of exhaustion made her feel like a fiend, yet she couldn't afford to waver. "I can only imagine how tired you must be, but Alice, I believe doing so will help the baby to come."

Alice could only stare at her in return, her glassy eyes shrouded by doubt.

"Please." Eliza took both of her hands now, holding them firmly in her own. "I promise to assist you every step of the way. We must act quickly before the next pains come. I know you are strong enough. I'm certain of it."

Alice continued to lie still, and Eliza let her shoulders sag. Had she made a truly impossible request?

But then, Alice made the slightest movement forward, and Eliza tugged on her hands until she came into a sitting position. That much accomplished, she set to work on shifting Alice's legs toward the floor, finishing just as Alice began to cry out from another surge of agony. The sound no longer startled her, despite how it cut her to the core, and she resumed her soft words of encouragement while putting an arm around Alice's shoulder to keep her from collapsing backward. When Alice's yelps diminished, the pain easing off once more, she waited just a few seconds before saying,

"You're doing very well, Alice. It's now time to try rising to your feet."

She continued supporting Alice with her arms, ready to help lift her the second she made even a slight movement forward. In truth, performing this small task terrified her. She had only to look at Alice to realize how close she was to her breaking point. Soon, she would have nothing left to give. Yet if she could find just a shred of remaining strength and use it to rise to her feet, perhaps the baby could be urged along with the assistance of gravity.

"Come, Alice. I know you can," she urged, not able to prevent her voice from cracking. She turned her attention away long enough to glance out the window, longing for the sight of the doctor or midwife hurrying toward the cottage. Instead, she was met with the view of an empty road, revealing that they remained entirely alone.

Then, Alice shifted slightly. The moment had come to help her stand. There was no one else to assist, to offer other remedies, to ensure the safety of Alice and her child. The two lives before her rested solely in her hands.

Chapter 15

Edward raced down the road as if the flames of hell licked his heels. He hadn't stopped rushing since earlier that afternoon when he had seen Eliza, looking wild-eyed and determined, speeding away from Highfield Park with barely a glance in his direction. That triggered his haste, and while he had briefly considered spinning Apollo around and following her, his vague sense of unease instead prompted him to continue his journey back to Highfield Park, albeit at an accelerated pace. His mind swirled with a number of unsettling possibilities, but nothing prepared him for the sight that met him as he had burst into the drawing room.

Catherine sat on the sofa with her arms encircling the waif Jenny Turner, the girl's tearstained face eagerly watching as Catherine read aloud from an old book of children's stories. It had become clear in an instant that something was amiss with the Turners, the family Eliza had developed such an attachment to. After a few whispered words in the corner with Catherine, he rushed back out to his horse and hastened for Rochester in search of a doctor.

Thankfully, he had tracked one down in short order, and aided by his offer of a large bag of coin, the middle-aged man now galloped alongside him. The doctor was an adept rider, which made Edward extremely grateful, for he had no time to stop or slow his pace while knowing that Eliza and Alice were alone.

It still amazed him that Eliza had sped off to Alice's cottage unaccompanied at the news of trouble. He supposed, though, that her willingness to assist someone in need, no matter the circumstances, should have come as no surprise. She had proven, time and again, how deeply she cared for the wellbeing of those around her. He only hoped she had not placed herself in a situation where fixing the problem went beyond her abilities.

Knowing they neared their destination, Edward coaxed Apollo into one final burst of speed, thankful the doctor's horse could keep up the pace until they reached the front of the cottage. Eliza's own horse stood tied up near the fence, confirming her presence inside. He urged the doctor to go on ahead, taking a few extra moments himself to call for a boy walking on the other side of the road to come and see to the horses. Then, he braced himself for the possibility of a chaotic scene and inched the door open.

However, the inside of the cottage lay in stillness, except for the doctor's quiet rustling, and the first thing that caught his eye was Alice Turner, tranquilly lying in bed. Her eyes drifted open as the doctor approached her. Edward diverted his gaze, not wanting to intrude, and as his eyes traveled to the other side of the cottage, he spotted her. There was Eliza, sitting in a flimsy kitchen chair pulled close to the hearth, cradling a small bundle in her arms. Her face was etched with weariness, yet a slight smile crossed her lips as she swayed the little bundle.

His chest constricted at the sight, and an odd lump formed at the back of his throat. He had no idea of all that had transpired in the cottage that afternoon, but he felt certain that somehow, Eliza had managed to make things right.

"Would you like to come and meet the newest Miss Turner?" she asked in a soft voice, turning slightly so he could better see the tiny baby in her arms.

He walked over and stopped behind her chair, peering down at the baby's sleeping face and wisps of dark hair. "Pleased to make your acquaintance, Miss Turner," he whispered, running a finger over her soft cheek. Then, he moved his hand upward to squeeze Eliza's shoulder. How he wished he could take her in his arms and not let go. Instead, he leaned down to plant a light kiss in her hair, inhaling her familiar floral scent.

She shifted the baby into the crook of one arm and reached up to clasp his hand atop her shoulder. "You came." She sounded tired, but a note of gladness still rang in her words. "You brought help."

"Yes, as quickly as I could. Although it seems to me you already had the situation perfectly in hand."

She had no opportunity to reply, for the doctor approached her looking to examine the baby. After passing over the little bundle, she went over to sit on the edge of the bed, where Alice lay drowsy but awake.

"Are you well?" Eliza asked as she reached for a cup of water to offer her.

Alice took a sip and nodded. "After a bit of rest, I'll be fit as a fiddle." Her eyes suddenly widened, and Edward realized that, for the first time, she must have noticed his presence. "Why, Lord Ashton," she exclaimed as she began struggling into a sitting position.

"Please, do not rise on my account," he interjected quickly. "I merely wanted to congratulate you on the arrival of your new daughter."

"Thank you kindly, m'lord." She glanced to the other side of the room where the doctor still held the baby, and a proud smile crossed her face, the circumstances of the difficult birth and the challenges that loomed in the future currently forgotten.

"Have you decided what to name her?" Eliza asked, flashing the baby a fond look of her own.

"Yes, without a doubt. She'll be called Elizabeth, after the person who helped bring her into the world. I thought she could be Beth for short."

Eliza had kept herself highly composed from the moment he had stepped into the cottage, but at this, her eyes began to shimmer with the hint of unshed tears. However, before her emotions had the chance to intensify, a commotion by the door caught her attention. Everyone turned to stare as a stout, red-faced woman burst into the cottage. He vaguely recalled Mrs. Parker telling him, just before he had rushed off to Rochester, that she had sent servants in search of local help, per Lady Ashton's command. Presumably, then, this was the midwife making an appearance at last.

Sure enough, she said, "A footman from Highfield Park tracked me down just as I was finishing up with Nancy Hill and bid me come here at once, at the request of Lord and Lady Ashton." She leaned over to catch her breath and motioned to the baby, who the doctor was in the process of handing back to Alice. "It seems, though, I'm too late."

"Yes," said Alice, "although I thank you for coming all the same. As it turned out, the one who acted as my midwife today was none other than Lady Ashton herself."

The woman's mouth gaped as she took in Eliza's appearance, and then her attention turned to Edward. "Why, Lord Ashton! And Lady Ashton? I had no idea … But why … and how … But forgive me. Meg Thorpe, at your service, m'lord. And m'lady."

"It's rather a long story, Mrs. Thorpe," said Eliza, stepping forward to greet the obviously flustered midwife. "All that matters now is that all is well, and everyone is in good health, I believe?" She turned to look questioningly at the doctor, and he offered a reassuring nod.

"Quite, my lady. In fact, I do not believe my services are required here any longer."

Alice smiled at the news as she stroked Beth's fluffy hair, but suddenly her expression changed, and a mumbled word escaped her lips. "Jenny."

"Oh, of course," exclaimed Eliza, hurrying back to Alice's bedside. "We can send word to Highfield Park and arrange to have her brought home at once. She'll be so pleased to learn the good news."

"Why don't you head home yourself, m'lady?" Mrs. Thorpe urged gently. "If you'll forgive my saying so, you look tired out, and I can't say I blame you. Midwifery is not for the faint of heart. I'll stay to see that Alice and the wee one are settled and well."

"An excellent idea," said Edward before Eliza had the opportunity to protest. "That way, you can tell Jenny the good news yourself and perhaps arrange to have Catherine and Miss Martin accompany her home in the pony cart."

She looked hesitantly at Alice and Beth, but seeing that the baby was fast asleep and Alice looked on the verge of drowsing herself, she nodded her assent. "Yes, I suppose you're right. I'll just take the time to say my farewells."

"Of course. I will wait for you outside. Good day, Mrs. Turner. Mrs. Thorpe." He inclined his head to them and headed outdoors, allowing the women a moment alone.

He was outside only long enough to settle up with the doctor and untie the horses before Eliza emerged from the cottage, her hair instantly turning fiery as it caught the early evening light. She appeared so beautiful, so confident, so entirely awe-inspiring, but there was also a slight sag to her shoulders, betraying the inner weariness she must feel.

He held out a hand to her, but instead of taking it, she launched herself into him, burying her head against his shoulder. He wrapped her in his arms at once, rubbing a soothing hand along her back as he felt her tremble against him.

"I'm so glad," she said, her voice muffled. "So glad, yet I was so afraid."

"I know, sweetheart." He pulled her against him even more tightly, still trying to fathom the day's events and what she and Alice must have gone through. "I think even the most formidable beings must experience fear on occasion. In any case, you were marvelous."

He continued to hold her, vaguely aware of the looks they attracted from curious passersby. He wished to say so much more on how greatly she amazed him, but this wasn't the place. "Let's go home," he murmured into her hair, anxious to have her back at Highfield Park where he could tend to her without prying eyes.

Slowly, she pulled herself away from him and allowed him to help her onto her horse. He then jumped onto Apollo's back, nodding curt greetings to his staring tenants before they set off. As tempting as it was to break into a gallop that would convey them home without delay, he settled for a trot, recognizing that after an afternoon of rushing around, a more serene pace would benefit them all. Indeed, the leisurely ride in the fresh air seemed to do Eliza good, for she relaxed into the saddle, turning her head upward to the weakening sunshine hitting her face.

"It looks like your actions today caused quite a stir," he remarked as they turned onto the road toward Highfield Park, finally away from the company of others.

Eliza turned to him abruptly, her face becoming tense. "Does that bother you?"

"No," he rushed to say. "Not at all." And as he mulled it over, he was surprised to find just how little he cared for the opinions of others. What difference did it make if his wife's behavior was viewed as unbecoming of a proper lady? She had acted out of genuine compassion, and that mattered far more than living by a series of unspoken societal rules.

"Anyone who thinks you are lacking in some way is a fool," he muttered, and despite his prior resolution to ride slowly, he urged Apollo to quicken the pace before waiting to see if Eliza had heard him. She easily caught up to him but made no comment, and they spent the rest of their journey home in silence.

Somewhat revitalized after the ride, Eliza was quick to jump down from her saddle as soon they came to a halt by the steps of Highfield Park, although the air of fatigue about her hadn't entirely vanished.

"I should go to Jenny without delay," she said, but as she began to hurry forward, one foot tangled with the other, causing her to make a small stumble. Reflexively, he reached out to grab her arm, reminded of the previous instance when they had been in this position. This time, though, her misstep seemed the result of pure tiredness.

"Go tell her the news," he agreed, "but then will you come upstairs? I'll arrange for a bath and dinner tray to be sent to your room."

Fortunately, she didn't object to taking some time for herself and said, "Yes, that sounds lovely. Thank you. I won't be long."

With Eliza hurrying off in search of Jenny, Edward wandered into the house himself, giving instructions to a servant before heading upstairs to the quiet of his room. He took his time removing his rumpled clothing and dousing himself with water from the washstand, rinsing away the dust from his long ride. From next door came the rustling of servants as they hauled up pails of bathwater, and finally, he detected a feminine voice that could only belong to Eliza. After donning a pair of trousers and a simple linen shirt, he tapped on the connecting door between their rooms and pushed it open, eager to see her again and ensure her well-being.

She was already reclining in the tub of fragrant water with her eyes closed. Her lady's maid scurried around the other side of the room, picking up her discarded articles of clothing.

"You can go," he instructed her quietly. "Lady Ashton will ring if she requires additional assistance from you."

The maid curtseyed and made a hasty departure, mercifully leaving them alone. Eliza's eyes flew open in surprise to see him standing nearby. "Edward ..."

His name on her lips always did strange things to certain regions of his body, but he attempted to push those sensations away as he knelt beside the tub. "Just relax," he murmured, pulling the pins from her bedraggled hair knot so the strands tumbled down and swirled beneath the water's surface. "Let me take care of you."

He picked up the bar of soap beside the tub and eased her forward so he could glide it in circles around her back. Feeling her relax against his arms, he continued by running the soap across her chest, wishing that with each stroke, he could wash away all her remaining tension and worry. He didn't stop his ministrations until he had reached every part of her, and she made small sighs of contentment, sending a surge of heat through him. With great difficulty, he reached for the towel her maid had left and extended his hand to help her out, his resolve hanging on by a thread.

"You should dry off and eat something," he instructed brusquely, motioning to the tray of food that waited on her bedside table.

She accepted his hand and stepped out of the tub into the waiting towel, but she gave her head a shake. "I have no interest in the dinner tray at present."

She pressed her damp body against him, torturing his aching arousal. "You have had a trying day," he said, the words coming out husky and strained. "You need to rest."

She stepped back just far enough to let the towel fall to the floor. "No. That is not what I need at all."

With that, his final shred of restraint vanished, and he scooped her into his arms, carrying her through the open door and depositing her atop his bed. She lay sprawled out like a tantalizing water goddess, her skin pink and glistening, causing desire to pound through his veins. He reached out to touch her dewy, heated body, starting with the curves of her hips and running his hands inward until they reached the apex of her thighs. Finding the folds of her intimate flesh drenched with evidence of her desire, he ripped at the buttons of his fall front, too impatient to struggle with discarding the rest of his clothing, and plunged into her with a moan of relief. Her welcoming cry urged him forward, and they swiftly developed a rhythm, her hips rising to meet each of his frantic thrusts.

Some part of his fevered brain alerted him that he was dangerously close to catapulting over the edge and should slow down to prolong the bliss, but Eliza's grip on him was like iron, her movements relentless. He lacked the will to pull away from her. Mercifully, she found her release quickly, her clenching muscles promptly sparking his own burst of pleasure as he poured himself into her.

He stayed inside her for a long time afterward, savoring her encircling warmth. For as long as they remained in this position, he felt as though the world comprised nothing but the two of them, as though nothing and no one else mattered, as though no force could possibly upend the connection between them.

Eventually, though, Eliza's need for sleep became more apparent, and he rolled to the side so he could tuck her under the brocade counterpane. He waited until she curled up in the opposite direction, and her breathing turned soft and even, to cast off his damp shirt and crawl under the counterpane with her. Only then did he allow all that had transpired during the preceding hours to replay in his mind. His breaths came fast and heavy, and he reached out his hand to brush against her shoulder, just to assure himself that the angelic figure beside him was more than an apparition. When his fingers met with soft skin, he pulled himself against her, so his chest was pressed to her back and his arm draped over her like a shield. If he could just lie here a while, inhaling her comforting floral scent, perhaps his heart would stop pounding and he, too, could sleep.

Eliza's hand reached up to squeeze his, making him imperceptibly startle. "I'm sorry," he whispered into her ear. "I did not mean to wake you."

He tried to pull away so he could give her back her space, but she maintained her grip on him and turned so they were facing one another. "Whatever is the matter? I can feel your heart racing." She brought her free hand to his chest, her brow furrowing.

He shook his head, attempting to keep his expression neutral. "It's nothing. Go back to sleep."

She fixed her green-eyed stare on him. "Tell me."

He hesitated a moment, then sighed. "I suppose I was thinking of how you never cease to surprise me, how I never know what you might do next. And of how, when I saw you galloping away this afternoon, I thought you had taken a notion to depart Highfield Park permanently. That I had succeeded in driving you away, although I assure you ... that is not what I desire at all."

He regretted his honesty immediately. No sooner had the words left his mouth than he cringed at how weak, how insecure, and how absurdly pathetic he sounded.

Eliza, however, smiled before pressing her lips to his in a quick caress. "I promise that no such notion has ever crossed my mind. If you do develop a wish to drive me away, I'm afraid you'll have to work much harder." She gave an uncertain giggle at her jest before pulling herself into a sitting position, her face turning serious. "Edward, you have made it perfectly clear how much you dislike bringing up the past. I have therefore avoided the subject as much as possible, but I cannot continue to do so. You have been subjected to rumors of my involvement in scandal since even before our first meeting. If I were to explain the truth of what happened, perhaps it would help us avoid such misunderstandings in future."

The pounding of his heart only increased in intensity, as it always did when he was forced to confront old memories. "No. No explanation is necessary."

"Yes, it is." Her catlike eyes never left his, and she crossed her arms in a determined stance. "I no longer want a relationship tainted by speculation and rumors. You should know what really occurred during my time in London. If nothing else, you can use what I tell you to form your own opinions of me based on fact."

He wished to hear none of it, especially if it meant she expected a similar disclosure from him in return. He wanted, no *needed*, to forget every miserable detail of his life before he had met her. It had been bad enough, during the brief period between Julia's death and his departure for the Continent, enduring all those inquisitive, pitying looks. Having Eliza *know* and then look at him that way, too, would be more than he could bear.

Yet after all she had done, not just that day, but throughout the entirety of their short marriage, how could he deny her such a simple request? At the very least, she deserved to tell what obviously weighed heavy on her mind. Maybe he couldn't return her openness, but he could listen.

"Very well."

She didn't begin speaking right away. Rather, she picked up his discarded shirt and tossed it over her head before hugging her knees to her chest as if ensconcing herself in a protective cocoon. The apprehension in her eyes shone clear. But when she gazed directly at him again, her lips held just the slightest trace of a smile.

"Very well."

Chapter 16

London, five months earlier

At the other end of the ballroom, the terrace doors beckoned, offering the promise of a reprieve, if only Eliza could find a way to reach them. Despite the chill outdoors, the overcrowded room had turned stifling, and the overwhelming scent of assorted perfumes combined with sweat made her head ache.

Unfortunately, slipping away meant bypassing the numerous guests who stood at the side of the room, circling the footmen wandering about with trays of champagne, and pushing past the sea of couples who glided around the floor in a quadrille. She supposed she should be used to such things by now, for this was not her first ball of the Season. However, knowing that this ball was being held in her honor to celebrate her recent debut made it all the more overwhelming.

As she glanced across the ornate room in search of the most direct escape route, it occurred to her, for the first time, that perhaps her mother had done her a disservice by never bringing her out in society. Her mother had undoubtedly intended it as a kindness, an attempt to shield her daughter from a lifestyle she regarded with disdain. But now her mother was gone, and her remaining family insisted she be brought out, leaving her to feel rather like she had been thrown to the wolves with no means of self-defense.

"Eliza, remove that frown from your face at once," said a sharp voice, distracting her from her unsettling realization. "It will not do for you to be seen standing alone, scowling at your own ball."

Eliza turned to see her aunt Frances's stiff, silk-clad figure standing beside her, accompanied by her daughter, Louisa.

"No," added Louisa, who had an unpleasant sneer plastered across her own narrow face, "it will not do at all. She's so old to be having her first Season that she will need to display all the charm she can muster if she ever hopes to succeed with it."

A biting retort flew into Eliza's mind: "*At least it* is *only my first Season.*" She choked it back, though, recognizing the futility of engaging in a petty conflict born of jealousy.

Louisa's envy had been apparent from the moment talk of Eliza's upcoming debut began floating around Riverton Hall. For while Eliza had passed the previous winter at home in Lancashire, sitting by her mother's bedside as she watched the life drain out of her, Louisa had spent that time in London making her own debut. Much to her chagrin, she returned to Riverton Hall without a suitor. And now that the Season had begun anew, she was on the hunt for a suitable gentleman once more. The fact that Eliza was now here and experiencing a first Season far more opulent than her own, on account of her father's excessive wealth, seemed to put Louisa in a constant state of pique.

"Twenty is hardly ancient," replied Frances, at least seeing fit to support her niece in this one small matter.

"Besides, you should consider how Eliza's position benefits you. Any gentleman who, attracted by her wealth, comes to call on her will have the pleasure of encountering you as well."

And with that, Eliza's gratitude to her aunt dissolved as quickly as it had materialized. Her cheeks burned from hearing them speak of her in such a manner while she stood mere inches away. Even worse was the uncomfortable churning in her stomach as she considered the truth behind the words. She knew her hair was just a shade too red and her features just a touch too sharp to garner her the distinction of being a true beauty, and her father was too low born to make her lineage attractive. She could opt for naivete and assume that any gentlemen who made her acquaintance had a true desire to know her as a person, but the reality that all these eloquent suitors likely thought only of her large dowry was too obvious to ignore.

These troubling thoughts made erasing the frown from her face increasingly more challenging. On the other hand, Louisa had no such difficulty, for her sneer suddenly changed to an exaggerated grin. Eliza turned her gaze in the same direction as Louisa's, quickly detecting the reason for her cousin's abrupt change in temperament. Strolling in their direction was Mr. Reginald Walker, one of the ton's most coveted bachelors.

Eliza had to stop herself from rolling her eyes. On account of Mr. Walker's perfectly groomed appearance and charming manners, not to mention the barony he stood to inherit, many unwed ladies of her acquaintance found him desirable, Louisa included. In a way, she could recognize the appeal of his neat chestnut hair, elegantly tailored clothing, and pleasant way of speaking. Yet his smile never seemed to quite reach his eyes, and something about the even tone of his words made her doubt their sincerity. Why he had made a point of seeking her out at the last few events they had mutually attended, especially given her lackluster attempts at expressing interest in return, exasperated her to no end.

"Good evening, Lady Havelock, Miss Havelock," he greeted as soon as he reached them, offering a smooth bow before turning his focus to Eliza. "And Miss Wright. I hope you do not find me too forward in saying how well you look this evening.

She dropped into a stiff curtsey, wishing he would return his attention to Louisa—or anyone else. Her pearl-adorned bodice felt almost indecently low, and she resisted the urge to tug it up to avoid the downward darts of his eyes. "You're too kind."

He awarded her one of his superficial smiles. "Might I request the pleasure of the next dance?"

Her eyes flashed to the terrace doors one final time, watching the promise of freedom slip away before coming back to Mr. Walker as she feigned gratitude for the offer. She could have claimed she was unwell and would dance no more that evening, but even spinning about the floor with Mr. Walker was preferable to remaining with her aunt and cousin and suffering their additional insults.

As the previous dance was just ending, she allowed the gentleman to lead her to the floor, where the glittering light from the chandeliers made her feel as though she were on display. She was then obliged to concentrate on performing the correct steps while simultaneously responding to his attempts at conversation. Even so, she could still detect Louisa's steely glare following her from where she remained, partnerless, at the side of the room. It was suitable revenge, in a way, though it brought Eliza little satisfaction.

When the dance mercifully came to its end, she couldn't help but glance behind her to the terrace, wondering if there was some way she could now make her escape. When she turned back to Mr. Walker, however, something in that direction caught her attention instead. From the open doors behind him that led to the corridor, a set of slender arms darted out, making frantic gestures as if they were beckoning someone.

"Miss Wright?"

Mr. Walker's placid face held just a note of perplexity, indicating he must have said something to which she had made no response.

"Yes?" She tried to make it seem like he held her undivided attention when in reality, she kept one eye on the doorway.

"I asked if you would care for a glass of lemonade and perhaps a stroll on the terrace."

The face that belonged with the set of arms emerged for a split second, revealing eyes wide with terror and a mouth that formed a single, soundless word: "Help." Eliza could hardly contain her astonishment at realizing the face belonged to her lady's maid, Polly. More surprising still was how Polly clearly wanted her attention, right in the middle of the ball. That could only signal something had gone truly awry.

"If you will excuse me," she said, not even pretending to look at Mr. Walker now, "I—I must use the necessary." She caught a glimpse of his disgusted scowl before she hurried away, but she was beyond caring if he thought her indelicate. Thankfully, when she reached the corridor, it sat empty except for the two of them, and she pulled Polly into a shadowed alcove beneath the stairs before anyone could come along and see them.

"Oh, thank goodness you came, miss," Polly exclaimed, her voice shaking. "I need help and didn't know what else to do. It's Jim."

"Jim?" Eliza turned the name over in her mind, trying to place it.

"The new footman," Polly clarified, exasperated.

Her brief explanation evoked a conversation Eliza had overheard the week before between tittering housemaids, in which they praised the merits of Jim, the handsome new addition to the staff. "What of him?"

"He was perfectly well until suddenly he started gasping for breath. I've never seen anything like it. You're so clever, miss, with all your tonics, that I thought you might know what's to be done. Please."

Eliza stared at her blankly, trying to make sense of the information. "Did you alert Mrs. Woods?" she asked, alluding to the housekeeper. "Or did someone not send for a doctor? And where is Jim, exactly?"

Polly's face turned crimson, and she stared at her feet a moment before crying, "With all the commotion up here, we thought we could slip away to his room for a while, without notice. He's just so charming, miss! But I can't tell Mrs. Woods what happened, for then she'd know I'd been in the footmen's room and would dismiss me on the spot. Maybe you want to dismiss me too, but you've always been kind, and I thought you might help."

Eliza was torn between wrapping the girl in an embrace or shaking her. "How could you do something so reckless …" she snapped before trailing off, realizing that chastising Polly would accomplish nothing. "Never mind. I'll head below stairs directly and do my best not to attract notice, although I may have no choice. Go up to my bedroom, as if you are fetching me something, and stay there so you will not be associated with what happened. I will send word as soon as possible."

"Thank you, miss," Polly whispered as tears began sliding down her cheeks.

Eliza gave her hand a gentle pat before rushing toward the servants' stairs and peeking down to ensure they were unoccupied. With no one in view, she scrambled to the basement and down a dim corridor until she reached the stillroom. She tiptoed inside, mindful that Mrs. Woods's room was just next door, and pulled a bottle from the medicine chest with as much speed and stealth as she could manage. With the bottle in hand, she poked her head back into the corridor and, seeing it remained empty, hurried off toward the back of the house in search of the male servants' room.

Her slippers hit the stone floor with quiet thumps, although the sound got drowned out as she neared the bustling kitchen. She kept herself pressed near the wall, hoping to escape detection when a strange wheezing sound from behind one of the doors suggested she had reached the right place. She opened the door just a crack, in case someone else happened to be inside, but the room was empty except for a man who lay writhing on one of the narrow iron-framed beds.

"Jim?" she called in a soft voice, cautiously approaching his bedside. At once, she recognized him as the youthful new footman who often assisted in the dining room. So this was the man who had led Polly to an indiscretion. He possessed little charm at the moment, with his face contorted as he rapidly inhaled and exhaled, trying and struggling to force air into his lungs.

His panicked expression intensified when he noticed her, and she attempted to smile reassuringly, knowing his problem was far more likely to abate if she could find a way to calm him.

"Let me help you up," she murmured, extending her hand to him. "You may find it easier to breathe if you're seated."

He stared at her gloved hand in horror, as if, despite everything, he couldn't fathom the notion of touching her.

"Go on," she urged, for if she were to have a hope of assisting him, they would need to discard the boundaries between them. "I want to help you."

She breathed a quick sigh of relief as his desperation overtook his discretion, and he reached for her hand, allowing her to pull him into a sitting position. However, the way the candlelight now hit his face revealed his complexion to be ashen and his lips an alarming shade of blue. Her body threatened to begin trembling, but she clamped her hands down firmly on her shoulders, refusing to let panic get in the way.

"Please, although it may be very difficult, try to relax your breathing, and take slow breaths in and out as much as you're able," she instructed, sitting beside him on the bed. His heavy blue coat had already been removed, presumably during his time with Polly, but his cravat remained tightly knotted at his throat, no doubt adding to his distress. Before she could overthink it, she set to work on unfastening the knots, trying to keep her fingers from connecting with his heaving chest.

The cravat fell away in short order, and she reached for the bottle she had laid on the bed beside her. "I have something for you to take if you're agreeable," she said, casting off the lid of the honeysuckle tincture.

He nodded, still wheezing too much for words, and she pressed the bottle to his lips so a little of the liquid could trickle in. She peered at him intently, afraid he might choke it out, but he managed a labored swallow and continued his attempts at deep breathing.

"Good," she said, smiling again in encouragement. "Keep calm, and this will pass." And indeed, his breaths did seem to come with more ease now, giving her the first glimmer of hope that her efforts had done good.

And then, his words came, low and rasping but filled with gratitude. "Thank you, miss. Truly."

The worst of the crisis over, she inhaled deeply herself and gradually exhaled, releasing her pent-up tension. "Has this happened to you before?" she asked after giving him another minute to compose himself.

"A handful of times throughout my life. Exertion seems to bring it on, like when I'm running, or when—" His face reddened, and he abruptly stopped speaking. "But you won't tell anyone, will you? I'd lose my place for sure."

"No," she confirmed before he had a chance to grow agitated and suffer a setback, "as long as you promise never to do such a thing with Polly or any other member of the staff again.

"I promise," he replied, at least having the decency to look shamefaced. "Thank you, miss."

She began smoothing her rumpled skirts, grateful beyond words for the favorable outcome to the situation. Now, she needed only to slip upstairs and back into the ballroom before her absence attracted notice. She didn't anticipate any great difficulty, for she hadn't spent too lengthy a period below stairs, and if anyone questioned her whereabouts, she could always claim she had been strolling on the terrace.

"So, this is where you rushed off to in such a hurry."

The deep, harsh voice cut in from behind her, and with it, her previous sense of optimism swiftly vanished. Her body seemed to become impossibly heavy as she forced herself to turn and face the intruder in the doorway.

"Mr. Walker!" She couldn't contain her gasp as her eyes locked with his, although instead of wearing his usual placid expression, he looked like he could breathe fire.

"You're a terrible liar, you know." His measured tone was gone, replaced by a quiet, unsteady voice that sounded on the verge of erupting. "I knew you must be up to something, although I must say, your depravity goes far beyond what I imagined."

Her own voice turned frosty. "One of our footmen was ill. As I have some knowledge of medicine, I came to assist him."

Mr. Walker laughed mockingly, gesturing toward the bed where she and Jim sat and then to Jim's discarded coat and cravat on the floor. "Yes, I can see you provided just the cure."

It was fortunate that Mr. Walker remained in the doorway, for it prevented her from acting on her urge to slap him. She glanced at Jim, whose face was beginning to crease with nervousness.

"Please, do not worry," she whispered, pressing the bottle of honeysuckle tincture into his hands. "Keep this in case you require it again. I must go."

"I'm so sorry, miss," he mumbled. "Truly, I—"

However, she jumped up and dashed out of the room before he could say any more, marching down the corridor while the sound of Mr. Walker's heavy footsteps echoed behind her. As they approached the servants' stairs, she abruptly spun around to face him, causing him to stumble back to avoid bumping into her.

"How dare you!" she hissed. "You had no right to follow me about my own house, and a gentleman should never question a lady's word."

"And how dare you accuse me of inappropriate behavior, you shameless slut, when *you* are the one cavorting with a servant of all people!"

She flinched as the spittle from his acerbic words hit her cheek. The swine she had always suspected to linger beneath Mr. Walker's pleasant façade had emerged, and in turn, a fierce, fiery feeling bubbled within her until she could no longer contain it.

"You are despicable!" she shouted in a tone highly improper for a respectable young lady. If he had already made up his mind about her immorality, it made little difference how she acted. "You know nothing about what happened. Absolutely *nothing*. You should take your misguided assumptions and heave them up your—"

"Eliza, why on earth are you yelling?" Her aunt Frances descended the servants' stairs, eying her with a puzzled frown. "I stepped out of the ballroom to speak with a footman and could hear your ungodly racket all the way from the corridor upstairs. And Mr. Walker?" She turned her notice to the irate gentleman next to Eliza, her look of bewilderment intensifying. "What is the meaning of this?"

"Go on, Miss Wright," urged Mr. Walker, his voice dangerously gentle. "Tell your aunt how you traveled below stairs to seek more diverting company."

Eliza was tempted to pinch herself, just in case it would wake her from this nightmare. But something about the vividness of the unforgiving eyes glaring at her, along with her heart's insistent pounding, confirmed that this was more than just a horrifying dream. "I was only trying to help Jim when he became unwell," she exclaimed, unable to mask her exasperation. "There was nothing more to it than that."

"Indeed, Miss Wright," said Mr. Walker, flashing another sardonic smile. "I'm sure you had helped him very much by the time I discovered you on his bed while he sat next to you in a state of undress."

Frances drew her wiry frame up so tightly that it looked like a single touch would snap her in half. "Surely, Eliza, you would never do such a thing. Confirm to me this instant that these accusations are untrue."

"But they *are* true, Mama."

The grating feminine voice cut into her, and she gaped at her stony-faced cousin as she joined them below stairs. "Louisa," she tried to gasp, although no sound came out.

"I saw her in the same position on my way to the kitchen several days ago." Louisa stared directly at her, her eyes glittering with spite. "At the time, I was simply too shocked to say anything of it."

"But I didn't," Eliza insisted weakly, although the protest died on her lips. She peered at the three figures before her, all regarding her like she was some sort of pariah. And suddenly, every ounce of anger flowed out of her. All that remained was the icy sting of defeat.

Frances let out a strangled cry, allowing her taut shoulders to slump. "Oh, my nerves cannot handle such torment. Louisa, go upstairs and fetch my vinaigrette at once. Mr. Walker, if you will kindly escort my daughter up the servants' stairs."

She clutched Eliza's arm as if requiring support, but the second Louisa and Mr. Walker disappeared from view, she dug in her nails so harshly that they clawed through Eliza's glove, and she dragged her down the corridor until they reached the privacy of the wine cellar.

"How could you, you stupid, selfish girl?" she shrieked as she slammed the door behind them. "You may very well have ruined us all."

Eliza no longer had the energy to provide explanations that would only fall on deaf ears. Her slippers pinched her feet, her stays had grown painfully tight, and she wanted nothing more than to return to her bedroom and sleep away the next week.

"I should have known this would happen," cried Frances, on the verge of hysterics. "With your lowborn father and ridiculous mother who insisted on shutting herself up in the country, you could hardly be expected to properly mingle in polite society. Well, one thing is for certain. You will never show your face in London again. I only hope you have not entirely ruined Louisa's chances at attracting a suitable husband, for I will never forgive you."

The insults rolled off her now, and Eliza allowed her mind to wander. Nearly every day, she had looked out the window of this rented London house to the bustling street below and wished she was instead peering down at the rolling meadows of her Lancashire home. It seemed her wish might soon come true. Funnily, the realization brought only cold comfort.

Chapter 17

For some time, Edward sat on the bed with Eliza in his arms, saying nothing. The sun was sinking low in the sky, and the room's candles had not yet been lit, leaving them alone in shadowy silence. In this darkened sanctuary, free from distractions of the outside world, her story tumbled through his mind, each detail so disconcerting that he hardly knew what to think.

Eventually, she stole a glance up at him, her expression imploring and tinged with nervousness. "Edward?"

He gritted his teeth until he could no longer keep the words from bursting out. "If I ever have the misfortune of crossing paths with Reginald Walker, I cannot be held responsible for what happens." Perhaps it was the wrong thing to say, coming out as cold and uncomforting, but among all the sensations rolling within him, anger had pushed its way above the others. "And as for your so-called family …" He trailed off, unable to come up with words fit for a lady's ears. The idea that her own kin, the ones she had relied upon for support, had treated her in such a manner made his blood boil. He had long recognized his parents as selfish and unfeeling people, but slandering and casting aside an innocent relation went beyond even their level of callousness. No wonder Eliza had agreed to her father's marriage scheme when the alternative was to remain with the people responsible for her ruin. She had previously explained her desire to avoid living on her aunt and uncle's charity, but he had never fully comprehended the force behind that desire until now. For her, anything would have been better than depending on the people who betrayed her, even an unwanted marriage. The realization hit him like a blow to the stomach.

Eliza, however, appeared calm. "I would be untruthful in saying I never felt resentful toward them or that I was never tempted to put all my efforts into returning Louisa's spitefulness. Ultimately, though, I did my best to forgive them, if for no other reason than to avoid spending the rest of my days burdened by bitterness. In any case, I suppose I was foolish to place myself in such a compromising position, and I can understand how it must have appeared—"

"Perhaps, but that doesn't mean you deserved the treatment you received," he interjected.

She managed a small smile. "Do you believe me, then? About what happened? For I've grown so accustomed to having my words doubted."

"Of course I believe you." He pulled her a little more tightly against his chest, hating the apprehension that remained in her voice. "I saw how you rushed off to help Alice and her child without a second thought. I do not doubt the plausibility of you doing something similar on a previous occasion. What I cannot comprehend is why you protected your maid's reputation at the expense of your own."

She made a soft and resigned sound. "I saw no point in incriminating Polly. Not when my aunt and uncle had already made up their minds about my guilt, for they would have never accepted my word over their own daughter's. By saying nothing, I thought I could at least ensure that one of us came out of the night unscathed. In the end, though, it didn't matter. There was nothing I could do to prevent Aunt Frances from dismissing Jim, and a couple days later, Polly followed him to seek out a factory job in London. She said they intended to marry, although I'm unsure if they went through with it. By that time, Papa was already escorting me back to Lancashire."

"I see." Edward had been absentmindedly running his hand over her shoulder, and it was only then he realized how hard his fingers were digging in. He pulled his hand away from her and clenched his fist, then abruptly released it as if he could cast his fury away. "And what was your father's stance on what happened?" he asked, thinking of Thomas Wright's smooth exterior and calculating interior. "Did he at least have the decency to believe you?"

"Truthfully, I do not think he cared one way or another what really occurred. He only cared how society's perception of what happened would affect him. Angry doesn't begin to describe his reaction when he thought I had ruined my chances for an advantageous marriage. But then, as he so often does, he was able to turn the situation to his advantage. His feelings toward me warmed considerably after that." She had that look in her eyes again, the mixture of awe and shame that often appeared when she spoke of her father.

Once more, Edward stayed silent. Eliza may have accepted how she'd been wronged, but that didn't stop his outrage on her behalf. How could a supposed gentleman, and then her own family, have used her empathy against her? How could she have found it within herself to excuse so readily what they had done? Furthermore, how, despite everything, had she come to Highfield Park retaining more than a shred of her compassionate nature? Especially when he started the relationship by making no great effort to show her kindness or acceptance ...

"I'm sorry," he finally said. "I'm sorry your cousin took no issue with maligning you. I'm sorry your earnest desire to help brought about your ruin. And most of all, I'm sorry you were forced into marriage as a result."

"No, do not be sorry." She let her fingers brush over his forehead and into his hair, her touch light and calming. "At least, not for the final part you mentioned, because I'm not. In fact, I'm not sorry for any of it, for, without the scandal, I likely would not have ended up here. Initially so disagreeable to us both, this marriage arrangement has benefited me more than I could have ever imagined. Getting to know your tenants, especially Alice, Jenny, and now my little namesake, Beth, has helped fill the void I felt when leaving Riverton. In Catherine, I have found a cherished friend and sister. And then, Lord Ashton, there's you." She flashed him a coy smile, the kind that made him want to tumble down to the mattress with her and not get up for the next several days.

"But I don't just mean this," she added, gesturing to the bed sheepishly as if somehow reading his thoughts. "Although this is indeed very nice, I—"

"*Nice?*" he cut in, arching a quizzical eyebrow. "You think our time together has merely been *nice?* Why, Lady Ashton, I believe we can do far better than that." He grasped her shoulders, ready to lay her beneath him and replace his frustration with a far more enjoyable emotion.

Eliza, however, gave him a playful shove away. "I misspoke," she conceded with a little laugh. "Nice does not begin to do justice to how I feel when we're alone together. But it's not just that." Her expression suddenly turned serious, and she gripped his shoulders so he was forced to remain seated and look her in the eye. "I have come to care for you in a way I didn't think possible. And I have come to feel something I didn't believe I ever would." She took a deep breath before bringing her hand down to clasp his. "Love."

Edward experienced a split second of elation before coldness began seeping through him. Had he possibly misheard her? No, the word echoed through his mind as plainly as if she were still speaking it. *Love.* She peered at him expectantly, clearly awaiting a response, but all he could do was gape like an idiot.

The silence between them hung heavily in the air for what seemed like an eternity when in actuality, it was more like just a few seconds before her face fell. "You needn't look so horrified." She pulled her hand away from his and folded her arms across her chest. "I will not try to force a similar admission out of you when clearly you do not return the sentiment."

He was no stranger to moments of self-loathing, but none so great as right now, when he was forced to confront the great hurt he had caused her. Yet her revelation paralyzed him, rendering him incapable of offering a satisfactory response.

Love. The word he had never thought he would hear, and never wanted to hear, again. A familiar memory flooded his mind, and despite its relation to a long-past event, it still cut into him like a rusty knife.

"Why did you think it necessary to go about the ballroom flirting with every man in sight? For God's sake, Julia, we have been married for merely a week. You could at least pretend to have a shred of deference for your status as a newlywed."

"Ha." Her laugh rang out with a cold musicality. "Do not tell me you are jealous, Lord Camden." Even in the dimness of the carriage, her pale eyes pierced him as she lounged nonchalantly on the opposite seat. "I have spent the Season thus far as the jewel of the ton, and I see no reason why that should change just because I am married. If I choose to remind others of my charms on occasion, then what of it? It will only accentuate your position as a man to be envied. The other men mean nothing. You're the one I love."

"It isn't real," he exclaimed, desperately wanting to return to the present and escape the memory, although its implications still rattled within him. "In any case, I have yet to experience any evidence of it." *It.* He couldn't even bring himself to utter that particular four-letter word out loud. "It is just something besotted young couples say to one another to try to explain the jumble of things they feel. Over time, though, the sensation fades, and at best, all that remains is a companionable partnership."

Eliza sat before him saying nothing, and judging by her stony expression, he wondered if he had shocked her into silence.

"I thought you would understand," he muttered weakly, "having grown up with a mother whose supposed love match brought her a lifetime of misery. You and I have begun to get on well together. We have come to care for one another. Can that not be enough?"

"Indeed. I'm sure you are right," she replied in a steely tone he had never heard her use before. "It's likely just a fleeting notion of mine. It will pass."

Her words should have appeased him, but instead, the sinking feeling deep within him intensified. He longed for the Eliza of just a few minutes before, the woman of indomitable strength who also displayed such warmth and compassion that he felt like all was well with the world whenever he was near her. However, the Eliza sitting before him now had grown detached and frosty. Even worse was the resigned look in her eyes that suggested she had succumbed to defeat. And worst of all was the damnable knowledge that he had caused it all.

She wriggled herself farther away from him. "I think I have said quite enough for one day. If you'll excuse me, I'm going to retire early this evening."

She tugged down the shirt she wore to ensure it covered her and pushed herself off the bed, leaving a void where her soft body had warmed him. Ever since their first night together, they had always slept in the same bed, either his or hers, but she was currently walking toward the connecting door, alone.

"Stay," he called out, causing her to pause, although she didn't turn back toward him. After all she had gone through with Alice, followed by all it had taken to explain the story of her scandal, he couldn't stand the thought of her lying in bed by herself. He wanted her to fall asleep cradled in his arms, knowing she was protected and esteemed and cared for.

"Stay," he repeated, quietly but insistently. "Please."

She hesitated a moment longer before spinning in his direction once more, her face devoid of expression. Without a word, she tiptoed back to his bed and crawled between the sheets, rolling to her side so she faced the wall instead of him. Tentatively, he stretched his arm across her and rested his hand at her waist, half-expecting her to shake it off. Instead, she remained perfectly still until suddenly, he detected the faint movement of her fingers skimming over his. He allowed himself the tiniest flicker of hope as he pulled her closer to him so he could bask in the heat of her body and inhale her rosewater scent once more. Something, though, was different. Her body seemed wrought with tension, and aside from the gentle motions of her fingers, she kept herself uncommonly still. She was right next to him, in his arms, just as he had so desperately wanted. Why, then, did she feel so far away?

Chapter 18

Once again, Edward returned to the fields to join the laborers. The uncomfortable heat of summer had given way to the first hint of an autumn chill, and each day brought them closer to the completion of the harvest.

On that front, things had been going as well as could be expected. While the yields were undoubtedly not what they could have been, the corn they did have seemed of decent quality, and the reapers made good time bringing it in. He remained hopeful the estate would turn at least a small profit so he wouldn't need to completely depend on Eliza's dowry or further generosity from Thomas Wright.

As for the matter of Eliza, things hadn't been going well at all. And though he pushed himself physically, heaving stooks onto the cart without repose, the throbbing in his back and burning in his lungs were no longer enough to distract him from thoughts of her.

Outwardly, nothing about her behavior had changed. For the past five days, she had still come down to the breakfast room with a smile and bid him good day before he headed off on business about the estate. She had also chatted with him and Catherine at the dinner table and then in the drawing room each evening with as much amiability as ever.

The difference, though, was that he no longer saw her alone. She had taken to sleeping in her own bed without him, saying she had her courses and didn't desire company.

He supposed he could take that as an explanation for the faint shadows under her eyes and the way she continued to carry herself with a slight rigidity that contrasted with her usual carefree stance. However, he felt certain the real reason extended far beyond that. The truth was, he had hurt her. He had taken the fragile connection between them, the reason he had felt shreds of happiness return to his life, and shattered it. He hated himself with every fiber of his being for doing it and yearned to make things right again. But as for how he would do that, at least without uttering idle words that meant nothing, he hadn't the faintest clue.

When he finally took a moment to stretch out his cramped muscles and wipe the beads of sweat from his forehead, an auburn-haired figure in the distance caught his eye. He shook his head, annoyed that in addition to overtaking his thoughts, Eliza had also begun appearing to him in visions. However, as he continued to stare, the figure came closer until he had no doubt that the real Eliza was heading in his direction. His heart lurched at the sight as if he were some ridiculous green boy awaiting a meeting with his first sweetheart. He ran a hand through his disheveled hair and tried to appear nonchalant, although the pangs in his chest wouldn't cease.

She soon came close enough to attract the attention of the other laborers, for the song they had been in the midst of singing died out, and they, too, began standing up straight and doffing their caps.

"Good day," she called with a smile, although her hands twisted uncertainly around the bunch of leafy herbs she held. "I apologize for the interruption. I was out for a walk and thought I would come this way to see how the harvest is getting along. I see you have all been quite busy, so please, don't delay your work any longer on my account."

Then, just as quickly as she had appeared, she spun on her heels and began hastening in the opposite direction, her airy yellow skirts fluttering behind her.

Edward tossed his pitchfork to the ground and dashed toward her. "Wait," he exclaimed before her hurried footsteps had the opportunity to turn into a full run. "There's no need to leave in such a rush. I can assure you that your presence here is far from an intrusion."

"In any case, I didn't know you would be here, and I won't take up any more of your time. I'll see you at dinner later," she mumbled, looking at him only briefly before continuing with her walk.

"Are you returning to the house now?" he called after her. Based on the sun's position in the sky, he judged it to be late afternoon, the time when she often sat with Catherine and Miss Martin in the drawing room.

She turned around long enough to give him a nod. "Yes, I planned to."

"Let me walk back with you." He strode to her side and gestured to the other laborers, who had already started back to work and were quietly resuming their song. "I do not think I'm needed here any longer." For that matter, Eliza clearly didn't need him, or perhaps even want him, to accompany her either, but the possibility of spending time alone with her was too tempting to let slip away so easily.

"Please," he added gruffly, noting her hesitant expression. "That is if it would be agreeable to you."

She slightly inclined her head. "As you wish."

It wasn't the most enthusiastic invitation, but if it were all she had to offer, he would take it. He strolled beside her silently, contenting himself with just being near her. A sweet, lemony fragrance emerged from the herbs she carried, mixing with her usual floral scent to form a new combination that was entirely alluring. At present, it was all he needed to feel satisfied.

After a few more minutes of traipsing in the direction of the house, her eyes fell upon him. "You know," she said with just a shadow of a grin, "if you, the earl, spend your days in the fields like this, you run the risk of being labeled an eccentric."

He couldn't stop his own smile from breaking through. "And would it trouble you to have an eccentric husband, Lady Ashton?"

"Not at all. If anything, people would probably say I made you that way."

He laughed at her return to good humor, his trepidation beginning to dissipate. And then the words rose in his throat. *"I'm better that way."* They crept to the tip of his tongue, but another unsettling lurch deep within him caused them to die off unspoken.

They continued walking without saying anything, the light swishing of the grass beneath their feet and the melodic ringing of birdsong overhead providing the only break to the silence until Eliza turned to him once more. "Now that the harvest is nearing completion, I think we should plan a harvest home celebration for the laborers and tenants. Perhaps nothing too elaborate, given the recency of your father's death, but those who stayed with the estate despite the challenges of recent years deserve some sort of recognition."

"You are correct, of course. I was remiss not to plan for it sooner." For as much as he dreaded the thought of being surrounded by a large group of his tenants, people who had known him in the past, he realized he also had a duty to erase the former earl's legacy of neglect and start his management of the estate off on the right foot.

"Good. I'm happy to see to the arrangements. Maybe Catherine can help me. She doesn't seem to care much for large gatherings, but if she's to undertake a London Season in the new year, it might do her good to gain more exposure to them, at least in some fashion."

"Whatever you think is best. I will leave it in your hands." She already appeared deep in thought, and he had no doubt she would see to it that the celebration was just as it needed to be. "Thank you," he added, although the word was insufficient for all he needed to convey.

After that, he allowed her to mull over arrangements without interruption, walking slightly behind her so the edges of her skirts licked at his trousers. He wished he could have more of her, that he could reach for her hand and whirl her around to him and take her in his arms. However, knowing they had not returned to that level of comfort with one another, he kept his hands firmly pressed to his sides until they climbed the imposing stone steps that led to the front door of Highfield Park.

"There's still some time left before dinner. You should ring for a bath," she suggested after Higgins ushered them into the entrance hall. "Get rid of some of this dirt from the fields."

Mindlessly, she brushed her fingers over the dusty front of his shirt, and before he could stop himself, he clasped her hand in his. "Join me," he murmured, leaning close to her ear.

She inhaled sharply, and was it just his imagination, or did he detect desire glittering in the emerald depths of her eyes? She made a slight movement in his direction before suddenly stumbling backward, snatching her hand out of his grasp. "I should bring this lemon balm to the stillroom and lay it to dry," she mumbled, squeezing the limp leaves of the herbs she still held between her fingers. "I'll see you at dinner."

As she scurried away from the entrance hall, a stem of the lemon balm slipped from her grasp and tumbled to the floor, providing a shock of earthy green against the cool black and white marble. He bent down to retrieve it, breathing in the citrus scent that made it seem like Eliza was still next to him. He enclosed it in his palm, pinching the leaves between his fingers as he climbed the stairs and waited for his blood to cool.

The unsettling heat within him remained even after dinner as they all assembled in the drawing room. Without delay, Catherine seated herself at the pianoforte and started in on a Haydn minuet, her fingers traveling deftly over the keys as Miss Martin tapped her foot in time to the music while eagerly perusing a book of poetry. Eliza, too, sat on the sofa with a book in front of her, but after nigh ten minutes had passed, she had yet to turn a page. She had been unusually quiet at dinner as well, making it impossible to ignore that something was wrong. Foolishly, upon seeing her in the field that afternoon, he had allowed himself to hope they were heading toward a reconciliation. Instead, it became increasingly apparent that Eliza was only drifting farther away.

He picked up a newspaper and began leafing through the pages, although, like Eliza, he couldn't seem to absorb the words in front of him. His eyes kept drifting to her tense frame, and he wished he could tell what she was thinking. On the end table beside her sat a full brandy decanter, shining invitingly beneath the candlelight, and because he didn't know how to approach Eliza, he eventually approached the decanter and helped himself to a generous glass. Instead of providing comfort, the first sip slid uncomfortably down his throat and roiled in his stomach.

"Will you pour me one?"

He started at the soft voice and looked to see Eliza peering up at him. He couldn't help raising his eyebrows. "Are you certain? I have never known you to drink after dinner brandy."

"Yes," she asserted, "please."

Something about her ramrod posture and the firm set of her mouth made him disinclined to argue, and wordlessly, he handed her a filled snifter.

She swiftly pressed it to her lips, showing no reaction as she took a large swallow of the burning liquid. "Yes," she repeated, running her tongue against her lips to brush away a few remaining drops, "I thought I might try doing as you do."

"And what is it I do, exactly?" he asked. Something about her low, steely tone set him on edge.

"I thought I might wash my troubles away with brandy."

He shoved his snifter back to the end table, its contents suddenly repulsing him. Words escaped him, and all he could do was meet her challenging expression with a blank stare. He didn't like this new Eliza, so taciturn and sharp. Yet how could he dare complain when he had helped bring about this change in her behavior, and she had spoken nothing but the truth?

The air between them hung heavy with tension. It occurred to him that the room had fallen silent, and when he looked toward the pianoforte, he noticed Catherine sitting with her hands in her lap, a bemused expression plastered across her face.

"I believe I'll retire early this evening," she said, just as Miss Martin uttered, "I think I'll go up to bed now."

They both rose from their seats, shooting each other a furtive glance, and without another word, they scurried from the room. Now it was just him and Eliza with nothing left to focus on but each other, and although neither of them spoke, the gaze they shared became almost a challenge to see who would look away first.

Ultimately, Eliza broke the silence first, but she kept her eyes fixed on him as she said, "Perhaps I'll retire now as well."

"*Stay a while longer*," he wanted to implore her, for he didn't know how either of them would sleep restfully with all this unresolved strain between them. But he also knew he was no longer in a position to ask anything of her, and so he said, "By all means, if you are tired."

He had thought his bland words innocent enough, but something about them seemed to make her snap. She tipped back her snifter and swallowed down the remainder of its contents before tossing it on the table beside his. "Yes," she said, her voice troublingly low. "I'm very tired." With slight clumsiness, she gestured around the room, ending by pointing at him. "I'm tired of all of this."

He could have questioned her, but there was no need. He knew exactly what she meant. He was bone-weary himself. And as he stood there, absorbing her lividity, a realization dawned on him. He had to tell her the truth. The details of his past marriage, the ones he had so adamantly concealed, needed to come out in the open.

The very idea of explaining all that had happened between him and Lady Julia Carmichael made him want to retch. What a grotesque bedtime story that would make.

Once upon a time, there lived a young lady whose beauty and charm made her the coveted prize of every unmarried gentleman in the ton. There also lived a young gentleman, a viscount poised to inherit an earldom, who was raised to believe he deserved to have his every whim fulfilled, and he, therefore, decided this prize should be his. Luckily for him, his status and perceived wealth (for he wouldn't discover until much later that the wealth was an illusion) enticed the young lady to accept his proposal. If, throughout their engagement, he noticed her disappearing during balls and soirees or acting just a little too familiar with other gentlemen, he didn't pay it much notice, for he knew he was her chosen one, and together they were the envy of the ton.

When they married and her free and easy way with others continued, he grew somewhat troubled, although her pretty words assuaged his fears, and he was too consumed with lust to notice how she dangled him on a string. In any case, he assumed this unfortunate situation would be remedied when they departed for their honeymoon in Brighton, for there, it would be just the two of them, removed from the bustle of society.

But of course, they were not the only visitors to Brighton, and of the people with whom they soon became acquainted, the young bride took a particular interest in a Captain Adamson. The newly married viscount found the captain agreeable enough and even passed evenings with him at the card table. That is, until one evening when the bride remained in their hotel suite with a megrim, and Captain Adamson was noticeably absent from the card table.

Out of concern for his wife's welfare, the viscount retired early from the evening's entertainments, only to be greeted by the sight of Captain Adamson warming his wife's bed. As the viscount observed the scene, shouting outraged obscenities but finding himself frozen in place, the captain grabbed his personal effects and hastened from the room, and the errant bride wasted no time in following him. The scorned husband *forced motion back into his limbs just in time to dash down the stairs and see the illicit lovers climbing into a waiting curricle.*

He tried to catch up with them, too blinded by fury to know what he would do but wanting to reach them nonetheless, but they were quicker, speeding away with insistent flicks of the reins. How unfortunate that in their haste, the captain paid no heed to the street before them until the shouts of the approaching coach driver caused him to swerve suddenly, sending the horse and curricle crashing to the ground. All at once, the scene erupted into chaos, filled with terrified shrieks of passersby, but the viscount hardly noticed as he rushed to the site of the accident. For there, he saw his wife, as lovely as ever, except that her cerulean eyes had turned glassy and lifeless.

His attention rested solely on her, although he later discovered that Captain Adamson had succumbed to the same fate. Therefore, the wicked received their due punishment, and the viscount, gaining freedom from his wayward wife, was left to live happily ever after.

As the memories flooded him, he had to choke back a sickened laugh. His father had viewed what happened as rather simple. Julia had scorned him, she had paid for her deception with her life, and that meant he was free to pursue new and better things. But for Edward, it had never been that simple at all. As much as he had tried to convince himself that dwelling on the situation was beneath him, the bitterness, the misery, and the utter shame surrounding what happened had weighed him down like Sisyphus's boulder.

He had cut himself off from society and his family. Why, he had even left the country and wandered the Continent aimlessly for years in an effort to forget. Nevertheless, here and now, he was going to confront the past again. For how else could he make Eliza understand?

He lowered himself to the sofa, relieved when Eliza remained seated beside him, for he doubted he would have had the resolve to call her back had she fled. His heart pounded, leaving a sharp, steady ache in his chest. He stared at her hands for a moment, letting his fingers skim over hers, before forcing himself to look her in the eye once more. Her weariness and frustration, and maybe even a bit of tipsiness, were plastered across her face. But behind that, there looked to be a hint of concern, giving him hope she hadn't stopped caring for him altogether. In any case, it made him trust she would hear him out, for better or worse.

He took a deep breath and released it in an unsteady exhale. "Might I speak with you?"

Chapter 19

A bead of moisture trickled down Eliza's cheek and dropped onto her sleeve. Edward had spoken for a long time, and now that he was through, he slumped against the sofa with a look of trepidation. His words tumbled through her head as she frantically tried to process all he had told her. His beautiful wife ... his wife's unthinkable deception ... the horrific accident ...

"*I'm sorry.*" The apology echoed through her mind until she wanted to shout it out over and over. "*I'm sorry, I'm sorry, I'm sorry.*"

She knew, though, that Edward didn't want her pity. And so, she said what lingered beneath, the truth he needed to realize. "It wasn't your fault."

He made a sound approaching a laugh but shrouded in bitterness. "No. The earls of Ashton, past, present, and future, are never to blame for anything."

"You are not to blame for your former wife's duplicity," she insisted. "Nor are you to blame for her death."

He flinched at that and turned to gaze aimlessly at the darkness outside the window. "Maybe. I hardly know anymore. All I know is I was a damn fool, and I will *not* let that happen again."

The irony of the situation began to dawn on her. Throughout the course of her turbulent relationship with Edward, she had thought the problem lay with her inferiority to his first wife. Then, when he had rejected her declaration of love, she assumed his aloofness stemmed from the fact his heart would always belong to another— the one he had lost. As it turned out, his first wife, the being who had gained such an elevated status in Eliza's mind, had not been her superior in morality and goodness. Furthermore, while Lady Julia had indeed helped close off Edward's heart, this stemmed from her unfaithfulness—not her perfection. Much to Eliza's shame, a pang that felt suspiciously like resentment vibrated through her as she considered the damage the dead woman had done.

She impatiently brushed away the wetness from her eyes and gripped Edward's shoulders, encouraging him to look at her once more. "I'm not Julia." She stared into his troubled blue eyes, silently imploring him to understand.

"I know." He ran his finger across her cheek where a couple of stray tears remained. "You're different from her in so many ways. I would never want that to change, which is why I have no wish to complicate things between us with declarations of … love. Surely you can see that."

She should have seen that. After all the years she had spent observing her mother's unhappiness and vowing not to let the same fate befall her, she should have seen that. Yet something about Edward led her to change her mind when it came to love. Maybe it was due to the thrilling sensations he had awoken in her body. Maybe it was the way he cared for his estate and those close to him, even though he tried to conceal it beneath a brusque facade. And even more likely, maybe it was how he accepted her for who she was, despite her parentage, her unconventionality, and her past.

Whatever the reason, she had developed feelings she never thought she'd experience. And if she could find a way to push past her fears and open her heart, why couldn't he?

"No," she said. "Funnily enough, I don't see that." By now, she knew Edward well enough to recognize his inclination to avoid difficult conversations. However, they could no longer afford to circumvent this issue between them. He had taken a huge step by finally opening up to her, and she would be damned if either of them left this conversation while still holding things back.

"Perhaps at the time of your first marriage, you were a vain, arrogant fool," she continued. He looked at her with mild surprise, but in her desperation to get her point across, she lost the ability to choose her words delicately. "Perhaps you now have a thousand regrets, but Edward, regretting a bygone situation will not change it! All you can do is take your past mistakes and learn from them to make yourself better. Regardless of how she wronged you, Julia's death was a tragedy, but you were given the gift of living on. It might not have always felt like a gift, but I think it was, and I hate seeing you waste it. There is good you can do in the world and love you can give. Do not let the memory of the woman who wronged you close you off from that forever."

She had wanted to bring him comfort with what she said, or at the very least help him to see reason, but instead, he sat beside her looking like a broken shell of himself.

"It's not as simple as all that," he muttered, his voice dull and expressionless. "You do not understand."

Maybe she should have softened her approach with him or even retreated from the conversation altogether. But at this point, her days of frustration and heartache, her months of dealing with her own grief, and her newfound shock at Edward's revelation had combined into some powerful, unnameable emotion that kept her pushing forward. "I understand that the situation is what you make of it," she exclaimed, surprised by the forcefulness of her tone. "Running from the past won't make it disappear. You need to acknowledge it. You deserve to let yourself mourn, and heal, and find happiness."

"Eliza—" he began to say, but she held up her hand to stop him. There was something else she had to make clear to him, and while the mere thought of it made her stomach churn like she would be ill, she couldn't leave it unspoken.

"If you find you do not have feelings of love toward me, then so be it." Remarkably, her voice only wavered slightly as she uttered the words. "But you do yourself a great disservice by closing yourself off to the possibility of love altogether. And frankly, if you insist on keeping yourself at arm's length forever, I fail to see how we can even hope of continuing successfully together."

Edward stared at her like she had just thrust a knife into his chest. "Eliza, surely you must realize …"

She waited this time, careful not to cut him off, but he didn't resume his speech. Suddenly, that force that had driven her forward, giving her the strength to reason with him and hold nothing back, vanished. She had poured everything she had into listening and trying to understand him, and trying to make *him* understand. Now, she had no more left to give.

"I'm going to bed now." She forced her weary legs to propel her off the sofa. "Perhaps you should reflect awhile on what I said."

"Eliza." He said her name one more time, although it crossed his lips as a shaky rasp.

She thought back to all the times she had wanted to talk to him about important matters, and he had remained silent, or changed the subject, or even departed the room. Few things had aggravated her more. Now, though, it was her turn to walk away. As much as she despised herself for doing it, she feared even one more word would shatter her. And so, she fled.

***

"My, Alice, she gets bigger by the day." Eliza peered down at Beth's sleeping face as she relished the feel of the baby's warm weight in her arms. While the preparations for harvest home had taken up much of her time over the past week, she now felt confident that everything was in order for the evening's celebration, and she had therefore slipped away to see Alice. Cuddling Beth helped calm the sense of frenzied unease that had overtaken her lately, making her immensely grateful she had made time to visit.

"They grow too fast, m'lady," said Alice, rustling around by the hearth to prepare tea. "It seems like no time at all since Jenny was that size and sleeping in my arms."

For an instant, the image of rocking her own baby, golden-haired like Edward, filled Eliza's thoughts. However, recognizing the diminished possibility of that happening, she pushed the vision down as quickly as it had risen. Five days had gone by since her conversation with Edward, and between his farm work and her planning, they had barely spoken. She had no doubt Alice was correct about the rapid passage of time. Did that mean she would wake up one day, still not reconciled with Edward, and realize years had passed?

"Will you, Jenny, and Beth attend the harvest supper this evening?" she asked, eager to distract herself.

Alice frowned as she seated herself at the table with the teacups. "I don't think it wise. I doubt very much we'd be welcome additions. Although …" Her mouth twisted into a semblance of a smile. "I had a visit yesterday from an old friend of mine, Ellen Davies. She brought her daughter, Ruth, and allowed her to run about outdoors with Jenny. I'm sure I have you to thank, m'lady, for if you don't think you're too grand to associate with me, I suppose she can't either."

"I'm so glad," said Eliza, and although she still had many concerns surrounding Alice's situation, she felt the tiniest shred of hope that things could start to improve for her. "Will you come, then, to the harvest supper? Lord Ashton, Lady Catherine, and I would certainly welcome you there, and I imagine others would follow suit."

"This evening would be too soon, I think. For now, 'tis best I remain here. But maybe, in time, things will be different."

Eliza smiled at the hint of brightness in Alice's expression. But as happy as she was for her friend, and as much as she continued trying to absorb Beth's peaceful presence, she couldn't stop the angst, which had been her constant companion of late, from remerging.

She stared at Beth's tiny form, and then out the window, and then at her untouched tea, desperate for a distraction when she felt Alice's gaze fall upon her.

"A penny for your thoughts."

Eliza snapped her attention back to Alice, but as she did, the threat of tears stung at her eyes. What on earth was wrong with her?

"M'lady, I hope you'll pardon my boldness," said Alice, using the same gentle tone as when she soothed Beth to sleep, "but we're well enough acquainted now that I can tell when something's troubling you. I hope you know that, whenever you like, you can talk with me in confidence, just as you did before. Anything you say, I'll take to my grave. I swear it."

"Did you ever meet Lord Ashton's first wife?" The words escaped Eliza's lips before she had a chance to think them over. The answer would change nothing, but she had a sudden desire to know. "The Viscountess Camden," she clarified, feeling her cheeks flame.

If the question surprised Alice, she gave no indication of it. "Not when she was the viscountess, no. I remember one time, though, after their engagement, I believe, when Lord Ashton, or Lord Camden as he was at the time, brought her riding through the village."

"Was she very lovely?" Perhaps the question reeked of jealousy or pettiness, but once more, she couldn't stop herself from posing it. She had built up Julia, the Lady Camden, so much in her mind that she still had trouble reconciling what Edward had told her about the woman with the flawless being of her imagination.

"Do you mean, was she lovely to look at? Then yes, her beauty was the talk of the village," answered Alice bluntly. "But while she inclined her head to me all proper-like, I never saw her smile, and no one I know heard her speak a word to them."

Eliza propped her free elbow on the table and sunk her head into her hand. "Oh, Alice, I think she may have closed him off from ever loving another."

"From ever loving …?" Alice trailed off as her face took on a look of confusion. To Eliza's shock, Alice then broke into a grin. "Let me tell you something, m'lady. The day Beth was born, when Lord Ashton came to seek you out, I felt wearier than I ever have in my life. Even then, I could see the way he looked at you. If that wasn't love, I don't know what is."

Although she was wary of letting it get carried away, a trace of optimism sprang up within her. "I just don't know."

"I do. Please believe me, m'lady." Alice's voice lost its mellow edge and turned more commanding. "His lordship's adoration for you was plastered across his face, as plain as day. I know that look because John used to set his eyes on me that way. Someday, maybe some man will again. Stranger things have happened."

She finished her speech with a rueful smile, and Eliza reached out to clasp her hand. Her tears slipped out now, silent and heavy, and instead of trying to shut them back in, she let them fall. Alice had experienced her own unspeakable tragedy, had gone to hell and back as a result, but still, she had found a way to persevere and hold on to hope. And if Alice could do that, why couldn't she?

She craved Edward with every fiber of her being. Before knowing him, she had thought the term "heartbreak" to be a metaphor, but now, whenever she imagined living life without him, a physical ache spread through her chest. However, she couldn't continue to accept this closed-off version of him. She would take either all of him or none of him. And if the choice was to be none of him, as much as it would make her feel like the world had shattered and the sun would never come out again, she would find a way to carry on.

She rocked the gently stirring Beth in one arm while her other hand continued to grip Alice's as if through their connectedness, she could impart some comfort in Alice while absorbing her strength in return. They stayed that way for a long time.

Chapter 20

With many tenants already on their way to Highfield Park for the harvest home celebration, the village streets lay nearly deserted. It was just as Edward wanted. Soon, he would return to Highfield Park as well to witness the last cart of corn being brought in and take part in the harvest supper. However, there was something he needed to do first, a task he had neglected for far too long.

He continued down the quiet street, gradually slowing Apollo's pace as they approached the church. Upon reaching the front of the gray stone structure, he glanced around him, checking again to ensure no one was near before jumping down from Apollo's back. He began walking across the lush lawn of the churchyard, accompanied only by the sounds of the gentle rustle of leaves from the nearby oak trees and the pounding of blood in his ears. The ground turned uneven as he passed stone crosses and monuments, and although his pulse seemed to turn more rapid with each step, he willed himself to keep going, stopping only when he reached an impressive, intricately carved gravestone. The stone hadn't been in place the last time he had been here, on the day of the burial, but the location had always stuck with him, and so finding it had presented no difficulty.

He allowed himself to sink to the ground and take in a few deep breaths of the crisp air. Then, he reached out and ran his finger over the engraved letters that denoted the gravestone's owner. *Julia*.

They had spent their time together engaged in an inane flirtation, which they eventually turned into a marriage based on trivialities. How unfortunate he hadn't recognized that seven years sooner. The time to rectify the situation with Julia had long passed, but if he could only speak aloud what he should have said years ago, then maybe … maybe …

"I'm sorry." His words came out as a vanishing whisper in the breeze. Ironically, he couldn't recall ever uttering this phrase before meeting Eliza, and God knew he owed it to her a thousand times over. But being back in England, and being confronted with truths he had tried to run from for so long, made him realize he owed it to Julia as well.

"I'm sorry," he repeated, "for never seeing you as more than a trophy to be won. Had I looked past my infatuation and grandiosity for a mere moment, I would have seen how we did not suit. I don't think you were ready to be tied down to any one man, were you? Perhaps that wouldn't have stopped you from accepting an offer of marriage from another had I not made you an offer first. However, I should have known better, and for that, I'm sorry."

His voice had gained more power, making his speech echo down to the ground and up to the heavens. Here he was, a solitary man speaking to the air in a graveyard, yet with each word, a speck of his apprehension melted away, encouraging him to continue.

"We both got things horribly wrong, you and I. And because you are not present to speak for yourself, I want you to know something." He stilled his hand, letting it rest on the cool surface of the marble. "I forgive you."

They were only three small words, but somehow, it felt like a stone had been unchained from his neck. And so, he repeated them. "I forgive you."

He had made more mistakes than he could count, mistakes he had thought would follow him for the rest of his life, but then, unexpectedly and for reasons unbeknownst to him, he had been given another chance. By setting Eliza in his path, fate had gifted him with a true partner. A desirable lover, yes, but she was also so much more than that. In her, he had found someone who would always seek out the best in him while also encouraging him to do even better. She didn't judge or scorn him for his past, just as he didn't condemn her for hers. Together, they could heal from old hurts while looking to a brighter future. That is, if he hadn't already pushed her so far that she possessed no remaining desire to forgive or carry on with him.

He lowered his voice to a whisper once more. "I forgive you, and I wish you peace."

Then, he pushed himself back onto his feet, brushing blades of grass from the black legs of his trousers. It was time to return home.

***

The back lawn of Highfield Park was adorned with numerous long tables, all laden with roasted meats, pies, fresh loaves, bowls of fruit, cakes, pastries, and an endless supply of ale and cider. Edward peered out at the crowd before him as they helped themselves to food and drink and merrily chatted amongst themselves.

They indeed had much cause to feel merry, him as much as anyone. The first harvest to occur during his time as the Earl of Ashton had been successfully brought in, unafflicted by excessive rain or cold. Despite Mr. Hunt's inexcusable neglect, the land had provided them with enough, and now that the competent Mr. Locke had taken his place as land agent, there was every reason to hope that things would only improve from here.

He turned toward the sound of animated female voices beside him and smiled to see Eliza conversing with several of the farmer's wives.

"Alice says the poultice you gave her did wonders for her backache," said one, a woman he believed went by the name of Ellen Davies. She rested her hands atop the swell of her belly, made heavy with child. "Do you think you might offer me something like that, m'lady?"

"And might you know a remedy for sleeplessness, m'lady?" asked an older woman whose name escaped him. "There's times when I spend half the night pacing the floor, and 'tis giving me no end of frustration."

"Of course," Eliza replied, grinning at them as if she were in the company of close friends. "Perhaps I could call on you tomorrow, Mrs. Davies, and bring you a poultice similar to what I gave Alice when she was still with child. And Mrs. King," she added, addressing the woman whose name he'd forgotten, "I have a valerian tonic you might like to try. After supper, I'll go to the stillroom and fetch it for you so you can try it this very night."

"Thank you, m'lady," the two women uttered in unison, admiration shining on both their faces.

It was obvious to him how well she fit in here just by witnessing this brief exchange. Unlike the former Lady Ashton, his mother, who had worn a look of distaste every time an event had necessitated her association with the villagers, Eliza clearly enjoyed the companionship and paid no heed to rank. There was nothing artificial or forced in the way she carried on a conversation; the caring she displayed was genuine.

He gave a small smile again as Eliza posed a question to Mrs. King about her grandchildren, and the woman launched into a lengthy reply, plainly flattered at being asked. Viewing Eliza's sense of ease helped quell his discomfort as he considered what he needed to do next.

He sat quietly in his seat for a few moments longer, just observing, before finally rising to his feet with a mug of ale in hand. He cleared his throat and forced his twitching foot to be still. "If I might have your attention for a moment."

Instantly, a hush fell over the crowd, and dozens of sets of eyes turned upon him. The sight made him freeze. How quickly it took him back to the day of Julia's funeral when he had felt the eyes of the numerous acquaintances who crowded the church bore into him as if by staring hard enough, they could ascertain whether the scandalous whisperings surrounding Lady Camden's death were true.

However, these faces held no judgment or malice, only happy anticipation. They gave him the determination to resume his speech. "I would like to start by welcoming you to

Highfield Park and thanking you for your hard work this season. As you know, I am newly returned to the estate, and while things were not kept as they should have been in my absence, thanks to your dedication and hard work, we still brought in a successful harvest, one I know we can only improve in coming years. For that, you have my undying gratitude, and I toast to you."

Murmurs of appreciation rang out before they all placed their mugs to their lips. He took a long mouthful from his before adding, "I indeed have much cause for gratitude this year, for I had the good fortune of finding a woman who consented to marry me."

As he paused for the few rowdy cheers the revelers emitted, he took the time to glance down at Eliza. She tilted her head to the side, a slight smile crossing her lips. "Those of you who have met her are no doubt already aware of what a welcome addition to the estate she has proven herself to be. I cannot begin to describe all she has contributed; I can only say I consider myself among the luckiest of men. And so, Lady Ashton, I toast to you."

Eliza flushed at the applause and raised glasses pointed in her direction, but then a wide grin spread across her face. She was accepted here. She was home. And she was so wanted. He hoped he had helped her see that.

"To conclude," he said once the noise died down, "I hope you will all enjoy yourselves this evening and partake of the bounty before us. May it be a sign of more prosperous times ahead. I toast to your health and to the health of the estate. God willing, we will all join in celebration again for next year's harvest."

"And a toast to you, m'lord," called a voice from the crowd, "and your good health and good fortune."

Edward gazed a moment at all the cheering, laughing people in front of him before turning his attention back to Eliza. She focused on him, too, her eyes shining, and ever so slightly, she tipped her mug in his direction. "To you, Lord Ashton," she murmured, her voice nearly drowned out by the commotion from the crowd.

As he took his seat, surrounded by his tenants, his land, and most importantly, his wife, a realization dawned on him. After all these years of running, he, too, was home.

He wished he could whisk Eliza away at once and tell her everything he wanted her to know, but no sooner did the thought cross his mind than Ellen Davies's daughter came to present her with a posy of wildflowers, and instantly, her attention was diverted.

Suppressing a sigh, he settled back in his chair and turned his focus to conversing with those seated near him. He couldn't see himself ever being fully comfortable with engaging in idle chatter, but somehow, the idea had become significantly more tolerable.

Before long, several of the men brought out fiddles, which led to singing and dancing. Catherine came to sit beside him, both of them observing rather than joining the revelry on account of their mourning period. But where was Eliza? He had noticed her talking to the Morgan family and then to Mr. Hughes. However, her blaze of auburn hair was decidedly absent from the group performing a country dance. He peered at the people who lingered around the tables, squinting as he tried to make out features in the deepening twilight. Still, none of the faces stood out as the one he most wanted to see.

"Catherine," he said, leaning toward his sister's ear, "have you noticed Eliza about lately?"

"I don't believe so," she replied, glancing around at the crowd. "Around the time the music started, she passed by me and said she was going to the stillroom to fetch a tonic for Mrs. King, but I cannot recall seeing her since."

"Perhaps something delayed her there. I think I will go to the house myself, just to verify. Regardless, I could use a few moments of quiet."

Catherine flashed him a half-smile. "I understand. I will be in before too long myself."

He squeezed her shoulder before crossing the expansive lawn toward the house, the thought of having Eliza to himself for a moment quickening his step. Assuming she was still gathering her medicines, he slipped through the back servants' entrance, but upon reaching the stillroom, he found it dark and empty. He stepped back into the corridor, peering up and down, and was relieved to catch sight of Mrs. Parker heading in his direction.

"Mrs. Parker," he called to the housekeeper, "has Lady Ashton been here?"

"Yes, she's come and gone, my lord," she replied, approaching him with a curtsey. "I happened upon her just as she was leaving the stillroom, and I'm sure she said she planned to rejoin the festivities. Did you not catch sight of her outdoors?"

"Perhaps, amongst all the merriment, our paths did not cross. Or perhaps she had something else to attend to inside." Both scenarios were entirely plausible. Why, then, had tension knotted its way into his stomach?

"Sarah, her lady's maid, just came into the servants' hall," offered Mrs. Parker. "She might know something of her ladyship's whereabouts. Shall I fetch her?"

"No," he answered quickly. "No, I will seek her out myself. Thank you." He just caught sight of Mrs. Parker's bemused expression as he turned to make his way down the corridor. He must have appeared incredibly foolish, yet he couldn't shake the sense that something was amiss.

With the festivities still in full swing, the servants' hall was mostly empty, although the few servants who lounged around the table scrambled to their feet at the sight of their master.

"Sarah," he said, eying the young woman whose face remained flushed from the exertion of dancing, "have you seen Lady Ashton recently?"

She dropped into a curtsey. "No, m'lord. I saw her come in for a moment, but I thought she meant to head back to the celebration. I was just in her bedroom to fetch a shawl in case she needed one, and she wasn't there."

A light clattering noise drew his attention from Sarah to the opposite end of the table, where Mary, the scullery maid, had been clearing dishes. Her hands shook so much that the plates she held clinked together, and her downcast eyes had become wide saucers.

He approached Mary very slowly, not wanting to add to the girl's obvious terror. "Mary?" He kept his voice as low and mild as possible. "Is it possible you know something of Lady Ashton's whereabouts?"

One of the plates slipped from her fingers and crashed back onto the table, cracking cleanly in half. She bit her lip so tightly that it turned white as she moved her unsteady hands to retrieve the broken pieces.

"Leave it," he commanded and then added more gently, "It's of no matter. Please, just tell me if you have seen Lady Ashton."

The girl still trembled as she lifted her face to look at him. "I did see her, m'lord, not long ago when I went outside to shake out my dustpan. It was growing dark, but I'm sure it was her, for she had on that pretty green frock with the lace, and her hair was done up so nice with the little rosebuds in it, and she wore those shoes with—"

"Yes," he interrupted, impatience getting the better of him, "I believe you. Could you tell me what Lady Ashton was doing at the time?"

At this, Mary instantly dropped her gaze back to the floor and began shuffling her feet. "She ... she ... she was with a man, m'lord."

"I see." Given the hundred thoughts simultaneously racing through his head, Edward's voice remained surprisingly calm. "And do you know the identity of this man, Mary?"

She shook her head vehemently. "No. He was unfamiliar to me, and as I said, it was growing dark, and he had his back turned to me, and—"

"That's fine," Edward said cutting off the flustered girl once more. "And do you know if Lady Ashton and her companion were making their way back to the festivities?"

Again, Mary gave her head a little shake. "No, they weren't." Her voice quivered just like the rest of her. "That is, they looked to me to be heading in the opposite direction."

"Thank you," he managed to choke out. "You have been most helpful." The last thing he heard as he dashed out of the servants' hall was the girl's loud sigh of relief.

He ran until he burst out the servants' door through which he had entered, letting the night air wash over him. He inhaled deeply, taking in repeated heavy breaths as if the extra air would help make his vision stop swirling. His forehead burned, but at the same time, his blood felt like it had turned to ice. What the hell was happening?

The scullery maid's admission kept echoing through his head. *She was with a man, m'lord.* Was fate playing some kind of cruel joke on him? Had everything he believed about Eliza been a lie? Was he destined to live in a merciless world in which history kept repeating itself?

It didn't matter. He had run from England to escape his troubles before, so surely, he could do so again. Except … if he was entirely honest with himself, he didn't know if he could run anymore. He had changed too much since then. Eliza had changed him.

Which led him to a new train of thought. In the months since he and Eliza had first met, she had never given him the slightest reason to doubt her. Could there have been an innocent explanation for why she walked off with another? Could Mary have misinterpreted the scene?

Then, another possibility occurred to him, a possibility a thousand times worse than Eliza having a liaison with another man. What if something had happened to her? It just seemed so *odd* that she would willingly leave in the midst of the harvest celebration. Could she possibly be in danger?

Not wanting to waste another second, he bolted in the direction of the stables. Perhaps he would come across her dancing merrily around the lawn with the tenants, and he would then see how he'd succumbed to a ridiculous overreaction. Perhaps, after a little searching, he would discover her tucked away with this other man, confirming his old fears. Regardless, he had to search for her, for nothing was worse than not knowing, and he couldn't fathom sitting idly by if there was even a chance she found herself in trouble.

He needed to find her first and would worry about the implications of what he discovered later. None of it even mattered unless he knew Eliza was safe. He made a silent vow to keep looking until she stood before him once more.

Chapter 21

After visiting the stillroom to procure Mrs. King's sleeping tonic, Eliza had intended to return to the celebration and deliver it to her at once. However, upon stepping back outdoors into the cool twilight, she no longer felt an inclination to rush. From here, the cacophony from the party floated up as muffled background noise, and she found the relative quiet provided exactly what she needed.

She sauntered away from the shadow of Highfield Park, using these moments of peace to let the evening's events pour through her mind. For amidst the jumble of feasting, conversing, laughing, and dancing, something else stood out to her: Edward's speech.

She had barely spoken to him lately, including today, when amongst the flurry of preparations, he had absented himself until the moment the last wagon of corn came in, and the celebration started. Despite not seeing him, she found he never strayed far from her thoughts. At night, she had lain in bed, wondering if the completion of the harvest would bring about his departure for the Continent. His continued silence certainly suggested that as a possibility. And while she had repeatedly insisted to herself that she would carry on just fine either way, the thought of being without him made her whole body ache in a way that no amount of tonic could cure.

Tonight, though, something in his demeanor had changed. The subtle discomfort that lined his face when he had stood up to make his speech had given way to an easy confidence she couldn't recall witnessing in him before. He had actually looked happy to be there. Then, he had directed part of his toast at her, and once more, her assumptions about his feeling were turned on their head. A whisper of hopefulness fluttered in her chest as she remembered his words. Whether she should quash it down or allow it to soar, she hadn't the faintest clue.

"Evening, Lady Ashton."

The unfamiliar male voice snapped her away from her thoughts, and she peered around in the dim light, trying to detect its owner.

Her ears perked up as a low rustling emerged from behind the nearby beech tree, and she stared as an unfamiliar figure stepped out from behind it. It was difficult to make out his features fully, but she didn't recognize him as a tenant, laborer, or household servant, and she felt almost certain she hadn't seen him at the supper. As he approached her with unsteady steps, the acrid stench of alcohol filled her nose, and she took an involuntary step backward. "I don't believe we are acquainted, sir."

"No." He flashed a lazy smirk, and despite the darkness, she could make out his yellowed teeth. "Allow me to introduce myself. The name's Hunt, my lady, at your service."

The name didn't signify, and his obvious inebriation made her skin crawl. She stepped back once more. "It's very nice to meet you, Mr. Hunt, but if you will please excuse me—"

"'Fraid I can't." He took a large stride in her direction, standing far closer to her than the rules of propriety dictated. "Looks like you don't recognize me, my lady, so let me enlighten you. I'm employed as the land agent here at Highfield Park. At least, I was until the new master decided I wasn't good enough for him. I need to speak to you about that."

She recalled Edward telling her about hiring Mr. Locke after dismissing a previous land agent for incompetence, but she hadn't known any animosity lingered over the matter. In any case, there was little she could do to remedy the situation, and Mr. Hunt was in no state to conduct a meaningful conversation. "If you have grievances, you should take them up the earl," she insisted, spinning herself away from him. "Now, I really must be going—"

A quiet clicking noise caused the words to freeze in her throat, and she turned to face a cocked pistol that Hunt pointed squarely at her chest. "I must insist, Lady Ashton."

She stared, unmoving, into his wild eyes, barely able to hear her thoughts above the rapid thudding of her heart. She had to find a way to make herself focus. Even if Hunt were a skilled marksman, maybe his drunkenness would interfere with his accuracy, and she could run into the night while escaping his bullet. Alternatively, she could take him by surprise and knock the pistol from his hand before he had a chance to react. Moreover, did he truly intend to fire at her, or was the pistol just for show?

Hunt lunged at her, and before she had a chance to give it another second's thought, he clamped one hand over her mouth while the other hand, firmly clutching the pistol, pushed into her back. "How about we take a little walk?"

"As you wish," she muttered into his hand, trying not to gag as she was forced to inhale from his sweaty, gin-scented palm.

Much to her relief, he lowered his hand from her mouth, although he nuzzled the pistol tighter against her back. "You have no notions of screaming or running, do you?"

"Not at all," she answered dully. "Lead the way."

They stumbled together over the grass toward some unknown destination. She fought the urge to look back in the direction of Highfield Park in a last-minute attempt to signal help. She could only hope someone had peered outside at the right moment and seen them, but given the darkness and their distance from the house, she had to admit to herself the unlikelihood of that possibility. The strains of music from the party grew fainter, indicating that their haphazard route took them in the opposite direction from the festivities. Would some of the revelers eventually notice her absence? Or maybe Catherine, or even Edward himself? He had come searching for her once before. Did he trust her enough to do it again?

Her legs had turned to jelly, but somehow, she made them keep going, even as the hard metal wedged in her back provided a constant reminder of the danger she faced. Hunt himself had trouble walking in an orderly fashion, and she prayed silently that his intoxication would cause him to collapse before he had the opportunity to enact whatever part of his plan came next.

However, it seemed her prayer had fallen on deaf ears, for she soon caught sight of the oast house, standing dark and silent, and felt herself being dragged in its direction.

"In here," Hunt slurred as they staggered up to the entrance. He pushed them both in through the door before slamming it behind them with a low creak.

She was hit by the oast house's earthy smell and looked around frantically, trying to get her bearings. The only bit of brightness came from the slivers of moonlight that shone in through the tiny windows. "Why are you doing this?" she dared to ask as her eyes adjusted enough to make out his harsh features.

"Is that not obvious? Lord Ashton loves his wife. Lord Ashton's wife is rich. I have Lord Ashton's wife. Lord Ashton gives me money to get back his beloved wife. Lord," he said with a chuckle, "I could make a ditty out of that."

"Oh, shut up," snapped Eliza as he began humming tunelessly. "I'm afraid you have overestimated my value to Lord Ashton, so you should really let me go."

"No, you shut up," he snarled, "and don't go trying to fool me. I hear what they say about you two in all the taverns. You have great value to him indeed, and he cost me my wages, so he owes me. Now, put your hands in front of you." He withdrew a length of rope from his pocket, obviously intending to bind her wrists.

Bile rose in her throat, and beads of perspiration dotted the back of her neck as she mindlessly obeyed his command.

At least she could glean a speck of confidence from knowing that his plan would only succeed if he kept her alive, but still, her hands wouldn't stop shaking.

Hunt's own hands trembled as he attempted to tie the rope, and after several failed attempts, he set the pistol on the stuffed jute sack next to him. It sat just a few feet away from her, glistening invitingly. Perhaps this was her chance. If she could just drive her knee into him, enough to startle him for a moment, she could grab the pistol before he had an opportunity to react. Given Hunt's inebriated state, she could surely move faster than him.

She couldn't afford to hesitate this time. Without wasting another second, she slammed her knee into his gut with as much force as she could muster. At Hunt's outraged cry, she lunged for the pistol, feeling the cold metal brush her fingertips before she suddenly found herself crashing to the floor with a large weight on top of her and a sharp stinging in her neck.

She blinked a few times, her vision filled with stars and her head too heavy to form a coherent thought. The pistol. Mr. Hunt. Despite his tipsiness, he'd managed to overtake her. She put her hand on the throbbing spot on her neck and gasped as it connected with sticky wetness. Blood.

Her eyesight cleared enough to spot Hunt writhing on the ground next to her and the silver glint of a knife he managed to hold above her throat.

"I trust you won't be tempted to try that again," he panted, dangling the knife precariously close to her skin. She hadn't considered the possibility that he possessed additional weapons. By assuming his drunken state would prevent him from effectively executing his plan, she had done them both a great disservice.

She attempted to shake her head, but when bursts of light appeared before her eyes once more, she was forced to lie motionless. She became vaguely aware of his resumed efforts to bind her hands, and while her mind screamed at her limbs to move, she lacked the strength to make them obey. Her breath caught as Hunt reached into his pocket, but this time he removed only a flask, drinking from it eagerly before setting it on the ground and turning to examine his wounds.

A surge of clarity emerged from Eliza's clouded brain. It was merely a silly, farfetched idea, but it was all she had. And if there was any chance it could lead to her escape …

With Hunt's back still turned, she brought her hands to her pocket and plucked out the small bottle of sleeping tonic that rested there, clutching it tightly in her unsteady fingers. She tugged at the cap, willing herself to stop shaking long enough to unscrew it and let out a long, quiet breath as the cap came away in her hand. She gathered what scrap of strength she had left and heaved herself into a sitting position, although fresh doubt filled her mind as she debated how much of the tonic was needed to be effective while not overpowering the taste of gin.

She would just have to take her chances. There was no time to waste. She tipped the contents of the bottle into the open flask and shoved the empty bottle back in her pocket within a matter of seconds.

Hunt's head whipped around at the light swishing of her skirts, and his knife flew back to its position by her throat. "What do you think you're doing?"

Terror clutched at her insides and froze her in place until, all of a sudden, she rolled her eyes back in her head and toppled to the ground, feigning unconsciousness. It was a poor substitute for escape, but at least it put distance between her neck and the knife.

She lay perfectly still, although her heart thudded so rapidly it was a wonder Hunt didn't detect it and pick up on her ruse. Had he possibly seen what she did? She could sense his gaze upon her, and she pushed down the shriek that threatened to rise as she imagined him approaching her with the knife or the pistol, all while her eyes remained closed and unknowing.

He rustled around next to her, and she grappled with maintaining her charade of unconsciousness. Perhaps it would be better to open her eyes, to know what was coming next, to fight with whatever she had left …

And then she heard a loud swallowing noise. Hunt had imbibed from the flask. Her ears pricked, listening for any grunt of surprise or revulsion at the doctored gin. Instead, all that came was the sound of another vigorous swallow. She allowed herself a slow, subtle exhale, realizing she must have been holding her breath. Now all she had to do was wait and hope.

Her head grew heavier, threatening true unconsciousness, and she moved her fingers just enough to dig her nails into her palms. She couldn't lose focus now. She *couldn't*. She had to hold on a little longer.

At first, she took the low noise that crept up beside her for a groan from the floorboards, but then it sounded again and again, following a rhythmic pattern. Could it possibly be … snoring? She cracked one eye open, on high alert for impending danger. But when no threats swooped toward her, she opened the other eye, and as she readjusted to the dimness, the only thing that appeared before her was Hunt's sleeping form, propped against the jute sack.

The promise of freedom dangling before her was enough to cause an abrupt flood of energy that propelled her to her feet. She stopped only long enough to grab the pistol before bolting through the door and into the refuge of the night air. The back of her head throbbed like it was split open, and blood continued to seep from the slash in her neck, trickling down and soaking the front of her dress, but it didn't matter. Nothing would stop her from running.

Her legs took long, clumsy strides through the grass, filled with a newfound lightness that alarmed rather than reassured. Did this mean she was on the verge of fainting? She didn't even know what direction she headed, but if she could just continue a bit farther, maybe she would encounter someone who could help, or she would at least be beyond Hunt's detection whenever he awoke.

She brought her hands to her neck and applied pressure as an afterthought, but the effort was futile. She had already lost too much blood. The heaviness in her head turned to a strange weightlessness, and the world spun around her. A sharp ringing noise vibrated through her ears, but beneath it echoed whispers of her name. *Eliza. Lady Ashton. Eliza.* The ringing grew louder, but so did the whispers, until she let herself hope they were more than just figments of her imagination.

She stumbled blindly in the direction of the voice that called her name. *Eliza.* It became clearer, sounding more and more like the voice she wanted to hear above anything else in the world. Another noise joined in with it, almost like the thundering of hooves, and amidst the splotches of light that danced before her eyes, she could make out the form of an approaching horse.

"Eliza!" The voice shouted at her, frantic and insistent. It belonged to a tall figure who leaped down from the horse's back and rushed toward her, his hair glowing dark gold in the moonlight. "Eliza!"

She stopped in her tracks, fighting to process the scene before her, and as recognition set in, relief washed over her. She threw down the pistol and scrambled forward as fast as her wobbly legs would take her. "Edward!"

He had come looking for her. He had found her. He would protect her. His arms waited invitingly, just beyond her reach. She would curl up in them and explain all that had happened, but first, he needed to understand the danger that still lurked.

"Hunt …" she murmured. "The oast house …"

They were the last words she uttered before spiraling into blackness.

Chapter 22

When Eliza drifted back into consciousness, the world had turned perfectly still. The ringing in her ears abated, giving way to silence, and as her eyes struggled to focus, only indistinct shadows appeared before them. Was it dawn? Or perhaps nightfall? She pushed herself up with her elbows, seeking a better view of her surroundings, and was greeted by a renewed throbbing in the back of her head, instantly bringing back memories of all that had transpired with Hunt. She threw her hands out to the sides, half expecting them to connect with the floorboards of the oast house, but she was met only with softness. Upon closer inspection, she could detect the tiny blue flowers on the counterpane that covered her, marking it as her own. Somehow, she had arrived back in her bed and was wearing her familiar cotton nightgown. She inhaled and exhaled deeply, waiting for her pulse to slow. The danger had passed. She was safe.

"Eliza! Oh, Eliza, dear, thank goodness!"

Catherine's voice, which had taken on an uncharacteristic note of animation, rang out from the doorway, and she rushed to Eliza's side, settling herself on the edge of the bed. She peered into Eliza's face with dark, concerned eyes. "Are you all right?"

"Yes," she tried to say, although it came out as a croak. She gratefully accepted the glass of water Catherine handed her from the bedside table and took a few sips. "Yes," she repeated, more successfully this time, "I think so."

The candle Catherine held illuminated her smile. "I'm so relieved. I came in to insist that Edward get some rest while I sat with you a while, so seeing you awake is the best surprise. I will rouse Edward at once."

Eliza turned her gaze in the same direction as Catherine's, and then she saw him. Edward reclined in the chair in the corner, his eyes closed and his chest rising and falling rhythmically. He wore the same clothing as at the harvest supper, except his cravat, shirt, and waistcoat were stained with blood. Presumably her blood. She brought her hand to her neck, which was covered with a thick bandage.

"No," she called softly, holding out a hand to stay Catherine. "Let him rest a moment. He looks like he could use it. Catherine, how long have I been asleep?"

Catherine shot a hesitant look at Edward before repositioning herself on the edge of the bed. "A full night and day, for evening is falling once more."

Eliza rubbed at her temples as if doing so could help make the fog in her brain lift. "That long?"

"We were so worried," exclaimed Catherine, drawing her brows together and setting her mouth in a tight line. "After all that happened, Edward refused to leave your side for even a second, and ... Oh, I really think I should wake him. He would be displeased to know I hadn't."

"Soon," Eliza conceded. "Give him a few more minutes to sleep while I take a few more minutes to awaken fully. In the meantime, could you please answer one question for me?"

"Anything."

"Mr. Hunt …" Eliza trailed off, the name sticking in her throat like venom. She had a fierce need to know what had happened but couldn't articulate her question any further.

Fortunately, Catherine understood. "He was apprehended in the oast house, fast asleep, and is sitting in a prison cell as we speak. He poses no additional danger to you or anyone else."

Eliza let out a quiet sigh, allowing her pent-up tension to drain away. "I'm glad to hear it." She focused on Catherine's gentle, concerned face, letting it calm her. "Do you think you could still sit with me a while? For the time being, I truly just want to forget the events of last night, and I would welcome a pleasant distraction."

"Of course." Catherine smoothed the counterpane around her and carefully fluffed up her pillow. "Would you like me to tell you a bit of news? You will find it very good news, I think, and I've been so anxious to let you know."

Eliza gave a tiny nod, careful not to jostle her head. "That would be lovely."

"Miss Martin wrote to an old friend of hers recently, a Miss Everleigh. Miss Everleigh was once a governess herself, but over the past few years, she has turned her attentions to teaching at a school in London, an academy for young women who might otherwise end up in the poorhouse, or worse. These disadvantaged women are given an education and taught skills to help them make a wage for themselves. You once mentioned Alice's talent for sewing, and Miss Martin wrote to Miss Everleigh about it, and just today, she received a reply from Miss Everleigh saying that Alice would be welcome at the academy. She could have the opportunity to improve upon her seamstress skills and be given a chance for a fresh start. Jenny could go there to obtain an education as well, and Miss Everleigh also said the academy has a nursery." Catherine's eyes shone with excitement. "Are you pleased? And most importantly, do you think Alice would be happy with this arrangement?"

Eliza could feel her face breaking into a grin. "How wonderful that such a place exists. I cannot wait to tell Alice about it, and you and Miss Martin will have to accompany me on my visit, of course. But yes, I think that will please her very much indeed." She gave Catherine's hand a light squeeze. "My sincere thanks to Miss Martin, and to you, too, for caring enough to set this in motion. I truly couldn't have asked for a kinder, better sister than you."

Catherine's cheeks flushed at the praise, and she flashed Eliza a timid smile. "I feel the same. We're all so fortunate to have you, and I'm more grateful than I can say that you're home and safe. Now," she added, turning her attention to Edward where he still dozed in the corner, "shall I wake my brother?"

Eliza peered at him as well, watching the lines that creased his face as he slept. He must have been bone-weary to not even stir throughout the entirety of her conversation with Catherine. Nothing would feel better right now than lying beside him as his arms encircled her. However, she could stand to wait just a little longer. In fact, she needed to wait in order to collect her thoughts fully.

"Not just yet," she insisted. "Perhaps I'll rest for a few more minutes myself first. However, I have suddenly realized how famished I am. Would you mind ringing for a tray?"

"Right away," said Catherine. "In fact, I should go below stairs and speak with Mrs. Parker. The whole household will be relieved to hear you have awoken no worse for wear, and I'm sure Mrs. Parker will want to call for the doctor."

"That's not necessary," Eliza protested weakly. "Really, I'm quite all right."

"Nonetheless, you always see that we are all cared for. Now, let us take care of you." Catherine leaned in to plant an affectionate kiss on Eliza's cheek. "I will return to check on you soon." With that, she moved to exit the room, casting one last rueful glance at Edward before slipping through the doorway.

With the room silent once more, Eliza sank back farther into her pillow and closed her eyes. There was so much to process after everything that had transpired this past week, although one fact stood out above the others. Edward had come for her when she needed him most, and he hadn't left her side.

Her eyes flew open, prompted by the sudden fear that, in her confusion, she had imagined it all. However, the dim light of Catherine's candle, which remained burning on the bedside table, showed that Edward still sat in the armchair with his chin tucked to his chest.

"Edward." She uttered his name as little more than a whisper, just wanting to feel it against her lips. Surprisingly, he began to stir. His arms moved slightly, and his mouth twitched, almost as if he were trying to say something. Was he dreaming?

"Edward," she said again, in a voice just as quiet, and watched him intently.

His eyelids fluttered open, making him look like he was still in some sort of dream state, until he suddenly snapped his head up, his eyes darting from side to side. And then their gazes connected, his bright eyes piercing into her own.

"Eliza," he murmured, his jaw going slack, and in an instant, he was at her side. She reached out her arms to him, shuffling to allow plenty of room on the bed. He stretched out next to her, laying his head on the pillow and resting his forehead against hers. "Thank God," he said, his breath lightly tickling her cheek.

She pressed her palms into his shoulders, absorbing the warmth and security he provided. This was what she had missed and craved. This was exactly what she needed. She lay against him with her eyes closed for long minutes, feeling the rhythmic thumping of his heart against her chest. She was loath to break the spell with words or to bring this moment to an end. However, when she cracked open her eyes again, the sight of his disheveled hair, shadowed eyes, and bloodstained clothing came back to her. "Edward?"

He opened his eyes to gaze at her, brushing a stray lock of hair away from her face. "Yes, sweetheart?"

"Catherine came in and said you've been sitting in here since last night. Have you not taken a few moments to yourself?"

"I couldn't!" He looked appalled by the suggestion. "Not until I was certain you would be all right. I apologize for falling asleep. If Catherine was here, she should have woken me immediately."

"I assure you, she wanted to," said Eliza with a wry grin. "I thought you needed the rest. Now that we're both awake, why don't you go to your room and change and then join me back here for the dinner tray I requested?"

He peered down at his cravat with a grimace. "But I must speak with you—"

"And I'll be right here waiting when you return, I promise." How ironic that she was now the one deflecting conversations. However, they would surely communicate much better once he had washed away the grime from the previous night and returned to her at least partially refreshed.

The door opened, revealing a maid carrying a tray laden with hearty soup and bread, and behind her, in the corridor, stood Catherine.

"Go," she urged, "just for a few minutes. As I said, I certainly have no plans to go anywhere, and when you return, I may not want you to leave my side again for a very long time."

He pulled himself up to standing and glanced back and forth between the bed and the door. Eventually, he took a step toward the door, although he kept his eyes on her. "For a few minutes, then," he conceded with a sigh, "if you insist. I'll return shortly."

He stepped toward her to press a soft kiss to her lips and then hurried out of the room, apparently wanting to make good on his promise of only being gone briefly. Already she missed the warmth of his body. But after coming this far, what was the harm in waiting just a little longer?

So much had happened since that summer evening when they first met. They had disdained each other. They had built up a fragile sort of caring for each other. They had trusted each other until his reservedness had led her to believe they couldn't have a meaningful relationship after all. But over the past day, a realization had struck her. Edward's actions spoke to things he had never expressed aloud. Those were the things she should focus on. She would be foolish, of course, not to have lingering doubts and fears. But if he needed more time for his words to catch up with his actions, she could be patient.

Chapter 23

Edward had intended to rush through the connecting door into his room and attend to his tasks as quickly as possible, but seeing that Catherine lingered in the corridor, peering at him uncertainly, he stepped out to meet her there instead. He motioned for her to join him a little past the doorway, where they could talk without disturbing Eliza. "Is something amiss?"

Catherine frowned. "Not exactly. It's only that Thomas Wright is downstairs in the entrance hall, asking to come up and see Eliza immediately. He's being most insistent."

The thought of the sly, calculating Wright made Edward scowl. "Should he not be at home, sitting at his dinner table right now? Why the sudden urgency?" After all, Wright had yet to pay them a visit at Highfield Park. In fact, the last he'd heard, Wright had returned north on business.

Catherine threw her arms up. "I hardly know. Perhaps he has a genuine concern for his daughter's welfare."

"You and Eliza are both far too kind in your opinions," he grumbled. If he were being truthful, he deserved to have Wright come to his home and give him a good reprimand for not taking better care of Eliza's safety. However, that seemed an unlikely reason for the visit, for he couldn't imagine the social-climbing Wright admonishing an earl. Nor could he see him losing sleep over Eliza's wellbeing. He breathed out a weary sigh. "Go to Eliza, then, and ask if she desires to see him. The decision should rest in her hands.

I'm going to my bedroom to change and will return to her momentarily."

Catherine nodded in agreement and entered Eliza's bedroom, leaving him to go to his own room next door and clean himself up. He went over to the washstand and gingerly began unfastening the buttons of his waistcoat. His fingers still smarted from the blow they had dealt to Hunt's jaw as the men who had joined in the search dragged him from the oast house. It was far less than the bastard deserved, but he would see to that later.

He switched to unfastening his cravat, cringing as the bloodstained square of linen fell into his hand. To think that something could have happened to Eliza after he'd been such a fool … His chest constricted so intensely that he had to push the idea away. By some miracle, she'd been returned to him, and he would spend the rest of his life making it up to her.

A low-pitched murmur drifted from Eliza's bedroom, followed by the subdued tone of her voice. It seemed she had consented to her father's visit. With that being the case, Edward hastily threw off the rest of his clothing and splashed tepid water over himself until the physical signs of the previous night faded to just a bad memory. After redressing in a clean shirt and trousers and running water through his unruly hair, he pushed open the connecting door between the two bedrooms, eager to return to Eliza's side.

Thomas Wright loomed above the bed, his back to Edward. He was in the midst of such an animated speech that he didn't seem to notice anyone else had entered the room.

"When such a report awaited me upon my return to Hinshaw House, I thought for sure there had been a terrible mistake," he was saying, his tone incredulous. "But you don't deny it? You've really been showing favor to a fallen woman and her bastard child? By marrying the earl, you were supposed to be rebuilding your reputation, not tarnishing it further! And now, if word begins circulating that you disappeared with another man, there's no telling how people will twist that story."

Edward had heard quite enough. The memory of his father, red-faced and shouting at whatever happened to displease him, filled his mind. However, he refused to make such a spectacle of himself. Instead, he spoke quietly, in a tone hard enough to cut iron. "How dare you."

Wright stumbled back a step, turning to face him with bulging eyes. "Why, Lord Ashton, I didn't realize you had come in. I really must apologize for my daughter's behavior. I assure you—"

Edward shot up a hand to silence him. He stalked toward the wretched man, stopping inches short of his face. "Your daughter was forcibly taken, could have damn well been killed, and you merely wish to chastise her for her reputation?"

Wright opened his mouth to speak, but Edward was having none of it. "Quiet!" he snapped, low but menacing. "Furthermore, does it truly bother you to know that Eliza has shown kindness to all our tenants, regardless of their station? I should think you would be glad she exhibits decency and benevolence, traits it doesn't appear she inherited from you. I, for one, appreciate those qualities in her, amongst countless other things that make her the most magnificent woman I have ever known."

"Lord Ashton …" Wright said again, although Edward's steely glare quickly silenced him.

"You should know that you will forever have my gratitude," Edward continued, softening his tone just a touch. "I realize that in arranging this union, you thought only of how your daughter's position as countess would elevate your own station. However, in forcing us together, you have given me the most unexpected but best gift—a gift far greater than any size of dowry. You gave me a wife who means more to me than life itself.

"Now," he added, fixing Wright with another frigid glower, "if Eliza, with her generous heart, chooses to continue her association with you, so be it. However, you will not return to Highfield Park at my invitation, and presently, you have quite overstayed your welcome. Eliza?" He turned to her, seeking her consent to banish this offensive creature from their sight.

She sat tall in the four-poster bed with her arms crossed, looking very much the countess. "At present, I have nothing else to say to you, Papa."

Edward gestured to the door with a flourish. "Good evening, Mr. Wright. Higgins will see you out."

Wright glanced from Edward to Eliza, his mouth gaping. Then, without another word, he scurried from the room, leaving them alone once more.

With that unpleasantness over, Edward allowed himself to flop back onto the bed and encircle Eliza in his arms.

She gazed at him, wide-eyed, although she looked like she was trying to bite back a grin. "What on earth was that? I cannot recall ever seeing my father speechless before."

He scowled at the spot beside the bed as if Wright still stood there. "He chose a good time for speechlessness, for I refuse to allow anyone to speak to the Countess of Ashton in such a manner." He turned back to Eliza, the anger flowing out of him as he peered at her face. "Besides, I'm in no mood for visitors. As I said, I must speak to you myself, alone."

Eliza twined her fingers in his and gave him an encouraging smile. "You have my undivided attention."

His stomach began to roil, but he ignored it. Nothing would stop him from going through with his speech. "I must start, again, with an apology," he said with a sigh. Really, it was nothing short of miraculous she hadn't run away as he'd feared but instead sat here beside him. "Past actions of mine put you in danger, and words cannot express how much I regret that. If I had only been more aware, more vigilant—"

"What happened last night wasn't your fault," she cut in. "It sounds as though Mr. Hunt thoroughly deserved his dismissal, and no one could have known he would react in such a manner. Please, do not have regrets for something that was out of your control."

"But I do." He swallowed hard, trying to force down the lump that had risen in his throat. "I have so many regrets because something could have happened to you, and you would have never even known the truth of my feelings for you."

Eliza took in a sharp breath, her fingers tightening around his. "But nothing did happen to me," she whispered. "I'm right here. You can tell me now."

"I've been such a fool." He gave his head a rueful shake. "I've spent so much time avoiding and denying what was right in front of me. The truth is, I think I've loved you from the moment you played that godawful sonata on the pianoforte."

Eliza laughed, that melodious sound that tugged at his heart. "Is that so? Are you certain you didn't wish for someone who could charm you with her musical talents?"

"No," he answered adamantly. "I had no need of a wife who could play, or sing, or embroider, or paint, or perform any other sort of insignificant talent. I needed someone who could provide me with a remedy when I foolishly drank too much brandy. I needed someone who would welcome and befriend my sister. I needed someone who would care for our estate and tenants when I was too short-sighted to do so. I needed someone who would see me as more than just the hollow, evasive shell I felt myself to be. I needed someone I could trust and someone who would fight for our partnership when she was well within her right to walk away from it. That someone, Eliza, is you, and I love you for all these reasons and so many more."

Eliza's green eyes glittered with tears. "I cannot begin to tell you how wonderful it is to hear that."

He leaned in to brush his lips over hers. Despite everything, her skin still held the faint smell of roses. He pulled away enough so he could speak again. "It was idiotic of me to try to deny it. You bewitched me from the first moment I saw you. But after all those years I spent roaming the Continent, convincing myself that happiness and love were lies …"

"I know." She pressed a gentle kiss to his cheek before tilting back to gaze at him. "I understand. I hate knowing that your first marriage ended as it did. However, I'm glad I know because now we can move on from it together. I believe in you, just as you believed in me when most others saw me as a scandal-ridden disgrace. And I think we can press on and come out stronger and better than before. For Edward, I love you with my entire being."

He remembered his dread the first time she had uttered those words to him. Now, the declaration caused the rest of the world to melt away and leave only Eliza, the most wonderful sight he could imagine, sitting before him. It lightened him. It completed him. It made him feel like he could take on anything life demanded. He had spent far too long pushing it away, but going forward, he wouldn't waste another second.

"I think you're correct, Lady Ashton," he said, settling her to rest against the crook of his arm. "With you by my side, we could likely conquer the world. At the very least, I know we can conquer the difficulties here at Highfield Park and turn it into a successful estate once more. It will be our home. You will always belong here. Furthermore, I will spend the rest of my life showing you how very loved you are."

Eliza snuggled into his body more tightly, leaning her head against his chest. She smiled up at him but then raised her hand to her mouth, stifling a yawn. "I'll hold you to that, Lord Ashton."

He pressed his face against her hair, inhaling her floral scent as he kissed the top of her head. "You should rest some more," he murmured, closing his eyes. He could feel her slight nod against his chest, and before long, her breathing turned slow and even. His grip on consciousnesses began to lapse, but with Eliza now safe in his arms, he embraced his drowsiness rather than fought it. Soon enough, they would make plans for the future of Highfield Park, and then they would journey to London for Catherine's upcoming Season. Perhaps someday, they would even travel to the Continent together and make new memories there.

The future stretched out before them, filled with endless possibilities. But right now, they were exactly where they needed to be.

Epilogue

Eliza had never been so relieved to return to her bedroom in their rented Berkeley Square town house. Despite her thick cloak, her brief time in the winter rain chilled her to the bone, and the fire in the grate danced invitingly. She pulled her vanity stool close to the warmth and flopped onto it, kicking her sodden silk slippers from her feet. Next, she set to work removing feathers and unfastening the uncomfortable pins from her hair.

"God, that was tedious." Edward entered the room, already in the process of untying his cravat. He immediately came to the stool, squeezing onto it beside her and casting off his wet Hessians. That task complete, he pulled her into a deep embrace, tugging out her remaining hairpins as he went. When all the thick locks tumbled down her back, he leaned back to gaze at her, his blue eyes blazing intensely. "I've been waiting all evening to do this."

"I agree," she said, unfastening the buttons of his waistcoat, "that this is far preferable to anything else we experienced this evening." She thought back to the musicale that she, Edward, and Catherine had just attended in Lady Whitmore's drawing room. They had chosen to go based on the belief it would be a relatively subdued, unintimidating event compared to the numerous routs and balls to which they received invitations. However, while the event did have the advantage of being uncrowded, the music had been atrocious to the point of making her want to clamp her hands over her ears, and it had lasted a full three hours. A sudden giggle burst from her throat. "The only way the musicale could have been improved upon is if I had offered up a song of my own."

With his waistcoat discarded on the floor, Edward spun her so she faced away from him and began working on the row of tiny buttons traveling down the back of her dress. "You speak facetiously," he murmured, the heat of his breath creating a delicious tingle in the back of her neck, "but had you sat down to play, everyone would have been singing your praises."

Perhaps he was right, although it made her somewhat uneasy to think so. Her father's plan to have her restore her reputation through her advantageous marriage had succeeded. The same set who had scorned her less than a year before now made efforts to welcome the new Lady Ashton into their circle. And while she still had no desire to become one of the ton's top ladies, at least gaining acceptance made the Season somewhat easier to endure.

The silky material of her dress, along with her petticoat, slipped from her shoulders, leaving her sitting in her shift and stays. Edward's hands caressed her newly exposed skin with powerful strokes, easing away the tension that had built up over the evening. Any second now, the need to embrace him in return would overtake her, and they would be lost in each other, unable to think of anything but their growing desire. But before she allowed that to happen, she needed to ask him something.

"Edward?" Reluctantly, she moved away from his skill-ful fingers and turned back to face him. "Did you notice something odd about Catherine this evening?"

"Catherine?" The name didn't even seem to register with him at first, and he took a moment to slow his breath-ing. "Catherine ..." he repeated eventually. "She was rather quiet during the carriage ride home, was she not? And she went up to her bedroom without saying a word."

"I do hope she's all right. She hasn't seemed to truly enjoy any of the lavish events she's attended since her debut, but this evening, she seemed especially ill at ease. I realize the need for her to take her place in society, but I think an early departure from London may benefit us all."

Edward reached around to begin unlacing her stays. "You have no objections from me on that account."

"Good. In fact, our departure from London before the end of the Season may be quite necessary."

Her stays came away in his hands, and he tossed them to the floor. "How so?"

She couldn't stop her smile from breaking through. She had suspected something for some time now, but lacking certainty, she kept it to herself. However, the signs had be-come too obvious to doubt. "Edward, I'm with child."

His hands, which had been about to pull at the ribbon of her shift, abruptly froze, and he stared at her, expression-less.

Eliza's heart gave a little lurch. "Are you pleased?"

Suddenly, a wide grin spread across his face. "So pleased." He brought a hand to her stomach, still flat for the time being, and traced his finger across it as though touching her for the first time. "Imagine, a little lord or lady. And you will be the most wonderful mother."

She doubted she could contain another ounce of happiness without bursting. "I think this fits in nicely with our plans to continue improving Highfield Park."

"Yes," he agreed, "there could be no better improvement than that. You have turned the estate I didn't want into the only place I wish to be. A house filled with the laughter of our child, or if we may be so fortunate, children, and you by my side—nothing and nowhere could be better."

He ran his hand back up her body until it reconnected with the ribbon of her shift. He caused it to come open with a light flick and tugged the flimsy garment away. A moan rose in her throat as he resumed his kisses, traveling down to the sensitive curve of her breasts. "You, Lady Ashton, are the most marvelous creature." He breathed the words into her heated skin, forcing her cry of pleasure to emerge. "Words cannot begin to describe how much I love you. Allow me, though, to try showing you instead."

What happens next?

Sign up for Jane's monthly newsletter to access a free bonus epilogue for *Secrets and a Scandal*. You will also receive updates on promotions and new releases, including **book two** in the *Inconveniently Wed* series, ***Rumors and a Rake***.

For more information, visit www.janemaguireauthor.com.

About the Author

Jane Maguire is a Canadian author whose lifelong passions for history, writing, and love stories inevitably led her to begin penning historical romance novels. While her love of historical fiction spans all eras, she focuses her writing on high society in the glittering regency period. She enjoys crafting stories with lots of angst, which makes giving her characters their happily ever afters all the more satisfying.

When she isn't at her computer writing and researching, you can find her vacationing in the Rocky Mountains, playing classical music on the piano, or simply curling up with a cup of tea and a good book. She lives with her husband, two kids, a five-pound guard dog, and a foodie cat.

You can find Jane online at
www.janemaguireauthor.com.